# THE SURVIVOR

### THE ACES SERIES, BOOK #3

*New York Times* Bestselling Author
# CRISTIN HARBER

Copyright © 2020 by Cristin Harber

All rights reserved. This book or any portions thereof may not be reproduced or used in any manner whatsoever without the express written permission of the author and publisher except for the use of brief quotations used in a book review.

This is a work of fiction. All of the characters, organizations, and events portrayed in this novel are either the products of the author's imagination or are used fictionally.

www.cristinharber.com

## DEDICATION

*To my quarantine bubble,*
*You are the reason this book exists.*
*Thank you.*

"The opposite of anger is not calmness. It's empathy."

– Mehmet Oz

# CHAPTER ONE

**BEIRUT, LEBANON**

"AIN'T LOVE GRAND." Hagan Carter crawled through the dank, dark crawl space beneath their target location, a wealthy family estate. "Or is that money?" The expected cobwebs and varmint droppings could've been in any subterranean passageway, but Hagan had hoped for a little less rat shit in the underbelly of this protected, affluent enclave.

His teammate, Chance, one of those happy-go-lucky newlyweds, snickered into his mic as he led the team. "I think that depends."

"That's what they all say," Parker added from their Abu Dhabi headquarters. "Relationships are cyclical. In love one day, negotiating divorce settlements the next."

"Wow, bro." Liam brought up the rear of their underground assault. "You're a little young to be so cynical, boy genius."

"Maybe it's a numbers game," Hagan volunteered. "My mom wore a t-shirt once that said marriage was like a walk in Jurassic Park."

"Man, that's dark," Liam snorted as laughter filtered from headquarters.

"The more I know about you, the more I see what went wrong," Chance joked.

Hagan snickered, then added, "Once she wore a shirt for my dad that said, 'I love you with all my boobs because they're bigger than my heart.'" He shook his head. "Traumatized me for years." The guys laughed again. "She's big into t-shirts." He made a mental note to send his mom a new shirt. Something snarky that his sister would get a kick out of as well.

"Gotta collect something," Liam said.

"Like data," Parker said. "The numbers never lie." He shifted back to business. "You've reached the second marker. Check your position and confirm."

Chance paused their team to take a measurement, and Hagan dropped onto his stomach. A red laser beam flicked on and burned green through his night-vision goggles. Chance radioed back and forth with headquarters. Hagan rolled to his side and pressed his back against the concrete crawlspace wall as a bead of sweat trickled down his back.

"Confirmed," Chance finally relayed.

There had been concerns that their path might end at a cinder block dead end. Parts of Beirut lacked architectural records because buildings had been built on top of other buildings. Their target location was rumored to have been built during the Crusades, re-purposed during the Ottoman empire, and re-imagined into the estate that it was today when 1940s French architecture influenced the city.

Jared "Boss Man" Westin had summarized Parker's architectural history lesson as an infinite possibility of problems.

Hagan had already thought that of this job. Obstacles sprouted like weeds any time an international custody dispute resulted in an abduction. He knew Lebanon like the back of his hand, but this assignment made him feel like he was navigating a minefield.

"After the next piling," Parker said, "the access point will be on the right."

"Let's move," Liam muttered.

Their caravan continued at the pace of a hungover snail. The tight space narrowed like a concrete coffin grabbing for their weapons and gear. Dust and gravel rained on their backs. Their mics magnified every breath and grunt.

Finally, they passed the support pillar and made the turn. The passageway opened and gave them room to spread out. Sweat pooled on Hagan's spine as he waited for Chance to confirm their coordinates.

After Chance gave Hagan a thumbs up, he removed the cutting tool from his vest. They waited for the go-ahead from headquarters. Hagan's index finger tapped against the tool's on/off toggle, ready to put the blade and lasers to work. It could melt through drywall and plaster and grind through structural reinforcements like rebar.

Hagan's earpiece crackled with the communication from headquarters. "Aces, you're a go."

He powered the cutter and pressed the blade into the wall. Sparks jumped. Lasers smoked. Night vision goggles protected his eyes. He moved quickly and didn't cross a stray line of rebar. After making a final pass, Hagan flicked off the power tool. The silence thundered as loud as the cutter had until Liam moved the pneumatic ram into position.

"Go," Chance said.

Liam engaged the ram. With one strike, the outer wall shattered. A second strike exploded through the interior, where they hoped to find a basement laundry or utility room. But anything would be okay so long as it didn't shoot or bite when they breached the building.

Chance and Liam took a defensive position, and Hagan surged inside. He scanned the opening. "Clear."

This part of their job was unscripted. No blueprints. No intel on the layout. Surveillance reported that only a nanny had been seen with the minor. That wasn't much to go on.

Hagan spoke fluent Arabic and led the charge, eyes peeled for the nanny. They moved fluidly and reached the main level of the three-story structure without seeing signs that anyone lived in the home. Not a single personal touch or stray pair of shoes.

The well-appointed main floor showed that someone had spent lavishly on furnishings, but it still felt cold and unwelcoming.

They regrouped at the base of a marble staircase that wrapped from the formal entryway to the next landing as though its only job were to showcase a chandelier dripping with diamonds and crystal.

"Bet no one gets to play ball in the house," Liam muttered.

A house wasn't a home without football. At least that was what Hagan had been taught. He wondered if the kid had been abducted with the same calculations that the estate's furnishings had been acquired with. He couldn't imagine how life would've been if his parents treated Hagan and his brother and sister like a possession instead of a person.

The team summited the stairs and spread out, weapons up. Room by room, they swept until only one bedroom remained.

"Where's the nanny?" Hagan asked.

Chance lifted a shoulder and flanked the last door. "Let's find out."

"Great." Liam took the other side. "Sounds more like a guard."

Hagan agreed, ready for whatever they'd find on the other side of the door. He twisted the knob and pushed ahead. Chance and Liam flanked his sides. Hagan immediately sighted a large bed, and the sleeping boy half-under a blanket still clutching a Nintendo Switch.

Hagan crept into the bedroom more suited for diplomatic guests than a kid. Then he saw the nanny. She dozed in a wingback chair with a quilt over her lap. In a perfect world, they wouldn't have had to disturb her. But the world was far from perfect. That was why he had a job that paid the big bucks. To fix where society failed—and to pay down debts that threatened to bankrupt his family.

They spread out. Chance stepped toward the woman. Liam moved to the boy's bed. Hagan positioned between the boy and his nanny. Short of tranquilizing the kid, their consensus had been to quietly explain who they were and why they were there. Their target was old enough to understand and, hopefully, welcome their arrival.

The nanny kicked the quilt off and lifted a shaky grip on a handgun. "I will shoot you."

So much for not waking the nanny. Hagan turned his attention to her, trusting that Liam and Chance had him covered, and in his most trustworthy Arabic, said, "You don't need to do that."

He could see that she didn't want this responsibility, that she was unfamiliar with the gun in her hand. That didn't make the situation any safer. "We want to bring the boy to his family."

"You need to leave," she responded in her native tongue with more force. Still, the weapon wavered.

Hagan maintained a calm detachment as though he wasn't her intended bull's eye. Sheets rustled behind him, and the boy woke with a yelp. Hagan shifted to see both the woman and child, then spoke in English, "Your mother sent us. We work for her."

"You need to leave," the nanny interrupted.

"She wants you to come home," Hagan continued.

"I must shoot you," she pleaded. "You must leave, or I must shoot the gun—" Her voice cracked. "Go."

"I want to go home," the boy cried.

Tears trickled down the nanny's face. "This is my job. I must watch out for the boy. Protect him."

"We have the same orders," Hagan replied.

She wept. The handgun pulled at her hands as though it were as heavy as the concrete blocks that supported this house.

"I want to leave," the boy cried. "Please!"

"We both know he shouldn't be here," Hagan said.

Her lip quivered.

"Do you have children?" He holstered his weapon in a show of good faith. Her anguish reminded him of his own mother, of everything that she had faced. "What if you woke up and couldn't talk to your child? Couldn't comfort—"

"I do not want to do this."

"I know." He gestured for her to stand down. "You don't have to."

The reluctance to carry out a task that she wasn't capable of pulled her into the chair. Liam swept the boy and his covers off the far side of the bed. The nanny still had the gun, and Chance had his aim trained on her. Hagan held up his hands and approached her. It didn't take much effort to disarm her, and she fell into his arms, apologizing, explaining how she didn't want this for the child.

In the distance, Hagan heard Chance update headquarters and Liam readying the kid to move out. Hagan set the woman into her chair. He wanted to tell her she'd done the right thing, that she'd met a higher calling and done what duty and service dictated she should, not a job or a paycheck.

But all he could think about was when his mother had lost his brother and when Hagan had realized that pain didn't go away. It simply changed.

# CHAPTER TWO

**ABU DHABI, UNITED ARAB EMIRATES**

As SECURITY PROJECT contracts went, Amanda Hearst couldn't imagine a better company to work with than Titan Group, but as clients went, she didn't know a soul more aggravating than her friend Jared Westin. Though maybe that wasn't saying a lot.

As a rule, Amanda kept away from people. Of the few she was forced to interact with, she considered an even smaller number as friends. Jared had been a friend since she was an angsty, bleach-blonde, goth-makeup-wearing teenager.

It wasn't that Amanda couldn't make friends, but, rather, she knew better. Boss Man understood.

When he'd first asked her interest in designing a security system in Abu Dhabi, she hadn't known it would be for Titan's new headquarters in the United Arab Emirates.

When he casually mentioned the project would include two armored skyscrapers with SCIF rooms, Amanda salivated and crossed her fingers that he would see her as a security professional and not a family friend he had to protect.

Then, when he agreed to sign a contract that isolated her from all but essential personnel, she let out a loud whoop.

They'd worked together on smaller jobs before using her security parameters. It hadn't been easy, but they'd survived without strangling each other. Once again, the only problem with this project was Jared's infuriating habit of worrying about *her* security.

Amanda's stomach growled. She regretted skipping lunch to run an inspection with Parker Black, the brains behind Titan's intel and security. If the late afternoon sun was any indication, she was about to work through dinner. They'd found a glitchy pass reader and a loose wire outside the second tower's SCIF room.

Both were easy fixes that should've been corrected by now. But, as she approached the flagged pass reader, it only took a glance to see its yellow blinking light. The contractor hadn't fixed it before he left for the day.

Her stomach growled again as an alert pinged on her tablet. Amanda groaned at the preview of Jared's email.

*We need to talk.*

"Oh, fun…" She could tell he was in a mood and could've kicked herself for not eating earlier. There was no telling if Jared would harp on their ongoing disagreements or if he had another brilliant idea like bulletproof skylights. She made a mental note to keep snacks on hand and tapped out her reply.

*Sounds good. Come and find me.*

Amanda added a smiley face then hit send, confident that it would make Boss Man glower.

Now she needed to pick a location that would play to her advantage. She bypassed the malfunctioning door without swiping the necessary badge and walked to the nearest sky bridge. It connected the two hotel towers. The first tower's renovation was nearly complete. The second tower remained on schedule, though nowhere near ready for business.

She swiped her badge to enter the second tower, then moved through an area of unfinished steel-framed walls. One day, they'd be impenetrable meeting rooms. But the exterior walls and windows still hadn't been installed. It had taken an obscene amount of time to wire Titan's LIDAR security system. But Amanda, pleased with their progress, was infatuated with their multiple fields of vision. It offered a certainty of knowing what was where at all times—precisely her life goal too.

Amanda continued to one of her favorite places to think. Fresh air overtook the omnipresent smell of construction. She stepped through the plastic tarps that hung from steel beams. The thin plastic swayed as wind drifted off the city, comforting her almost as much as standing near the ledge.

Warning signs and a bright orange mesh barrier marked the perimeter. A mere four millimeters of plastic served as the only barrier between her, the open sky, and the streets below. It was only when she could look down at danger that she felt in control of her life.

Her parents would freak out if they knew how she found peace. They'd rain a security detail from the heavens, ready to catch her if she fell. On the opposite side of caution, Amanda's business partner and best friend Halle wouldn't even suggest a safety precaution. Halle's hard-and-fast trust in natural selection reigned supreme.

Jared was somewhere in the middle of the two extremes, depending on his mood and the day's headaches.

For now, she was alone and in control of her destiny. The city lay before her. Amanda breathed deeply, where she needed to be.

Familiar, heavy footsteps broke her meditation. Amanda turned from the gaping exterior wall and waited for Jared as he slapped plastic tarps out of his way, pursuing the fastest option from point A to point B.

Amanda gave a quick wave when he stormed into view. "You found me."

"Jesus fucking Christ, Amanda. Back the fuck up."

"I thought Army Rangers were trained to be sneaky and quiet," she teased. "Or was that too long ago for you to remember?"

He snorted. "If I didn't want you to know I was here, you still wouldn't know, *Sparkler*."

The corners of her mouth turned down. "Don't call me that."

"Then don't hang that close to the edge of my building." He cracked his knuckles, then crossed his arms over his chest. "Give me a couple more inches. If you trip and fall, do you know what you'd do to my insurance rates?"

"I'm glad you care about my safety."

Jared beckoned her closer. "A little more, cupcake."

"So long as you don't call me Sparkler." She moved then made a show of checking her distance from the fall zone. "I think I'm safe."

"*Thank you.*" A muscle ticked in his cheek. "Parker says there's a problem with—"

"Parker said the word *problem*?" She lifted her eyebrows. "Or did he say there were two new items on the punch list?"

A stress line deepened across Jared's forehead. "Same thing."

"Not really. I'll show you what's going on." They walked toward a plastic-wrapped pallet. Jared managed to stay behind and follow without blazing a path through unfinished walls or slapping plastic tarps. She laid her tablet on the makeshift desk. "There are two new items on the punch list. One's taken care of." She pointed to an update. "And this one"—she scrolled down—"should've been fixed already. But it'll be fine by tomorrow."

Jared harrumphed.

"Allergies?" she asked and continued to scroll when he ignored her. "This is the update I'm sending to Parker tonight."

Jared scrutinized the punch list. "You're still on schedule."

"Shocker." She returned to the top of the list. "Except, not really. You know I get the job done."

His nostrils flared. "Stay on schedule."

She gave him a playful salute. "Aye, aye, captain."

He grumbled. "And don't fall out of the damn building."

"I won't screw up your insurance rates." She crossed her

hand over her heart. "I swear."

"Not to mention, your father would kill me."

"Mom, too." She closed the project and let the tablet lock. "If that's all."

"How is your mom?" he asked, trying his best at small talk.

She cradled the tablet in the crook of her arm and thought back to her last conversation with her parents as they deplaned at Andrews Air Force Base. "She's fine. They just got back from an economic summit in Tokyo."

"Saw that."

"Mom's happy with the reception her communicable disease speech had with the press."

Jared nodded. "And your dad?"

"Busy, as always." She sighed. Jared wasn't one to make polite conversation. If he brought up her parents, she wanted to discuss security issues. Double standards infuriated her. After all, he'd contracted *her* security company. "Question for you, Boss Man."

"Shoot."

"How often do you ask your team to be careful near sharp drops?"

His dark eyes narrowed. "You might know if you ever spoke to any of them."

*Well, hell.* She should've seen that one coming. "I do—"

His hand went up like an NBA player blocking a shot. "Parker and Angela don't count."

"Then, never mind." Amanda gnawed on her lip. Titan's IT director and office administrator were the only people she'd communicate with besides Jared. He'd tried several times to brief her on his Abu Dhabi-based team, but Amanda always invoked her contract, which stipulated her right to privacy. She didn't want to know anything personal about anyone. It was a weakness that she'd never allow again.

His scowl deepened. "There's something you should—"

"No. There's not." If it wasn't mission-critical, she refused to listen. "I'm stubborn like that."

He glared. "That's a nice way to put it."

Seconds crawled by. This was the worst part of their ongoing disagreement. Jared could call her choices into question without saying a word. He didn't care that his attempts to broaden her world only unburied her pain. "I have to go."

"That's your choice to make," he said. "A stupid one."

Damn him. She refused to agree, and without a way to end the conversation, Amanda turned and rushed away.

# CHAPTER THREE

Hagan sprinted up another flight of stairs. His muscles burned as he concentrated on the endless slap of his running shoes. Sweat poured down his neck as he climbed the closed-for-renovations skyscraper. His vision tunneled. This wasn't just another workout. It was a regimen capable of clearing his mind days after the conversation with the woman in Lebanon. He still couldn't shake the sadness. Damn, he missed his brother.

Hagan growled and gulped for oxygen, pushing his body until darkness shadowed over memories of his death. Hagan re-focused on running. He could do another flight. "*Push.*" Push through the pain and aging memories. Push until he couldn't do anything except breathe.

He powered onto the next stairwell landing. Lungs burning, light-headed, and depleted, he didn't have the strength to stop his momentum. Hagan slammed into the cinder block wall like a runaway bulldozer. His pulse pounded in his ears. His forehead pressed to the gritty coarseness, and he rolled his head back and forth against it like it was an icepack.

For a blissfully delirious moment, he couldn't recall what had started him up the tower stairs. He basked in the endorphins that pummeled through his veins, furiously releasing their high and leaving every thought from the past in the distance. "Thank God."

He didn't know how long he stayed like that. Finally, Hagan wiped the sweat from his forehead, straightened, and rolled his shoulders. Lactic acid would knot in his muscles if he didn't move soon. With his breathing semi-controlled, he descended the first flight of many.

The hollow, metallic click of a stairwell door opening preceded a boom as it shut. Hagan froze, sure he'd been the only person in the unfinished tower. The construction crew had left hours ago. His teammates had no reason to be in this building. Hagan listened for Boss Man's hefty steps, but instead of the footfalls from a military muscle hound, Hagan detected a light, smooth gait rushing from above.

Curious, he backed to the wall and peered up. "Hello?"

The unknown person stopped, not answering.

*Well, hell.* His curiosity upgraded to suspicion. He climbed another flight and moved into a corner for a different angle, but he couldn't get a bead on the other person. He crept up another flight and kept to the corners—still no sight or sound from above. The rogue trespasser was a problem, and he was unarmed and unable to call for backup. Hagan had no choice but to investigate.

He edged up the stairs, forcing himself to move cautiously. He ignored the lactic acid coiling in his muscles and the dizzying need for water and calories. *Beep. Beep. Beep.*

Hagan slapped his hand over the exercise watch and muffled the notification announcing his heart rate had returned to a normal range. The gift from his sister, Roxana, had lit up his location like fireworks on the Fourth of July.

Finally, the notification stopped, but the damage was done. He remained still and listened. The intruder had the same wait-and-listen plan. Hagan shifted to keep his muscles from locking when he heard the unmistakable sound of a round entering a chamber followed by quiet steps.

Anticipation prickled down his neck. Hagan pressed against the wall and positioned for a better spot at the same moment that he registered a woman with a gun trained at his center mass. He pulled back.

"Stay where you are," the woman called. "Don't move."

Damn. Unlike the nanny in Lebanon, this woman's voice didn't hold a thread of uncertainty. With his location blown, no weapon or backup, and an inability to run away in his own damn house, Hagan didn't have many options. "I'm unarmed."

She moved into his line of sight, weapon still up, then eyed his clothing. "Why are you creeping in the stairwell?"

He scowled. "I wasn't creeping any more than you were." Her weapon didn't waver from its target. He extended his palms slowly in a show of good faith. "I could ask you the same question."

"Don't bother. Why are you dressed like that?"

He dropped his hands and pulled at the shirt sticking to his chest. "The local gym doesn't do it for me."

"Do *not* move," she ordered like she owned the place as

much as he did.

Hagan clamped his molars and tried to recall mention of a new teammate. Surely, he would've remembered hearing about a woman on their team. Especially a woman with dark hair and stealthy eyes that would've made any man take a second look. "Look, lady, I think this is a misunderstanding."

"Fine." She lifted her chin to dismiss him. "Leave."

His jaw sawed. "Like hell."

"Excuse me?"

He smirked. "If you were me—"

"I'm not," she snapped. "You crept up here. If this is a misunderstanding, go away."

A small part of him realized that he wasn't paying enough attention to her gun. "Say you were me, and you came across a beautiful woman—"

"Give me a break."

"With a gun," Hagan continued, "demanding that I leave my—"

Her brows furrowed. "Stop! I don't want to know anything about you."

Interesting. His curiosity returned. "If you were me, would you try for a conversation?"

She arched a single, disbelieving eyebrow. "Are you flirting with me?"

*Fuck yes.* "Why would I do that?"

"I don't know why you've done a single thing since I met you."

"That'd make two of us." Her training was evident, yet he

didn't see that hard edge recognizable in almost any operative in his line of work. "Who are you?"

Her nostrils flared. "You should leave."

Intrigued and apparently stupid, he didn't move from the woman with the gun. "Maybe you're the one who should go, Annie Oakley." Now, both of the dark eyebrows twitched. He held out a hand, willing her to lower the weapon, and make introductions. "I'm—"

"Stop," she demanded. "Leave. Go. I don't want to know anything about you."

His ego found the wrong moment for a stubborn streak. Hagan wondered if it would be as much fun to get her to laugh as it was to make her eyebrows dance. He stepped closer. "Lower your weapon."

"Fat chance."

He took another step. "I promise, it'll make for nicer introductions."

"I *can't* meet you."

A desperate bent in her voice made him take a harder look. Something inside him jumped. Something beyond a reaction to the gun or her looks. He couldn't place that faraway feeling of familiarity. "Have we met?"

"*No.*"

He didn't believe her but came up empty when he tried to place her face. "I think we have."

She scowled. "Trust me. You're wrong."

He studied her delicate features. She didn't look like any of the renovation workers he'd seen roaming, and there wasn't an overabundance of sexy women with steady trigger fingers in his building. Even if there were, he would have recalled Annie Oakley.

Stiffening muscles brought him back to reality—charmed or not, the lady still hadn't lowered her weapon, something he needed to take more seriously. Hagan licked his bottom lip and tried again. "I feel like we got off on the wrong foot."

Her nostrils flared.

"Do you work around here? Maybe Parker should look into name badges." Hagan didn't wait for her to respond. He'd already jumped into the deep end of a questionable flirting situation and might as well start swimming. "I could show you around."

As though he'd said the magic words, she lowered her weapon.

"You want a tour?"

"You know Parker Black?" she said.

"So, no tour." But he was making progress. "Though points for dropping Parker's name?"

She gave a microscopic nod.

Hagan couldn't help it and grinned. "Now, does that make us friends?"

"I don't have friends."

"Sounds like you live a small, sad existence." He nodded to the gun. "Though you gotta wonder if it has something to do with first impressions."

She rolled her eyes. "Why are you still here?"

"Hell if I know," he admitted, laughing, "but I'm coming up to introduce myself. Don't shoot me."

"No promises."

## CHAPTER FOUR

PUZZLES INTRIGUED HAGAN. Brutally honest women had always caught his eye. He couldn't recall a situation where these interests converged. If they ever had before, it hadn't come in the form of a dark-haired beauty packing heat. "At least you gave me fair warning."

Irritation pinched the corners of her eyes.

Given the mysterious entirety of their brief encounter, he decided to take her words as the simple truth. *No promises.* She might shoot him. He almost laughed. What the hell was he doing?

Hagan took his time as he climbed the stairs, watching her trigger finger and studying the way she dressed. He couldn't explain why, but her unremarkable attire seemed less a fashion choice and more a tool to hide in plain sight.

With minimal makeup and hair tied into a ponytail so severe that it almost gave him a headache, she hadn't downplayed herself enough to keep his pulse from skipping. Or maybe her gun and attitude were what had his blood pumping. Either way, he didn't care and wasn't walking away.

Hagan took the final step onto the staircase landing. Her apprehensive gaze stayed on his, though she had to tilt her chin up to maintain the connection. Her feet stayed planted, and her jaw clenched as she defiantly held her ground.

"You haven't shot me yet," he pointed out.

"The night's still young."

He grinned. "I've never been propositioned by a woman with a gun before."

A blush ignited on her cheeks despite her disinterested expression. "Trust me, you haven't been tonight."

His mind raced. She didn't shoot him or demand he leave, and Hagan couldn't stop wondering what made her tick.

The tint on her cheeks had cooled, and she stood straighter. He wanted to point out no matter how she stretched, he'd still have at least a foot on her.

She inched closer. "What were you doing?"

The corners of his lips quirked. "Nothing as exciting as this."

"Wow, you like to avoid direct answers, huh?"

"Depends." Hagan lifted a shoulder playfully, then admitted, "Running fireman sprints."

"Those aren't easy," she said.

"I wasn't looking for easy." He realized how much that still applied. He dipped his chin to the gun still clasped in her hand. "Are you gonna holster that bad boy?"

"No. I hadn't planned on it."

The irregular cadence of her breath made his hitch. "It's not a security blanket."

Her nostrils flared. "Which is why I can't understand why you're still here."

The faint outline of her nipples pressed against her shirt. Hagan swallowed hard. "We've come this far." His lips quirked. "I don't see the fun in leaving yet."

"I don't like fun."

He laughed. "Bullshit, beautiful."

"Do lines like that work for you?"

"Better question." He stepped closer. "Is it working now?"

Her eyes rounded, and her lips parted as though she didn't know what to say. "You're flirting with me?"

"I'd be a fool not to."

A two-count passed. He wasn't sure she was breathing until he heard the whisper of her breath. He sensed her hesitation then wondered how she knew Parker. The last thing Hagan wanted to do was flirt with a new teammate. He retreated. "I should head out."

Her eyelashes fluttered as though he'd caught her off guard. "Maybe—" She straightened. "*Yes*. That's what I've been saying."

*Maybe?* Had he read her indecision wrong? "*Maybe* we could run into each other again."

She solidified into a concrete wrecking ball of back-the-hell-up. "No."

*All right then, maybe not.* He gave her more room but still wanted to see her again. "We could make plans. How about dinner?"

"Dinner …?" She blanched as if Hagan had suggested they join the circus. "*No*."

"Shot down again." He laughed at himself and saluted.

"Message read loud and clear."

"Wait." She grimaced. "All I meant was—"

"You don't have to explain." He gestured to her weapon. "Even if you didn't have the gun."

She glanced down and then licked her lips. "I already explained, I don't do friends—" Her chin snapped up. "Nothing in the same vicinity as friends."

Was she warning him away from the hope of friends with benefits? His eyebrow crooked and his mind escalated the possibility in a nanosecond. "It'd be just my luck that you don't do buddies either."

Her gaze flamed. "I don't do buddies of any kind."

"Too bad." He winked.

She swallowed hard. "It's the best way to be."

"Very cautious of you." He leaned into their conversation. "Why are you so wary?"

"Why are you still here?"

Hagan smiled. "Because I'm not sure either of us wants me to leave."

Without disagreeing, she sealed her lips. "Friends are dangerous."

"Nothing a quick frisk and pat down couldn't help with."

Her lips parted as though a physical search hadn't crossed her mind before, and now that it had, she didn't know how to respond to the idea of her hands on his skin. "Are you dangerous?"

"Not to society." He moved with slow, purposeful steps until he'd closed their distance. "Not to you."

"That's what they all say."

Hagan dropped his tone to match hers. "I'm going to tell you a secret."

"I don't want to hear it."

He winked. "It's so cheesy and true that you'll thank me later."

A flicker of a smile betrayed her. "I doubt it."

"Ready?"

She tilted her head, almost rolling her eyes. "Sure."

"I'm nothing like you've ever met."

Her laughter was music to his ears—then a devilish dare of an idea danced over her face. "Turn around."

"Why?"

"You suggested a quick frisk." She signaled for him to turn. "Against the wall. Arms up, feet apart."

Hagan snorted. "Lady, it was a *joke*."

She didn't so much as blink.

"Jeez, tough crowd." He waited. There wasn't a popsicle's chance in hell that Miss Uptight-With-A-Gun would put her hands on him. Not even if Hagan prayed.

"Turn around," she repeated.

Hell, what did he have to lose? He stepped to the challenge and turned.

She shifted and holstered her weapon.

His stomach dropped, and Hagan glanced over his shoulder. "I don't know if I'm astonished or slightly turned on right now."

She positioned her foot between his and angled her position to protect her smaller frame.

"You know what you're doing." He gave her space to search him, slowly lifting his arms. He shivered at the possibility of her nimble fingers skimming across his stomach, hips, and thighs. And, if she came anywhere near his groin—he'd feel a lot more than a shiver.

"Of course, I know what I'm doing." Deftly, she tugged at his shirt. The fabric pulled from his post-workout damp skin. Cool air kissed his flesh. Goosebumps formed. His breath caught as she methodically searched him with a frightening level of professionalism. If the situation had been reversed, he wouldn't have been businesslike. "Am I clear?"

She ignored him, and her fingers skirted his waistband. If this little game didn't end soon, she'd learn exactly what he was packing.

Hagan glanced over his shoulder again. "*Now* are we friends?"

Mistrustful reservation had darkened her eyes. "Stand still."

"What do kids these days consider second base?"

Her hands ran up his ribs and in front of his arms until she returned to the front of his shorts.

"Because second base would make us more than friends," he explained, restraint waning. "Yeah, this is definitely, almost second base."

Without a word, she stepped back. "Guess you're not as dangerous as you look."

Hagan pinched his eyes shut and pulled himself together. He turned, and her cold expression might've castrated a lesser man. But that lesser man wouldn't have noticed the flush that returned to her cheeks. "Didn't know I looked that way to start."

She rolled her eyes. "If the games are over—"

"They're just starting." Hagan gave his most charming, distraction-worthy smile, then disarmed the woman and spun her to the wall before taking his next breath.

# CHAPTER FIVE

AMANDA COULD'VE KICKED herself a half-dozen times in the last fifteen minutes. But this time, she deserved it. Panic clawed through the thick fog of arousal that had drowned out the urge to run. But even as she freaked, Amanda couldn't escape this man's spell. She was thirsty for his company, and wasn't that just cause for irritation? "Asshole."

His mouth neared her ear. "I don't think that's what you wanted to say."

A full-body shiver prickled at the nape of her neck then rolled to the tips of her toes. His voice worked over her like the talented fingers of a masseuse. But it was the warmth of his whisper that made the fine hair along her back stand up like sharpened spears. "You're right."

"You know what I'm curious about?" he asked, sliding his hands down her arms.

She couldn't ignore his touch, and her goosebumps chased his strong hands. "Not really."

"I'm curious"—he skimmed his fingers up the underside of her forearms and bicep—"why you're still here."

She looked over her shoulder. "I'm pinned against the wall."

He took a step back.

She didn't move. "You have my gun."

He ejected the chambered round and released the clip. They clattered to the floor. Her nerves vibrated as if he'd stripped away her layers as easily as he'd rejected her reasons. This didn't make any sense. She had trained herself to be a machine. Never wavering, always following her strict rules. Amanda didn't take up with sexy strangers in remote hallways of construction sites any more than she would go on a date at a restaurant with someone she already vetted and knew well.

He waited for her to elaborate an explanation. The strumming beat of her pulse reached dangerous territory, and she didn't trust herself to speak. Amanda stared at the rough wall as if an answer might appear. Of course, it wouldn't. The last time she'd let a physical attraction sweep her off her feet, it'd almost killed her. Only the scars remained.

He leaned close, his chiseled face nearing her neck. "Is this game wrapping up or just getting started?"

Amanda didn't have an answer. Their tension thickened. This was insane, but she didn't care. In a careful, measured pace, Amanda lifted her arms above her head. She swore the man's breath caught. Arousal thundered in her chest, and impatient for his hands, she pressed her palms against the wall.

"You good?" He towered over her.

His question rumbled down her spine. "I'm terrified that I'm *not* terrified."

"Tell me if that changes."

She should say that she'd lost her mind; instead, she relished the new freedom. Unfettered liberty washed over her, clean and fresh and full of promise. "I'll let you know."

"Good." His powerful thigh nestled against the back of her legs, spreading her stance until he slid his foot between hers.

Heat bloomed deep in her belly. Breathless, she couldn't ignore the way his muscles pressed against her ass. Her pussy pleaded for the same attention. A long-forgotten, fevered thrill urged Amanda's back to arch.

His palms squeezed her shoulders. A shock wave of searing arousal swelled. She wanted to mewl but closed her eyes to indulge in the illicit touch. She imagined how his rough hands and herculean strength would fondle her body demanding her orgasms. A moan caught in her throat as he kneaded her neck and drifted down her spine, repeating the same noninvasive pat-down she'd given him, but with electrifying results.

He remained painfully unhurried. Her arousal spiraled, and Amanda vibrated on the edge of reckless mistake. Yet she was safe and certain that if she walked away, she'd never share an encounter as intimate and real as this.

He pulled away. "Now, we're both clear."

His voice was staggeringly unaffected. A torrent of shame twisted her stomach. Arousal had triumphed over prudence. She'd barely picked a side in their fight, preferring a fantasy. Worse, she'd defiled the reasons why she had protective limitations in the first place. Abasement gripped her thoughts and throat. She couldn't breathe. A black hole of reproach swallowed her ability to scream.

He touched her arm. "Are you okay?"

She exploded. Her elbow jerked back. The sharp angle connected with his gut, and as though she were a spectator watching, she knew what would happen next but couldn't stop. She twisted and knotted her hands into his shirt. Her knee slammed into his groin.

Violent pain exploded across his face.

"Oh, God." This wasn't his fault, but she struggled to gain control.

The man doubled over, coughing and cursing. He stumbled to the steps and collapsed.

"I'm so sorry." Tears ran down her cheeks. Damn it, she should've known better. "So sorry."

He wheezed in agony. "What the hell?"

"I didn't mean to." Though that didn't matter. Amanda pressed her hand to her throat. "I forgot how to breathe."

The man glanced up and glared, then returned to a self-soothing ritual that sounded like a dying bear.

Her legs trembled, and she reached toward him, hand shaking like she might pet his head but was too scared. "Are you okay?"

Groaning, he waved her away.

She didn't know what to do. Her guilt multiplied. "Do you need ice?"

Eternity passed. Then he laughed. "Are you serious?"

Another round of hot, embarrassed tears ran down her cheeks. "I didn't mean to do that."

Unmoved, he grunted, then uncurled himself, propping his hands on his knees like he might get sick. If he'd had a white flag to wave, he might've thrown it at her. "Game over. You win."

Amanda shrank back. "What?"

He managed a chuckle that quickly ballooned into stomach-clenching laughter.

Amanda's jaw fell. She hadn't meant to hurt the guy, but she wasn't about to watch her freak-out become his source of hilarity. "I should leave."

"Great idea." He winced and kept laughing. "The first good one either of us has had."

"It was an accident!" She wanted to disappear but couldn't shake her growing exasperation. "You're not dying."

He looked remorseful for flirting with a she-devil and tossed out a hand, half agreeing, half waving her away. "I'd rather you had shot me."

She flushed then swiped the unloaded weapon and clip. "Don't touch my gun again."

"Lesson learned, lady."

Guilt roared back. "Really, are you okay?"

"I'm not sure if I'll ever have kids …"

"Oh, God." She holstered her weapon and edged closer. "Honestly, I didn't mean for any of that to happen."

His head tilted up, and his eyes narrowed. "None of it, huh? Too bad."

"What?" She jumped back. "I thought you were dying!"

He winked, and she wanted to strangle him.

"Either way." The man pushed off the step, failing to hide a wince. "I'll survive."

He eyed the descending staircase, probably nauseous at the number of remaining floors until the ground level. Then he ran a hand over his face and returned his focus to her. The scrutiny made her feel as vulnerable as before but without the fantastic, fluttery light-headedness. "Why are you looking at me like that?"

His grin hitched. "Trying to decide if I'm going to puke or follow up on that invitation to dinner."

"*What?*" Her eyebrow twitched.

"I'm not much for games." He extended his hand like she hadn't just brought him to his knees. "But I dig puzzles."

Without thinking, she lifted her hand to his and floated when his grip swallowed hers. The handshake lingered and made her mind feel fuzzy. "I'm not a big fan of games." Their hands fell apart. "Or exchanging names."

His lips pursed as though processing what she'd said. Then he asked, "How do you feel about Majboos?"

"You're serious?" Her stomach clenched, and for a split second, the idea of a romantic dinner over spiced chicken and rice was enough for her to crawl back into his arms, where she had been safe and deliriously free. Then reality crashed her daydream. "No—I can't."

A heavy stairwell door opened and closed above them. A descending thunderclap of boots sounded a lot like Boss Man. She swallowed hard and heard the man next to her curse. Without another word, they faced the stairs and waited. Their encounter, for better or worse, had ended.

# CHAPTER SIX

HAGAN DIDN'T HAVE time to analyze the full range of the woman's reactions. He noted how she had sobered, damn well knowing who stomped their way. She knew of Parker, so why not Boss Man? Jared was the only person Hagan could think of who would be in the unfinished tower stairwell.

The bounding footsteps drew closer. He and the woman faced the stairs in strained silence as though they were waiting for a firing line.

Jared rounded the landing above them and froze. Surprise surfaced and then disappeared faster than Hagan could mutter, "Oh shit." He and the woman remained where they were like lead-lined statues. Jared's jaw ticked as he assessed them, and then without breaking the silence, he continued down the stairs until they were all on the same level.

Hagan couldn't read the situation. Jared and the woman ignored Hagan amid a silent argument. Was this a spat between spies? A lovers' quarrel? Envy pressed in Hagan's sternum. He'd never tread on another guy's girl, but hell if Hagan didn't feel a connection to this nameless woman with ninja moves.

Jared handed her a flat, dark package. She tucked it under her arm. "Thank you."

Hagan didn't care for her conciliatory tone and still didn't understand the dynamic playing out before him.

"Now that you two have met." Boss Man cracked his knuckles.

Something about the way he chose the words made Hagan uneasy. He lifted a shoulder. "Sorta."

Jared pinched the bridge of his nose. "This is a shitstorm of a headache."

Hagan raised his eyebrows. "Are we going to make legitimate introductions now?"

"*No.*" She even didn't look at Hagan.

He snorted. "Of course not."

Boss Man sighed, seemingly familiar with the woman's trust-no-one rules.

Again, a terse, unspoken conversation volleyed, pointedly leaving Hagan out. Betrayed spies? Fuck buddies? If Boss Man was the reason the woman didn't do friends or buddies, Hagan would have a tough time accepting that. Not to mention, it'd be awkward as fuck.

"All right then." Hagan had to go. He gave Jared a quick chin lift then caught the woman's stare. Her lips rolled together as her pupils flared as if she had just recalled his dinner invitation. Heat rose in his chest again. The corners of his lips quirked. "Until we meet again."

AMANDA WASN'T SURE if she was relieved or disappointed that Jared had interrupted. She hadn't wanted to look away as the handsome man meandered down the stairs, but she didn't have a choice. Jared was sizing up the situation. Could he tell that she'd swooned over a stranger in sweaty workout clothes? Jared was a human lie detector. If he asked the right questions, her answers didn't matter. He'd know something had happened—even if she didn't know what that had been.

She waited until the rhythmic slap of sneakers faded before facing Boss Man. "I didn't know the stairwell was such a happening place."

His jaw worked side to side as though he were grinding a scouring pad between his molars.

Amanda hated to be under the microscope. "Now that I know, it's another place I'll avoid."

"What the hell just happened?"

Even if she'd wanted to explain, she didn't know where to start. While Jared was a friend, he wasn't the kind of friend that she'd confess a secret to. "What does it look like? I ran into someone."

"I gathered." His eyebrow arched. "Have you changed the terms of our contract?"

"Absolutely not. I don't know a thing about that man, and I intend to keep it that way." She gestured to her tablet. "So, anyway, thanks for bringing this to me."

"Don't change the subject." He waited impatiently for her to explain.

Embarrassment warmed the back of her neck. "What do

you want me to say?"

He lifted a nonchalant shoulder. "You tell me."

She wanted to shake him. "Whoever that was—" Amanda raised a hand toward the stairs. "He remains an unknown, and yeah, I can see how a run-in with an unknown could've been a dangerous mistake. But given where we are, I realized he probably works for you—not that I want to know." The faster she spoke, the more Jared's stink-eye grew. She forced herself to slow down. "I ..."—*flirted, touched, closed my eyes and dreamed*—"had a conversation."

He smirked. "That's what you're going with?"

Her chin shot up. "That's what happened."

Jared rolled his weight back onto his heels and hummed in thought. "Well then, congratulations. Progress. One step closer to becoming a social butterfly."

Amanda balked. "Give me a break." If she weren't careful, he'd pivot from socializing to security. Though maybe he should. Her judgment was still hazy. She wouldn't have changed a thing—except the unfortunate physical attack that had nearly made the man pass out. "Can you stop looking at me like there's a mystery to solve?"

"Just wondering why you're on the defense."

Her jaw snapped shut. "You're wrong."

He chuckled. "And you're a little dramatic, kid."

Amanda clenched her jaw. "That's me, Boss Man. Wild and overdramatic."

She didn't expect him to recognize the throwback from their first conversation when he'd asked if she was the pain in the ass who'd stirred the press into a frenzy. Amanda had been bored and annoyed that she'd been forced to make a public appearance and had answered Boss Man—having no idea she'd find him to be an ally, she'd droned, "That's me. Wild and overdramatic."

Jared backed off, rubbed a hand over his face, taking a deep breath. He held it for a three-count before letting it out. "Amanda—"

"Please," she quietly implored, "drop it."

"Can't." He shook his head. "You two looked ready to fight or fuck."

"Jared!" A full-body flush burned through her. "We were just standing there."

Jared didn't counter and, given his human-lie-detecting talent, knew more of the truth than she could stomach. Amanda wanted to scream. Her fingernails curled into her palms, and she struggled to control her response. "Exactly. After passing in the stairwell, we put fucking or fighting next on our agenda."

"You've put me in a shitty position, Amanda."

"What's new?"

Tension ticked in his jaw muscles. "Fate's pushing my hand, and the fuck of it is, I don't believe in fate."

"Maybe you should see a doctor about that." Her fingernails dug into her skin. "That's what everyone tells me when—"

"Do not compare our contract that binds my nuts on goddamn introductions and pleasantries." His nostrils flared. "To what happened to you in college."

Her mouth went dry.

"There are things you need to know about people—about him—that person." Jared threw a hard glance toward the stairs. His fists curled at his sides. "It's not about your safety. It's about your sanity."

Apprehension curled down Amanda's back. It wasn't like Jared to speak in code, but then again, as he'd said, she'd tied his hands. "Sanity?"

"For lack of a better explanation, yeah."

The taciturn answer made her cagey. "What kind of clickbait bullshit is that?" She turned away. "Never mind. My sanity is fine."

"For now." With that, Jared left her clutching the tablet.

She'd made a mistake today, but it wasn't as if someone had died because of a harmless flirtation. She still had her meticulously crafted parameters that allowed her to exist in a bubble. Amanda waited until the cinder blocks and concrete stairs had dulled Jared's descent. Then, she sat on the top step and let the nameless man re-occupy her thoughts.

They'd flirted, and she'd liked it. Then she'd kneed him. Wasn't that the way every love story started?

# CHAPTER SEVEN

**TWELVE YEARS AGO**
**HOME OF THE VICE PRESIDENT**
**NUMBER ONE OBSERVATORY CIRCLE**

A MAN IN a dark suit and tie entered the far side of the circular library and approached Mandy as she sulked on the couch. He hovered. She ignored him, and when he refused to leave, she tipped her chin up and packed as much mistrust into her glare as she could manage. "Who are you?"

He didn't answer so much as he returned the smirk. She pushed aside her newly bleached hair, deciding that this guy annoyed her as much as the scent of the hair dye. Three showers and shampoos, and it still clung to her hair. Not that she'd let anyone know it was bothersome.

The man moved closer until he stood in front of the antique coffee table where she sometimes propped her feet. He sharply assessed her, then chuckled and slid his hands into his trouser pockets. "So you're the scary kid that sends grown men running?"

She rolled her eyes, then inspected her fingernails, which she'd colored with a black Sharpie marker. He didn't leave, and she planned to stare at her nails until he did or until someone else took his place, hovering by shelves of rare books.

Time ticked slower than Mr. Driech's chemistry class. Finally, she dared a quick glance. "What?"

He grinned. Not one of those professional, placating half-smiles taught to federal agents on their first day. No, this guy seemed amused.

"What?" she snapped again.

"You don't look that scary."

"Neither do you."

"It wasn't in the job description when I applied." He tilted his head with a knowing look. "But I can see why you might think that."

"Why?"

"Higgins's mustache?" He pretended to recoil. "Looks like a swamp thing lives on his face."

*Exactly!* Mandy had never been able to pinpoint why Higgins creeped her out, but this guy had nailed it. Not that she'd let him know.

"It'd help if he cut the thing back," the agent continued. "It'd make him look more like a spook from the eighties and less like a monster."

Mandy snickered. "Especially with that trench coat he likes to wear."

"Yeah, where did he find that thing?"

She caught herself from laughing and stared into her lap until she could keep a straight face, then eyed the new agent. He was younger and far more casual than the standard security detail assigned to the second family's detail, but she didn't trust him or the charade.

The corners of his lips twitched. "I don't recall your profile details including bleach blonde hair."

Mandy scowled, irritated at how quickly the agent had pivoted to her latest scandal. "Call the NSA and Homeland Security. Someone's slacking."

"Nah." He shrugged. "They're probably on it already."

She almost smiled, caught herself, and scowled again. His lack of a stiff upper lip made her wary.

"Do you mind if I take a seat?" Without waiting for an answer, the agent rounded the coffee table and sat down next to her on the couch. His gaze dropped to the style section of yesterday's newspaper folded between them. "They're relentless, aren't they?"

Relentless? That wasn't a good enough description if he was referring to the adults who made a living off of her misery. She'd describe them more as obsessed, nosy liars, but that was too kind, or maybe the agent meant the students at her school. The so-called friends and the classmates she'd never spoken to who provided anonymous anecdotes about her high school life. Angry tears caught at the back of her throat. Mandy clamped her molars together until the well of emotion peaked, then she bitterly added, "What would you know about that?"

"Not much," he admitted. "My family is the epitome of boring."

"Must be nice." Her family fascinated the world. Chatterboxes and rumormongers had rejoiced when a pretty-faced young couple and their gangly, awkward kid moved into the political limelight.

The agent picked up the newspaper, perused one side, flipped it over, then whistled. "This is brutal, Sparkler."

She didn't have to ask him which part, because she'd memorized every word before she walked into school yesterday. By the time Mandy had walked into homeroom, the few friends that she trusted had offered her pitying platitudes. The rest of her classmates had failed to hide their giggles.

> *With another breakout of teenage hormones, Mandy Hearst was seen at the pharmacy near school perusing zit creams. She left with a tube of Clearasil, a Hershey bar, and a high-end bottle of watermelon-flavored water.*
>
> *The newly-minted Second Daughter wore a school uniform of a khaki skirt and polo shirt emblazoned with the high school's coat of arms. Her typically unruly dark brown hair looked to be tangled more than usual and was secured into a low ponytail.*
>
> *Ms. Hearst's classmates reported that her hair debacle started in PE class while playing capture the flag when she tripped. Not known for her athletic prowess or gracefulness, the knobby-kneed teenager still managed to assist a classmate in a flag-capturing play.*
>
> *As always, we have omitted the name of Ms. Hearst's school and relevant locations to protect her privacy. In other style and entertainment news, celebrity chefs partnered with the A-List cast of ...*

Mandy didn't waste her time guessing which classmates had developed relationships with reporters. "I guess they'll have to take mention of my dark hair out of the newsroom rotation."

He leaned back against the sofa, then tossed the newspaper onto the coffee table that was a priceless gift from the English Monarch. At least, that's what her mother had said as if it had sat in Sir Isaac Newton's personal study.

"That's an antique," she pointed out.

"I'm sure you care." He leaned back. "Is that why you bleached your hair?"

Mandy lifted a shoulder. "I don't know."

"It's more interesting than a zit," he said.

Her jaw dropped, and she gaped at him. "That's rude."

"You should cut it short and wear makeup that'd match your nails. That'd be interesting." He held out his hands to frame an invisible headline. "Second Daughter gone punk rock." He chuckled. "Though I'm probably out of a job if you tell your mother that was my suggestion."

She could picture the headline as well as her parents' reaction and almost smiled, but the agent wasn't serious. "What would you have done if you were me?"

"Instead of bleaching my hair?" he asked.

She tugged her hair over her face and fidgeted. "Yeah."

He hummed as though giving her question serious thought. She had to commend his acting skills. It was more than she got out of the Vice President's office, the White House communications staff, or her mother's chief of staff when she complained. Everyone told her to ignore it. That was impossible when *it* encompassed everything in her life. Political pundits discussed puberty. Pseudo-psychologists offered unsolicited advice on raising teenagers in the public eye. Stylists suggested ways to make her uniform hipper. No one debated whether she'd signed up for this life.

"You could rip your braces off." She opened her mouth as wide as the rubber bands would let her and waited until he acknowledged the railroad tracks cemented to her teeth.

Unimpressed, he rolled his wrist like she should keep trying.

She closed her mouth and tried another tactic. "You could hike your skirt up." She waited for his discomfort level to rise. "Or go with everyone's favorite suggestion, buy a padded bra."

Undaunted, he hummed again as he thought. "I wouldn't stuff my bra. I don't think it would flatter my hips."

She couldn't help it. That time, she laughed. "I don't know if it works that way."

"Yeah, I don't know shit," he admitted.

A comfortable silence fell between them. He pulled out his phone—a definite no-no when on vice presidential babysitting duty—scrolled, then cracked up. She tilted to see what was so funny. The agent repositioned the screen. For the next five minutes, they laughed at clips of dogs.

A staffer walked into the library and stopped short. "I'm sure," she said with a heavy dose of distaste, "there is a more comfortable place upstairs for you to spend your free time."

"We're pretty comfortable here," the agent said. "But thanks for the suggestion."

The woman harrumphed and theatrically retrieved the

discarded newspaper from the coffee table. "Please don't put anything on the table again."

After they were alone again, Mandy turned her attention onto the agent. "I can't believe you said that."

"You warned me about the table." He shrugged. "Guess I should've known."

The corners of her lips quirked. "So you're the new guy?"

He nodded. "Yup."

"I don't know if you've been told." She picked at her cuticle. "But no one wants this detail."

"I've been warned about that, too." He put the phone down, then ticked off on his fingers as he said, "You cut school, ditch details, and somehow bleached your hair when no one was lording over you."

"And I'm just getting started," she warned.

He chuckled. "I'll tell you a secret."

Oh, joy. This was the moment when he became like every other agent. Maybe he'd regale her with tales about his adventurous youth or teenage angst or promise that nothing she could do would shock him. "What?"

"I've got a hundred bucks riding on whether or not I make it as your primary detail for more than a month."

Her eyes bulged. "You bet on me?"

"I'll split it with you fifty-fifty if we make it to day thirty-one."

Was he genuinely this chill, or had the Secret Service partnered with FBI profilers to determine a new way to handle her? "Double or nothing, you won't last the week."

He stuck out his hand. "Shake on it."

Mandy eyed him, waiting for the usual curl of dread that always arrived over the last few weeks when she saw her new bedroom, read the new rules, or met her new lead security detail. It didn't come. She didn't trust him yet and probably never would. But at least she could have some fun. Their hands clasped. "Bet."

# CHAPTER EIGHT

**PRESENT DAY
ABU DHABI, UAE**

WALKING DOWN THE stairs had been every bit as uncomfortable as Hagan had assumed it would be. Still, that balls-aching, depleted-muscle soreness didn't keep his red-blooded mind from wandering to the unknown woman. He wasn't one to search for hidden meanings in straightforward conversations, but he was curious. It was as though she had a list of archaic rules that kept her from society. Though not away from Jared. That realization bothered Hagan most of all.

He finally reached the final stretch of stairs, and a nagging sense of a missed opportunity made his spirit feel as heavy as his body. What would've happened if Boss Man hadn't interrupted? Maybe Hagan would've learned if she was a fan of Majboos.

Hagan was resting his hand on the heavy door's push bar when he heard Jared hustling down the stairs. Boss Man always hauled ass, but Hagan knew this time he wanted to catch up. He groaned and clutched the metal bar, considering if he had the energy to evade his boss. Even if he did, Hagan would rather get their conversation over with. Dutifully, he turned and waited.

Jared rounded from the staircase above, caught sight of Hagan, and slowed his roll. "You don't even know what you stumbled into, do you?"

"Guess not." Hagan leaned against the wall. "Just thought today would be a good day to run the stairs."

"Got that wrong, didn't you." Jared pushed open the door. "Come on."

Hagan followed into the unfinished first-floor lobby. The sub-flooring muffled their steps so that their heavy steps didn't make a sound. Jared stopped at the skeletal remnants of an old registration desk. A sense of foreboding made Hagan feel as exposed as the renovation site.

Jared rubbed a hand over his face. His lips pinched together as if he didn't like what he had to say. "Stay away from her. You see her, you turn the other direction. She walks into the stairwell, you walk out. She says hello, you don't even say goodbye. Do you read me?"

Hagan's scalp prickled. He wasn't sure what he'd expected from Jared, but that hadn't been it.

Jared moved into Hagan's personal space and growled. "Do you read me?"

He feigned nonchalance, unsure if a territorial urge or dehydration was the source of his growing irritation. Jared's face didn't show the hint of a joke. If anything, Hagan hadn't seen his boss this serious outside of a war room. Hagan leaned into the conversation. "That might be a problem."

Jared's jaw twitched. "And why the fuck might that be a

problem?"

"Because I'm taking her to dinner."

Boss Man blanched, then turned an unhealthy shade of pissed off. "Does she know that?"

"Technically—"

"Hagan," Jared managed. "This is above your pay grade. Stay away from her."

"Until when?"

Boss Man looked like a volcano ready to erupt. A vein pulsed on his forehead. "Until forever, until I say different. Until there's a damn good reason for you to see her again—and there won't be, so until *never*."

There wasn't a reason to pick a battle with his boss. Hagan needed this job. It paid better than he could have ever hoped, and his family needed that kind of cash. He liked his teammates and the work. Hell, he'd never been the asshole to escalate an argument over a woman. Not until today.

Still, Hagan couldn't force himself to back up and say okay. His fists curled as though they might go to blows.

Then Jared jerked back. He stuck a finger out instead of taking a swing. "Stay away from her." He jabbed his hand. "There are a million fish in the sea. Find any of them but her."

Jared rubbed his temples like the mother of all headaches had crawled up his ass and taken residence behind his eyes. Then, without another word, he left.

Hagan stared at the construction exit, speechless. Then, like a bad habit, he wondered where the woman had gone. There were several ways to leave. If she stepped into the lobby, would Hagan follow orders and ignore her?

He didn't know and waited to find out. Still, she was a no show. Too damn bad. Despite the crotch shot, she had been the highlight of his day.

# CHAPTER NINE

AMANDA WANDERED TO the closest skybridge and crossed into tower one, then took the freight elevator to the fifth floor. She figured no one from Titan would be on that floor. After all, one day, it would serve guests who didn't need armored safehouse suites or SCIF-level conference rooms.

From there, she used a back stairwell and slipped out of the building, checked her surroundings, and eased into the steady stream of foot traffic, keeping a vigilant eye out for problems.

Two city blocks later, she took an easygoing breath and ducked down an alleyway between two imposing skyscrapers. She swiped a pass and let herself into the hotel she called home.

Amanda entered and moved through the service corridor until she could access the hotel's marbled lobby. Cool, jasmine-scented air conditioning met her as she walked toward the elevators. The hotel catered to traveling mid-level business-people and families on vacation. It offered luxury without the type of clientele that would increase its security risk.

Once behind her hotel room door, she fastened the deadbolt and leaned against the wall. The day caught up with her at once, and Amanda slid to her bottom. Her focus softened until her eyes slipped shut, completely exhausted.

Still, as tired as she was, her thoughts slipped back to the mystery man and his brilliant eyes. The way he had watched her and whispered and made her feel alive. They'd been so close. So inappropriate. Amanda shivered, then shook her head like it had been a dream she needed to forget. But the man stayed in her thoughts, turning her insides to jelly. She recalled his raw, masculine power and the way he'd towered over her with the hint of a devilish grin. Her stomach flipped, and just that quickly, she recoiled at the memories from the last time she'd let her guard down. Amanda slapped her hands over her face. "Don't be stupid again."

The rules were there for a reason. Amanda pulled herself off the floor, searching for a distraction when her cell phone rang. *Small miracle.* She placed her tablet on the entryway table, then removed her gun and the concealed carry holster from under her shirt, wondering if the man had known what was wrapped around her abdomen. Like athletic wear that packed heat, it held her cell phone and hid her scars. She didn't leave home without it.

Amanda checked the incoming call, and the distraction she'd been searching waited for her to answer. She answered the call from her office. "This is perfect timing."

"What's wrong?" Halle asked.

"Nothing." The tight answer would do little to convince Halle to move on. Amanda inhaled slowly and let it out as she stared out the window and took in Abu Dhabi's surreal sunset. "I haven't had dinner yet."

"Hangry..." Halle seemed to accept the explanation.

"Hang on a second." She popped her Bluetooth earbuds in, then headed into the kitchenette. "Can you hear me?"

"Yeah—but you still sound off. Are you sure everything's okay?"

Amanda and Halle spent more time discussing projects than anything else. Relationships never came up. Halle was in a long-distance relationship that seemed about as exciting as watching concrete set. Shoptalk was their safe zone and the basis of their friendship, just as schoolwork had been when they attended college. "Jared was testy over the punch list."

"That man scares me." Halle laughed.

"Harmless as a puppy." Amanda grinned. "Unless you tell him I said that." She opened the small refrigerator and perused her options for making a quick meal, deciding on pasta leftovers. She tossed it with butter and Parmesan cheese and popped the bowl into the microwave. "What's new at the office?"

Halle groaned. "Shah argued with his computer all day and drove me crazy."

"So nothing new." The microwave beeped. She removed the dish and topped it with butter and cheese. Not a very exciting meal—but it was safer than Majboos with the mystery man. Her stomach fluttered. Had anyone asked her on a date like that before? *No.* A slow smile built that left her grinning and daydreaming. He'd been earnest and funny—laughing had made her like him all the more.

"Amanda?" Halle called. "Are you there?"

She pressed a hand to her throat. Her pulse jumped hurdles against her touch. "Sorry. Yeah, I'm here."

Halle explained that they'd won a competitive proposal. Amanda lowered herself onto a barstool and ate as she listened. A bank wanted a new security system. A famous horse breeder needed to upgrade a surveillance system that monitored rolling bluegrass pastures. Most of their jobs weren't megaprojects like Titan Group's hotel. Even with a Rolodex of interesting clients, Amanda had never interacted with anyone outside the contract's stipulation. Did that make her world small and sad?

She finished her dinner, questioning what the man had asked of her versus what she'd always believed. Her world was as safe as the rest of the world as long as she stayed away.

Halle finished, and they ended the call. The walls seemed to squeeze closer, and the beautiful hanging tapestries dulled. Living in a hotel room had never felt lonely before. Amanda was anonymous and hidden away. Except, right now, somber loneliness numbed her outlook.

She pulled her earbuds free and tossed them onto the counter. They skittered over the granite. One plopped into the sink, splashing into a glass of water as her cell phone rang again. "Shoot." She fished the bud out, then grabbed her phone with a wet, soapy hand. The caller ID read White House Switchboard. Thank God. Amanda answered on the fourth ring. "Mom?"

"Hi, sweet pea. Good time?"

"Sure." She wiped her hand on her pants. "But can you give me a sec?" She reached into a cabinet but dropped the phone. "Sorry, Mom! Hang on." Amanda wanted to save her pricey earbud and grabbed a box of boil-in-a-bag rice. Did it matter if the rice had been parboiled? Without another option, she tore it open over a bowl. Rice spilled everywhere but where it was supposed to go. "One more second," she shouted toward the floor, then swiped enough rice into the bowl to cover her earbud. Unsure if that'd work, she slumped, then remembered her mom and picked up the phone. "Sorry, I dropped you."

Her mother had been humming as she waited. "Must've been a long fall."

"Ha, ha, ha." Amanda swept rogue pieces of rice into the sink. "I bought new earbuds and then dropped one into a cup of water."

"Why would you do that?"

She rolled her eyes. "I didn't mean to."

Mom hummed again but sounded like she was wondering about life's meaning.

"What, Mom?"

"You're usually so…careful."

"It was an accident."

"I gathered that," Mom said. "Is everything okay?"

"Why do people keep asking me that—never mind." Amanda pinched the bridge of her nose. "I put it in rice. Maybe that will dry it out."

"Submerged electronics never come back from the dead."

"Don't use your professor voice on me." Amanda thumped her head against the wall that separated the kitchenette from the foyer. "I can't handle it tonight."

"What's wrong?"

If Amanda could've told her teenage self how close she'd grow to her parents, she'd have passed out. Funny how that had changed, and she hadn't realized it until now. "Jared Westin wants me to make a friend."

"Oh, the horror. That cruel, cruel man does such mean things to you."

*"Mom."*

"Halle's a friend who has never left your side, and, not for nothing, your dad was my friend before he swept me off my feet and into bed."

"Can we avoid that visual, please?"

"Jared will always have your best interest at heart. Give him a chance and try."

"I think that maybe, I sorta tried." Amanda squeezed her eyes shut and thumped her forehead against the wall again. "It didn't go well."

"Nothing's ever perfect the first time."

"It was a guy." She waited, unsure if her mom hadn't heard her or if she'd shocked the woman into an early grave. "Mom?"

"I'm here, honey." She faltered. "I think that's great news, and when a guy's involved, nothing ever goes exactly the way we hope. No matter what rules or contracts or—"

"I kicked him between the legs."

"Oh…was he pressuring you to—"

"No!" *Oh God.* Maybe she shouldn't have broached this landmine over the phone. "We were…" She gestured for a mom-appropriate description that wouldn't trigger a conversation about hormones and nuclear reactions. "Talking. I just freaked out and kneed him in the 'nads."

"The 'nads," Mom repeated.

"Do you know how much *The Washington Daily* would pay to hear the First Lady say that?" Amanda muttered.

"At least I know you were listening when I taught you the proper names for body parts." Mom laughed. "But honey, it's *go*nads."

"Okay!" She blushed. "Thanks for the reminder."

The laughter over the phone line quieted. "Will you see this gentleman again?"

"What? No!"

Mom hummed. "You can't go on a second date if you never see him for a first."

"I can't."

"You can do whatever you're ready for," Mom said. "Just remember that one day I would like grandchildren."

Amanda rolled her eyes. "It has nothing to do with what I'm ready for or what I want. It's—you know this—I can't." The back of her throat ached. "It's not safe for anyone." She bit her lip. "Can we forget I brought it up?"

Mom sighed, then yielded. "All right. A conversation for another day."

She played with the bowl of rice, swishing it over the earbud. "Thanks."

"Other than torturing you, how's Jared doing?"

Amanda half-laughed. "Oh, ya know. Snarling and growling his way through the day."

"Sounds like he's doing well."

She grinned and nodded. "The project is coming along nicely."

"Terrific. You know, your dad wants to visit."

"Please don't." Her parents' annoying habit of surprise visits always occurred at the worst moments. What if they'd waltzed into the stairwell with Jared? She'd have died on the spot. "I'll come home and visit soon."

"He wants to see your work," Mom added.

Amanda rolled her eyes. "No, he wants to play with Titan's toys."

"That, too—honey, I need to take this call."

The call ended, leaving her alone in the luxury suite. She turned toward her makeshift workstation that overlooked the city, but her work didn't lure her from the kitchenette. Amanda shook the bowl and uncovered her earbud. She tried to connect the Bluetooth to her phone, then tossed it aside. "I won't be able to save my earbud."

The empty room felt smaller than before. Her thoughts drifted to the mystery man again. She couldn't stay here, stewing in her companionless night like this hadn't been a decision she'd made. Amanda grabbed a headscarf and handgun, found her swipe card, and shoved it in with her cell phone. She'd replace her earbuds and be surrounded by strangers. Much better than sitting alone, wondering what might've been if she were someone else. At least tonight she could pretend.

# CHAPTER TEN

**TEN YEARS AGO
THE WHITE HOUSE**

MANDY SLUMPED AT the family dining room table and pouted. "It's not fair." She hadn't expected her request to be an instant slam-dunk, but at the very least, she'd expected her parents to hear her out. Wasn't that what the newest leader of the free world was supposed to do? Diplomatically listen and find a compromise.

Dad speared a slice of his roast beef with his fork, then offered the understanding look that had coaxed their nation through their grief. "Life's not fair."

If he had said that to the cameras after President Doddery's heart attack, the press would have called him heartless, which was how he was acting toward Mandy right now. "You don't understand."

"I do, kiddo."

She gripped the edge of the table so hard that the flesh around her purple metallic fingernail polish started to match. "There is literally no one on Earth that I want to meet more."

Dad swallowed his food. "You mentioned that."

Mom and Dad continued their meal as if the discussion

ended, *sine die*. "This isn't Congress," Mandy pointed out. "We're not just done talking."

"We are, sweet pea." Mom eyed Mandy as though she were one of her college students whispering too loud during a lecture. "It's time to move on."

"No." She stomped under the table. "I didn't ask to meet the German Chancellor or Stanley Cup guys—"

"Come on, kiddo," Dad tried. "Who doesn't want to meet the Capitals?"

*"Dad."* He wasn't being rational, and she wasn't a kid. Mandy turned to her mom. "I know you understand, don't you?"

"You have an exam," Mom said simply, like that stupid fact hadn't been shared a dozen times.

"I always have exams, and I will be miserable for the rest of my life!"

"I get it. I really do." Mom set her fork down. "But it's time to think like a proton and stay positive—"

"Do not tell me some stupid science teacher joke!" Mandy pushed away from the table as tears stung the back of her eyes. "I didn't ask to be in this family. I didn't ask to move from one stupid house into the next, or to go to that stupid school. I never asked for any of this!" Tears streamed down her cheeks. She mopped them away, smearing dark eyeliner and mascara onto her knuckles. "My absolute favorite singer in the entire world will be here, and I can't even stay home for the stupid luncheon to say hello."

Dad turned to Mom. "Any good news from the clinical

trials you're overseeing?"

"Nothing new, but we're still hopeful." Mom took another bite, then swallowed. "Either way, it's great experience for the Ph.D. candidates."

"You care more about them than me," Mandy shouted, feeling six instead of sixteen.

"Mandy," Mom said softly. "Sit down—"

She ran from the dining room and up the stairs. They were so stubborn! Maybe she should've kept her school uniform on for dinner instead of changing into the torn jean skirt, black shirt, and Doc Martens. The boots never seemed to make conversations with her parents any easier. Or perhaps she shouldn't have let them learn about her new eyebrow piercing through a tabloid the previous week.

She pulled her cell phone from the back pocket of her skirt and was storming down the center hall when a text message popped on the screen.

*Some people are meeting at Jaime's. You should come.*

Drink glass emojis trailed off the screen of her notification.

Amanda stopped next to a grand piano and swiped the message open. Tears swelled in her eyes again as she reread the message. Her friends would have fun tonight. They'd drink. They'd flirt with guys. Maybe they'd do more. But like always, Amanda would be at home, surrounded by books, art, and fancy things she wasn't allowed to touch.

*Not tonight.* She would join her friends. She'd be someone else. A normal teenager.

Easier said than done, though. Surveillance didn't track the family through the residence, though the Secret Service kept tabs. After stopping by her bedroom to fix her makeup, she set off to escape.

Mandy hadn't made it to the first floor before Agent McNally fell into line behind her. She didn't exactly have a plan and decided the best course of action was simple bullheaded determination. She walked through the halls as if there weren't an agent trailing behind. They weren't her babysitters and couldn't tell her what to do. Their jobs were simple: ward off the bad guys who thought that killing the First Daughter might send a political message.

Mandy stepped by the Marine who stood at the exterior door, then hurried onto the portico drive. An exhilarating rush tingled down her arms. Freedom had never been this easy.

She reached the north gate. The agent behind the bulletproof glass had obviously been alerted of her arrival. Unlike the Marine by the door, he didn't act like a statue, and Mandy didn't miss his semi-impassive expression that jumped to McNally. "Good evening, Ms. Hearst."

"Good evening." She tried for a casual smile, then eyed the still-locked gate. Another second crawled by. "I'm going for a walk." Her stomach tied in knots. Had her parents been informed? She'd die of embarrassment if orders were given to keep her inside the grounds. She focused on the gate, willing it to fly off the hinges—the locking mechanism released. *Victory!* She could hardly breathe. "Thanks."

With false bravado and a wild rush of adrenaline, she

stepped into the real world. A small group of tourists gawked from the sidewalk across from Lafayette Park. A businessman on his phone stumbled off the curb. Suddenly, Mandy realized how not in control she was. Just like always.

"Mandy." McNally stepped toward her side. "Let's head back and take a walk on the grounds."

Mandy glanced toward the East Wing. She didn't know how many snipers were stationed on the roof, but she was certain her unplanned stroll had caused them to reposition. Her cell phone buzzed, and she checked the text message instead of looking at the agent in the eye.

Pictures of her friends—*her crush*—scrolled onto her phone. Only one word accompanied the text.

*Coming?*

A light flashed. Mandy jerked from her phone. Agent McNally held up her hands to block a man taking her picture. "Give the kid her privacy."

Mandy snorted. As if that could ever happen. She strode down Pennsylvania Avenue without a clue of how to get to Jaime's house. First, she'd have to catch a taxi. She eyed 15th Street like it might be her salvation.

"*Mandy.*" McNally's Mama Bear tone warned her not to take her newfound freedom too far.

She glanced over her shoulder. Another handful of agents had arrived, warily watching Mandy as though she were a ticking time bomb. She swallowed hard and tried to play it cool. "You're welcome to come with me."

"Give us a few minutes to make arrangements."

Mandy closed her eyes, not sure if she would cry or scream. Her Doc Martens anchored her to the sidewalk. "I don't want anyone to make arrangements." She stared at the smooth, worn sidewalk, whispering, "I want to disappear."

"Mandy!" a child called. "Can we have a picture?"

She wrangled her emotions, nodded to McNally, and forced herself to smile. Two girls ran to her side. Their mother thanked Mandy before, during, and after she snapped the picture. After a moment of polite small talk, Mandy turned to see Dylan jogging their way. "Wow," she muttered. "They've called in for reinforcements."

"Hey, Sparkler." He reached her side and urged her to keep moving. "Where are we headed?"

She dragged her feet and eyed his street clothes. She'd never seen him off duty before. A light sheen of sweat peppered his temples, and she snorted. He must've run from wherever he'd been. She pictured him grabbing a beer with friends, or maybe just doing something totally, amazingly dull.

Dylan repeated his question.

"Nowhere," she mumbled.

"Obviously." He picked up the pace, then glanced over his shoulder. "You coming?"

She caught up—otherwise, someone might have scrambled F14s or swooped in with a Black Hawk to keep an eye on where she went. She and Dylan pretended they didn't notice gawking passersby as they crossed toward New York Avenue. "I wish I was someone else."

The light changed to yellow, and a crosswalk warning chirped. "Nah."

"I'm serious."

"Fine." Dylan held out his arm to block her from someone waiting for their turn at an ATM. "Who do you wish you were?"

"Someone who could just leave her house without the circus act."

He guided her around a happy hour that had gone late and spilled onto the walkway. "That's not a different person. That's different circumstances." He stopped at the corner. "I heard you can't miss your exam."

Her fingers curled into fists. "If Dad is supposed to negotiate peace treaties, he should be able to find a way—" Tears burned her throat. Her chin dropped. "I mean…" She gestured to a small group who watched as though she were a soap opera. "If I have to put up with all of this, then I should at least get to do the fun stuff."

Dylan nodded. "It sucks."

"And I want to go to my friend's house."

"I feel ya." He nodded again, then ushered her across the street. "Are you done complaining yet?"

"Hey!" She whirled on him. "You're supposed to take up for me."

"No, I'm supposed to keep you safe. Running off like this puts your life, my life"—he tossed his thumb over his shoulder to McNally and whoever else had followed them—"and their lives in danger. You know that."

Her ears burned, and she shuffled her feet. "I walked."

Dylan rolled his eyes. "I like it better when you pierce something or dye your hair. Makes the job more interesting."

Mandy bit her lip as embarrassment made way for an exhausting wave of guilt. "Let's get tattoos."

"That's the spirit." Dylan laughed and turned them back toward home. "Or, let's skip the tattoo and raid the kitchen for ice cream. You can figure out who you'd rather be another day."

# CHAPTER ELEVEN

**PRESENT DAY**
**ABU DHABI, UAE**

NEON LIGHTS DECORATED the entrance of an otherwise boring stucco building, turning an everyday shopping experience into something that only the United Emirates could have dreamed up. Well, the UAE or Las Vegas, though, Hagan could appreciate the difference between LuLu's Hypermarket and the Vegas strip.

He crossed the parking lot with his teammates, and they strolled into the megamart like a pack of prowling animals, each with their own agendas. Liam would always purchase diapers and fresh fruit for his wife's smoothies. Chance would search out specific cuts of meat to cook for his wife. Without fail, Sawyer and Camden would complain that they couldn't purchase a six-pack of beer and then fill their arms with energy drinks, jerky, and junk food. Hagan's grocery shopping habits leaned closer toward bachelor purchases, either way, their group was nothing, if not predictable shoppers.

They followed their usual routines. Liam and Chance secured shopping carts and left for the produce section. Camden hooked a bag of salted potato grills off of a sale display and then followed Sawyer toward the soft drink aisle. Hagan didn't need anything in particular except to see a different four walls. If he'd stayed home, he wouldn't have been able to ignore his questions about the gorgeous woman and Jared's warning.

Hagan nabbed a basket trailing Liam and Chance in the produce section. There had been a familiarity about that woman Hagan couldn't shake, but he still couldn't place her. Mindlessly, he grabbed a papaya and a sack of mandarin oranges. Even if Hagan could recall the woman, that didn't account for Jared's reaction.

"Hey, man," Chance called.

Hagan realized both men had been watching him blankly stare into the fruit. "What's up?"

A worry line pinched across Liam's forehead. "You're looking pretty serious over that citrus."

He tried to relax. "Big decisions, I guess." When they didn't loosen up, he added, "Long day. That's all."

"Right." Chance maneuvered his cart to the side and let another shopper pass.

A long day was the truth. Maybe not in the way their team might normally pull in a long day, but he was mentally exhausted. Not to mention, his groin was still sore.

Chance and Liam picked up a conversation, debating a trade in a fantasy sports league. Hagan realized he didn't need anything else from the produce section—or any other grocery aisles. He wandered away and let the lure of big-screen TVs pull him deeper into the store.

LuLu's Hypermarket reminded him of a Walmart Supercenter. It had food, plus everything else. The overhead speaker alternated announcements in several languages, notifying customers of freshly cubed Australian lamb, free trials of their home delivery service, and a sale on small appliances.

Even at this hour, the store had a steady flow of foot traffic with an eclectic crowd. Hagan spied Sawyer and Camden in the video game aisle with their items piled by their feet. Neither noticed him approach as they played the Nintendo Switch on display.

Camden pitched forward as though trying to assist the game controller with his physical willpower, then noticed Hagan. "Hey, man, you want in?"

Mindless gaming would probably be a good idea, but a restless urge needled his gut. "Nah."

"Suit yourself." Sawyer smashed the controller buttons.

Hagan watched for another minute and then left. Nothing caught his eye. Aimlessly, he turned into the next aisle stepping around a salesclerk stocking shelves, next to a scarfed woman studying the back of a box.

The display sign gave him pause. *Bluetooth for Bouncing Sports.* He smiled, and if the lady and the salesclerk hadn't been in the way, Hagan would've taken a picture for his sister. Roxana enjoyed the English translations that were unfamiliar to her, like 'sweet water' for soda and 'light' instead of diet.

Hagan pulled out his phone and waited for the woman to move, typing a message to his sister. *What the hell are Bouncing Sports?*

Neither the clerk nor the woman got out of his way. His

index finger tapped along the side of his phone. Hagan selected a box of earbuds from the shelf and mused over the possibilities listed in the product description. He skipped the Arabic and read the accompanying English summary.

*For exercise workout regimens such as running or outdoor training. Resists sweat and rain. Perfect to achieve athletic goals!*

Unwilling to wait any longer to photograph the display sign, he snapped a picture of the box, sent it to Roxana, and returned the earbuds to the shelf as the woman turned to her cart. Their eyes clashed, and the hair on his arms stood on end. Hell, every part of his body jumped to attention. Pinpricks of lust curled down his spine. A thousand questions came to mind. "Twice in one day…"

She dropped the box into her cart and gripped its metal frame. "Did you follow me?"

His head cocked. "Are you serious?" Apparently, she was. He studied the scarf draped over her head and her clothes from earlier, and it struck him again that she wanted to blend in and hide. A woman like that would have to do a lot more to dull her shine than simply cover up.

He soaked in the appeal of her pink lips. Their irresistible fullness made him weak in the knees. Her mouth seemed soft and sweet, like he could brush his lips against hers for hours.

But she wasn't drinking him in as well, and without the threat of a staircase showdown, he could see that she didn't miss anything. To hell with what she saw in him, what was she looking for? Her eyes were the darkest shade of espresso, not quite black and not quite brown. And just like the shot, he saw her as strong and robust. Bitter without the bite. Almost too hot to handle, but without the cliché of knowing it.

His chest tightened, and he wanted to know what made this lady tick. "We should exchange names."

For the second time in one day, he extended his hand.

She jerked the cart back.

"Or not." His hand dropped, and he waited for her to leave. She didn't, almost skittish as she inched to where she had been. "You're kind of jumpy to be in this line of work, aren't you?"

Her lips pinched. Their natural color paled. "What do you think I do? Wait. Never mind." She lifted her hand to stop his guesses. "Don't answer that. I don't want to know."

Hagan laughed. "I think you do."

She rolled her eyes but flushed. "I think you're wrong."

"Nah." He gave a semi-apologetic lift of his shoulders, unable to hide his grin. "I don't think so."

She fidgeted, as though she didn't know what to do next. Stay and talk? Run for her life?

He hazarded a step closer. The anticipation of what could be hit him like a bolt of lightning. "I guess we all have our secrets."

Her chin lifted defiantly. "You don't have secrets."

"You don't say?"

"Not the kind that matter," she challenged.

He crossed his arms but let his lips curl. "That's a little judgmental."

Stress tightened at the corners of her eyes. "You're too alive to have secrets like mine."

"Trust me, lady." He inched closer again. "You seem alive to me." He recalled the way his palms had slid over her warm curves; certain her mind had also slipped to their previous interaction. *"Very* alive."

Her pupils flared.

"The truth is," he added quietly, "I don't have any secrets, and I don't care about yours."

The salesclerk turned from his tedious shelf-stocking task, and suddenly Hagan remembered that they weren't alone. The overhead lights glared. Store announcements loudly grated over his senses. She yanked her shopping cart to face the opposite direction.

His pulse picked up. There was no telling if they'd cross paths again. "Not even a goodbye?"

He expected her to storm off and watched her knee carefully. But she simply stared into the cart and let her scarf obscure any facial expressions. An urge to move to her side nearly won out, but he forced himself to remain still. "If you're hiding from someone, I'm not that person."

The salesclerk looked between them and apparently decided it would be a good time for him to leave. Hagan waited until the man disappeared before stepping closer. "I'm not a threat. But if you're hiding from someone—"

Her shoulders squared. "I'm not hiding," she snapped. "I don't hide."

"Okay." He lifted his palms in surrender. "Just like you don't say goodbye or have friends."

"I operate within the boundary of specific restrictions."

"Yeah, that definitely doesn't sound like you're hiding."

"And," she continued, "even if I didn't abide by those rules, I wouldn't say goodbye to a stranger when I walk away."

"We're not strangers." The corners of his lips twitched. "We almost got to second base."

Her lips parted with a gasp that went straight to his groin. "I don't know you."

"You must've had one hell of a day not to remember pulling a gun on me." He inclined his head. "And we can't forget that little incident that may cost me my future children—"

Her cheeks flamed. "All right. We're not strangers."

"Glad we agree." He waited for her to storm off. For every second she remained, his confusion multiplied.

She rubbed a hand over her face, quietly laughing. "You're driving me crazy."

"Glad I'm not the only one feeling that way right now."

Her fingers pressed to the base of her throat as her lips parted, unintentionally setting his insides on fire as if his blood had turned to lava. Invisible sparks crackled. The air seemed heavy and hot. "Give me a straight answer about dinner."

She blinked hard and stumbled back, as though he'd shaken her from a dream.

"And don't tell me 'I can't'." He took a step closer. "Yes or no: I want to get to know you, and I want to take you out." He tried to get a read on her and had no idea what she'd say. "Would you like to have dinner with me this weekend?"

She licked her bottom lip, and for a half-second, his ego

readied for a swift shutdown. But she didn't say anything, as if she couldn't.

He had to look away, rubbing a hand over his face.

"I…" Her brow furrowed. "Well…"

*Hell,* he didn't want to make her squirm. "Wait. Different question." He changed tactics. "How about…do you *want* to go to dinner with me?"

She grinned, and Hagan almost threw his arms into the air. But then he saw the moment she pulled back. The sparkle in her eyes dulled, and her warm smile seemed a burden to hold in place. Something hummed in his chest. "I'll meet you again in the stairwell," he suggested with a laugh. "This time, I'll have showered and will bring food."

Her eyes softened. "Really?"

"Sure." He lifted his shoulders—then his skin went cold. Her bottom lip trembled, and he worried she might cry. "Are you okay?"

Her spine straightened. She reached for her shopping cart like it might roll away. "I have to go."

With a white-knuckled grip, she shoved off. Blindsided disappointment crashed over him.

She stopped abruptly and turned. "Have a good night." Tension pinched in her words, as if she'd forced each syllable out. She offered a small, painfully cute wave. "Goodbye."

Her struggle was painful to watch. Why the hell couldn't she hold a conversation or make a friend? Hagan balled his hands and shoved them into his pockets. "Are you okay?

"I appreciate what you said and the invitation—" Her voice

wavered.

"Seriously." The back of his neck tingled. "Are you okay?"

"I just wanted to tell you to have a good night. Goodbye." She hurried away, only slowing at the end of the aisle to sweep the perimeter, then disappeared.

*What just happened?*

"There he is," Sawyer bellowed. "You disappeared."

Hagan turned to Sawyer and Camden. They ambled down the aisle with a week's worth of junk food in their arms, then stopped short. Each man narrowed his gaze, as though Hagan looked as battered on the outside as he felt on the inside.

Sawyer repositioned a six-pack of energy drinks. "What the hell happened to you?"

Hagan rubbed a hand over his face. "No idea."

They took it as a joke and let it go. Hagan followed them toward the front of the hypermarket, half-listening to their debate over who would've won their game.

At the checkout, he tossed his items onto the conveyor belt, very aware that the nameless woman was gone. The air no longer crackled and sparked.

If he saw her again, he'd try his luck with an easier approach, like a simple hello, then let her take it from there. Answers would come—if they crossed paths again. More than anything, Hagan realized he simply wanted to know her name.

# CHAPTER TWELVE

AMANDA TOOK HER first vacation day since opening her security firm. She'd never had a normal nine-to-five job, never punched a clock, or counted the minutes until the end of her day. It wasn't only because she was the boss. Staying busy was her *modus operandi*. No one she knew would've believed it if she announced a personal day to tour a local attraction—though her mom might have celebrated taking time off. At least, Mom would have until she learned Mandy was hiding from reality and avoiding a handsome stranger.

It hadn't been *that* hard to ignore the real world while touring the Heritage Village, a reconstruction of a walled village from the pre-oil era. She'd spent the day with camels and goats, traders and craftsmen. It'd been fun, but it hadn't erased her run-in with the man at LuLu's. She'd never be able to use her new earbuds without thinking about him.

A swordsmith hammered metal into a curved blade. Amanda watched as he bent the sharp edge until it resembled the letter J. Maybe the mystery man's name started with a J.

John?

Jerry?

*Jeez,* this was as embarrassing as kicking him in the crotch.

She turned from the swordsmith and followed a sign for the museum. A display of ceremonial blades welcomed her under a sign that explained the khanjar blades and their hook-like, *J*-design. "Oh, for God's sake."

She stormed passed the display. It didn't matter what letter his name started with, and even if it were a J, the list of J names was endless. She sidestepped a family engrossed in the history of Emirati poetry and mystical interpretations. The mother read of a fabled curse—like a *jinx*. Amanda could've hugged the woman for putting the word in her head. *J stands for jinxed,* and jinxed had nothing to do with a man, because *she* was the living, breathing jinx.

How completely depressing and true. She gave up on the rest of the museum and followed the exit signs. They spit her back into the village's fray. Sun and the scent of camels rolled over her. The distant sound of swordsmiths hammering metal Js made her temples throb. She'd had as much as she could take of her day off.

After five minutes sidestepping merchants and artists, Amanda crossed the walled, gated threshold and found herself immersed in modern times. Her cell phone rang. "What timing…"

The weight of the world fell off her shoulders when she saw the call identified as the White House Switchboard. She didn't need a day off. Amanda needed her family. "Hello?"

"Hey, sweet pea."

An invisible hug wrapped around her from the other side of the world. "Hi, Mom."

"How's my favorite world traveler today?"

She tittered. "Yeah, that's me, and how many summits have you been to in the last month?"

"Which is why I'm calling." Mom briefly spoke to someone else, then returned. "I found a teapot in Japan that you would love, and I liked it so much that I got one for myself, too."

"You need new tea for the new pot."

"I was hoping you might say that—hang on a second." Her mother greeted someone. Amanda could picture her mother walking through the White House before her day teaching. She'd have on a pantsuit and stylishly, sensibly low heels. Mom interacted with the White House staff, treating everyone the same no matter if they were presidential policy advisers or longtime residence staff who would remain long after the Hearst family had left.

Occasionally, political pundits would remark on the First Lady's manners, which Amanda never understood. Acting like a decent person wasn't good manners. It was just something people should do…like eating and breathing.

And, as often as the news pundits mentioned Mom's manners, they would touch on Amanda's facial expressions. Sometime during her freshman year of college, a group of bloggers had decided she had a "resting bitch face," and that was that; a blogger had spoken. Amanda was no longer the rebellious, bored teenager. She was the bored blond bitch who wore too much makeup.

Amanda had never had a conversation with the so-called

journalists. They were the same as the reporters who decided that she was snobby or problematic. No wonder Amanda had been so quick to drop the name Mandy when she dropped out of public life. If only she'd given the gossip slingers a harder time earlier—at least she had Jared Westin to thank for that. He'd given her the phrase "tactical offensive maneuvers." Once she had that, Amanda had operated on a whole new level. Sometimes she'd drop anonymous tips on herself. Sometimes she'd send the gossip hounds on a wild goose chase for shits and giggles. Her offensive maneuvers drove her Secret Service detail to the edge. Only Dylan understood.

Her chin dropped. Sometimes she wished it were possible to go back in time so that she could listen to advice. Amanda tipped her head back and let the sun warm her skin. What would Dylan think of her stranger?

"I'm back," Mom said. "You still there?"

She bit back the melancholy and hummed, "Yeah."

"Sorry, that took longer than I thought it would." Mom paused. "Are you okay?"

"Mm-hmm." Amanda wandered to the taxi line.

"Where are you, honey?"

*Oh, nowhere. Just a popular tourist destination. By myself. No security detail to speak of.* Dylan would've lectured Amanda to kingdom come. "An outdoor market."

"Okay." Mom's tone dropped in that familiar worrying way. "Are you alone?"

Amanda glanced at the milling crowds. "Not really."

"You know what I mean."

"I'm fine." That wasn't a lie, though she hadn't taken nearly enough precautions to meet her parents' expectations for times when she was alone in public. Those expectations never squared with their request for her to mix and mingle in society again.

A tense silence hung between them, her mother's way of clucking disapproval without saying a word.

"Really, Mom. Besides, I'm heading home, anyway."

Mom hummed, unimpressed with her excuse. "Well then, how about you tell me where to send the teapot. Your office or the hotel in Abu Dhabi?"

The man directing taxis pointed to Amanda and then to the third car in line.

She walked to her taxi. "I'll be out here for a while longer. You can send it this way," she said, then greeted the driver and provided her destination before returning to her mom. "I'll be in and out for the next few months for smaller jobs, but this project remains my sole focus."

Mom paused. "About our conversation last night…"

Amanda picked at her cuticle. "Now's not a good time."

"I only want to point out that it might be nice to have someone to chat with other than Halle."

She'd never get away from thinking about that man. "Jared Weston's assistant is my friend."

Mom snickered. "Have you shared a conversation with his assistant about something other than work?"

Well…no. "Maybe."

"Then that, sweet pea, is what we call a *colleague*."

*Great.* Mom had jokes. "Friends can be colleagues."

"And so that you are fully aware," Mom continued as if Amanda hadn't spoken, "if you do lunch together with this person, you might be able to classify the relationship as a work *acquaintance*."

Amanda rolled her eyes. "You can't classify people like you do with elements in a science lab."

"Oh, sure you can," Mom sing-songed. "Hydrogen and oxygen come together and create something spectacular. Water."

"Seriously." The tips of Amanda's ears burned. "Please stop."

"The young man you mentioned? Separately, you and your romantic interest are like hydrogen and oxygen. Together—"

"Mom!" Amanda cringed as the taxi crossed into the business district. Another few minutes, and she could disappear into her hotel, swan dive into bed, and forget that she'd told her mother too much.

"You could make water."

"You're killing me."

Mom laughed loudly. "Maybe he's a not-so-romantic interest? When elements agitate, they can explode."

Her blush sped from the tip of her ears to the base of her neck. "I can't have this conversation."

"I'm simply reminding you, my dear, that you're not a robot, no matter how many rules and contracts you create. Human nature is human nature."

"Thank you, Dr. Hearst." She didn't cringe. Much.

Though, perhaps Mom had a point. Amanda had tried to ice him out. She'd learned that a watery middle ground wasn't possible. But steam? That kind of combustion was more than she'd allowed herself in a long time. Either way, this wasn't a conversation to have with her mother in the back of a taxi. "If that's all, this robot is going to go crawl in a hole and die of mortification now."

"Don't do that," Mom chortled. "At least, not before you figure out what you want from that man."

# CHAPTER THIRTEEN

HAGAN AND LIAM perched on a low cinder block wall on top of tower one. The wall subdivided sections of the roof. With their smartphones in hand, they read streams of data across from Parker as he typed into his laptop. A skyscraper's roof wasn't Hagan's idea of a good time. He could've sworn the building swayed. Slight shifts in the wind would shock the hell out of him. He'd much rather have taken a high-altitude job from a Chinook than sit on the top of this building.

At least Hagan had a decent reason to sit up here without a parachute. Titan had updated the adaptive abilities of their heavy-lifting drone, and if Aces wanted to repeat the benefits, they'd have to work out any bugs.

Work almost felt like playing video games as they tested the drone's newly updated adaptive abilities. Part artificial intelligence, part NASA-level algorithms, it could adjust to payload fluctuations, make decisions on takeoff, and run diagnostics while in flight. Meaning, once they calibrated the drone, their team had a very smart flying machine, capable of swooping into a battle zone for a rescue mission and initiating a health assessment.

But they weren't there yet and were currently stuck at the make-it-hurt-until-it's-better stage. Their million-dollar drone had regressed to a Wright brothers' level of technology, leaving collateral damage of bumped and broken security cameras, antennas, and lights in its wake—not to mention their poor test subjects.

Working out the bugs had helped Hagan ignore wind gusts and pigeons who didn't appreciate humans in their territory. Plus, they'd had their fair share of laughs.

"Careful with Doris," Liam warned.

Doris, their target on top of the other tower, was a tall, viney houseplant with a concrete pot that had to be heavier than his. She was their fourth rescue attempt. It wasn't as easy as they'd thought to liberate a living, breathing plant. If they weren't careful, they'd have to ask Angela to arrange for another assortment of weighted, potted plants to be delivered onto the roof again.

The drone was rated to carry two hundred kilograms, nearly four-hundred-fifty pounds, and she'd given them the stink-eye when Parker had requested the heaviest pots she could find. Angela did a damn good job with the variety of concrete, stone, and terracotta pots, coming closer than they'd expected to in maxing out the drone's carrying capabilities.

But the payload wasn't their biggest concern. They couldn't keep from dropping the plants during takeoff—rest in peace Alma, Beatrice, and Clementine.

The drone lifted Doris higher than any of her predecessors, but Hagan saw the same data points as Liam. He glanced at

Parker. Sweat beaded on his forehead. Hagan didn't want to give the guy a coronary, but Parker had asked them to monitor the data. Hagan grimaced when the corresponding line graph jumped again. "Careful."

"Please shut the hell up," Parker typed, as if the force of his keystrokes might help the drone lift Doris.

Lifting wasn't their problem this time. Hagan eyed Liam. Liam shook his head and almost laughed.

"Son of a monkey's—" Parker jerked his gaze from the screen. "Doris has one of those signs."

For a nanosecond, Hagan didn't know what Parker meant. Then he understood. The timing might send Parker into an early grave. Someone within the company had covertly hung notes and signs throughout the towers. No one admitted to orchestrating the funniest, most passive snark Hagan had ever seen, and even with Titan Group's surveillance capabilities, the culprit hadn't been smoked out yet.

Liam and Hagan tried not to laugh.

Parker returned to heavy-handed typing. "This is not the time, dickheads."

"We didn't do it," Liam volunteered.

Hagan kept an eye on Doris's statistics as the drone almost reached their altitude goal. "Angela arranged the plants."

"Everyone knows about the plants," Parker bit out.

"Yeah," Hagan agreed. "It's not her. Too obvious—Easy." The drone's AI adjustment added too many pounds of pressure. "You're red-lining."

"I see that," Parker muttered, ratcheting down the pressure

units. The drone's claw-like manacle reported an immediate positive effect. The AI system learned from Parker's input and adjusted its hold on the rucksack-sized pot. "There it goes."

Parker let out a breath, and they watched the drone and Doris level out and start the diagnostic sequencing.

"It's going to work this time." Parker set his laptop to the side and let the drone continue with its real-time adjustments.

Hagan and Liam's phones beeped, and Hagan reported the plant's temperature. "Doris is nice and cool despite the heat. Seventy-seven point nine degrees Fahrenheit."

"And no heartbeat to speak of," Liam added.

Parker pumped a fist in front of his chest. "And that's how it's done."

The drone recalibrated as the concrete pot swayed, but it continued, reaching the air space between the two towers. Hagan squinted to see the note on the plant but couldn't.

Their phones beeped with pressure warnings. Parker moved back to his laptop. Too late, the concrete pot shattered. Chunks rained between the hotel towers. Doris dangled and swayed. The drone rebalanced as the payload changed. Dirt sprinkled from her roots as the drone smoothly sailed toward the landing zone.

Parker cursed. Hagan choked on his laughter. Liam didn't bother to hide how funny he found it and slapped his leg.

"Doris isn't dead," Hagan pointed out as the remaining chunk of the pot dropped to the safety net that spanned between the buildings. The area below had been closed off with temporary barriers adorned with warning signs and hard hat notices that they'd borrowed from the construction crew.

Liam wiped at his face. "She could be." The roots dangled in the wind. "Crushed to death."

The graphic and data indicated a drastic shift in the plant's temperature but that the grip had corrected its pressure problems. Warnings flashed, then the AI recognized that Doris had sustained damage during transport.

Hagan chortled. "At least it's learning."

"At least we started with plants," Liam added. "Betcha Camden volunteers to go first when we graduate to people."

Hagan agreed. "He'd dare the thing to crush his ribs."

Parker growled. "It just needs a little finesse."

The drone reached the landing zone, sent a final diagnostic report on its cargo, and delicately released Doris into a crumbled pile of leafy vines, roots, and dirt. It purred quietly as it retracted its claws, hovered, and searched for a safe spot to put itself down, then landed.

The wind blew Doris, and the note fluttered and caught Hagan's attention again. "Parker gets to do the honors."

Parker muttered under his breath and closed his laptop. He crossed the roof and snagged the paper from Doris, unfolding it as his forehead creased.

"What's it say?" Liam called.

The corner of Parker's mouth tightened. He held up what looked like a photograph and returned to their station.

Hagan's gaze narrowed. It wasn't a picture. It was a meme. White, block-lettered text framed a picture. As the meme came closer, Hagan clearly saw the photograph was of Parker—with his eyes closed, possibly about to sneeze.

Hagan read the top line out loud. "Do you want a safety briefing?"

"Oh, shit," Liam said, then read the bottom line. "Because that's how you get us a safety briefing."

Two superimposed arms had been photoshopped onto Parker, along with two thumbs up. Hagan couldn't keep a straight face.

Parker crumpled the meme. "Those aren't my arms."

"Ya think?" Hagan slapped Parker on the back. "What about those hands?"

Liam doubled over. "It's like they knew this would be a disaster."

Parker scowled. "It wasn't a disaster."

"Doris didn't die," Hagan pointed out. "One out of four? Not bad."

"It's a potted plant," Parker snapped. "They break, asshole."

"Just like ribs," Liam deadpanned.

"And femurs," Hagan added.

Parker pinched the bridge of his nose. "Go away."

Their hysterics grew.

Parker dropped his head back, as though he were praying to the Drone Gods that Hagan and Liam would disappear. "*Go.*"

As funny as Alma, Beatrice, Clementine, and Doris had been, it probably meant that Parker had a shit ton more work to do. Hagan glanced at Liam, who seemed to be on the same wavelength. "We'll help you clean up this mess. Go get a beer."

"Hagan will clean up. I'll help." Liam checked his watch. "I have to meet Boss Man in less than twenty minutes."

"Sure you do," Hagan laughed.

"You, go." Parker waved Liam away, then nodded to Hagan. "Let's go. Then we'll clean up and grab some beers."

For such a high-tech, nimble-in-the-air piece of machinery, Hagan had always thought this drone was a pain to secure. Thirty minutes later, and after more cursing than conversation, Hagan dusted off his hands as Parker closed the compartment that housed several drones.

"Now, about that beer." Parker led the way to his laptop and packed his remaining gear.

Hagan propped Doris in several spots. She fell over every time.

"You ready?" Parker called.

"Absolutely." He gave Doris a pitying glance, then followed Parker into the tower. He didn't want to think about the mystery woman anytime he used the stairwells, but damn if she didn't pop to mind. Hagan wanted to hurry Parker. One more flight and they could access the elevators. He might never take the stairs again.

Parker reached for the access door as it swung open. "Shit."

There she was. The dark-haired beauty who hung out in stairwells and megamart aisles. Her eyes went wide when they met Hagan's, and a line of fire traveled down his sternum like she'd set off a tripwire in his chest.

Parker pulled her from the door and kept himself as a separating barrier, lifting his arms to block Hagan. "Give me a second."

The message was clear. Go away. Hagan didn't budge.

Parker glared over his shoulder. "I need a minute. Privately."

"Yeah, I don't think so."

Hagan sidestepped Parker. "Third time's the charm?"

A dawning realization of *something* hit Parker. He faltered, and his face snapped back to the woman.

She didn't smile, but that wasn't exactly a frown, either. "That's what they say."

Parker edged into the conversation like an unwelcome third wheel. "You okay?"

"She's fine," Hagan answered. Piss and vinegar threatened to flow through his veins if Parker continued to guard this woman like Hagan was a threat. "Think I'll take a rain check on that beer."

"You don't understand," Parker said, still running interference.

Hagan cocked his head and pointedly caught her eye. "No shit."

A curse caught under Parker's breath. "This is above—"

"My pay grade." Hagan laughed. "Yeah, I've been told."

The woman's demeanor softened. "I'll be fine. Thank you for staying, but we won't be long."

Tension ticked in Parker's jaw. With a lift of his chin, he backed away, pausing only to warn Hagan, "Careful."

Frustration mounted just the same as it had during Hagan's conversation with Boss Man. "Always."

Parker packed another warning into a lethal glare, then took his sweet time to depart. Hagan and the woman remained quiet well after the heavy door swung closed. He wanted to press her about the way Jared and Parker had warned him. Hagan wanted an answer on why men he trusted didn't want to leave her alone. He didn't think she'd give him a straight answer.

Hagan decided to toss her a softball. "How are the new earbuds?"

"They're distracting," she admitted, like they had an inside joke, then gestured to their surroundings. "Is this your favorite hangout?"

"We took the elevator most of the way. Work project."

"The drone?"

He nodded, apprehensive. "How do you know that?"

"Several newly installed LIDAR cameras were damaged." She frowned but raised a curious eyebrow. "I don't suppose you know anything about that?"

"I'll never tell." He laughed. "What do you know about those cameras?"

The frown melted away. "I'll never tell."

"Forget the cameras. Tell me what you know about LIDAR."

She grinned. "Everything."

"Is that so?" Peeling her layers away was the most fun he'd had in a long time. Forget that she was a knockout looker. He nearly tripped over himself when she offered clues about herself that he didn't expect. "I'll give you a hand to fix what we broke, and you can teach me a thing or two—" His cell phone buzzed with a message. He drew a tight breath at the timing, certain he didn't want to read the text, but duty called. "That's work. I have to—"

"I understand."

How much, he wondered. Hagan checked his phone. A text from Parker had been marked with high importance. Hagan grated his molars and opened the message. It had one single word. *Careful.*

There was nothing to do but laugh and shake his head.

"Not work?" she asked.

He held up his phone so that she could see the screen. "Jared and Parker do not like that I enjoy talking to you."

A light blush colored her cheeks. "They're protective."

"That's one way to put it," he mumbled.

She lifted her shoulders.

"Whatever this is about," he shook his phone, "you need to know that you're safe with me." He put his phone away and stepped closer. "And I want you to tell me if you don't feel that way." They were close enough to touch. His hands craved her curves again. "Do you read me?"

Her hesitation was difficult to read. Nothing about her showed fear. But that wasn't enough. "I promise." Hagan brushed his fingers against her chin and waited until she tipped her head back and met his gaze. "You're safe with me."

She dropped her gaze and murmured, "But are you with me?"

His fingers fell away. "Want to tell me what you mean?"

"Never mind." She wouldn't look him in the eye.

He eased back and took a deep breath. He smelled her light perfume, recalling it from before. Hagan had never paid attention to those kind of details until now, and he hadn't known it was possible to smell like sunshine and goodness. "What's your name?"

She stiffened and reached for her ponytail. Her fingers knotted into the dark strands. "Does it matter?"

*What an answer!* He reached for the hand that played with her hair. After a beat, Hagan let his touch drift to her shoulder, then elbow, then fall away. "What's in a name? You tell me."

"Nothing's in a name. It doesn't matter."

"Anything to keep the conversation anonymous, huh?"

She shrugged.

He grinned. "That doesn't bode well for taking you out to dinner."

"*What?*"

"How about you tell me. What do you want?"

She faltered. "What are you talking about?"

Seemed like a simple question to him. "What do you want from me?"

Her hand pressed to her throat. "That's pretty blunt."

"Nah, babe. Blunt would be if I asked if you wanted to go to bed for a nameless fuck." He grinned. "But I think we have too much chemistry to waste on a one-night stand."

Her breath jumped. "That's more than blunt."

"It's the truth, though."

"It's—" She blinked hard and edged back. "I should check on the cameras."

At least he'd learned that she worked with Titan and wasn't a client. A sense of déjà vu or a touch of familiarity squeezed at the back of his neck. He rubbed at it and shook his head. "I still can't shake the feeling that we've worked together before."

Hesitation settled over her like a sober blanket. She squared her shoulders. "No."

*Hell.* "I didn't say that to upset you." He struggled with what to say next that wouldn't sound like a cheesy line. "All I meant was—hell, I don't know. Different company, same time frame? Joint ops, somewhere, sometime ago? You work with LIDAR and—"

She pressed her back to the wall. "Stop talking."

"Damn it." Jared and Parker already wanted to jump his shit over this woman. But he wanted to know what was wrong. "I'm trying to explain—"

Like he'd lit a firework under her feet, she sprinted away. A simple question about the past—*their* past?—had sent her running again. What the hell was he missing?

## CHAPTER FOURTEEN

AMANDA BOLTED UP the flight of stairs, swiped her access badge, and threw the door open. She couldn't see straight, couldn't breathe. She'd tried to control that awful feeling but couldn't. For every second she'd stood there, hot water had risen. From her feet to her knees to her chest—it squeezed and squeezed and squeezed.

She gasped for another breath, angry her throat had twisted and knotted the air from her lungs. Her eyes closed, and she wanted to believe she wasn't dying, that this was a simple, stupid panic attack. *But the heat?*

Rubbing her temples, reminding herself that this was a mind game, she forced her eyes to open. Amanda blinked. Her brain processed. The heat…was the baking sun. There were no fires, no explosions, no places where she couldn't breathe. None of that was real. At least, it wasn't right now.

The water tower loomed overhead, and she let its shade draw her closer until she propped herself against a cool cinderblock wall and took in her surroundings. The city. The sky. This was what she needed to see. What she could control.

Her chin dropped. The adrenaline faded, and she laughed. At least she hadn't kicked him in the crotch. Embarrassed, she massaged her temples again. "What the hell am I doing?" She watched a bird soar above her, then muttered, "Why did I even try?"

A thud echoed from across the roof. A flock of birds took off and then re-landed. The man had come back to the roof. Why did he keep trying?

Amanda didn't know how to explain her triggers without triggering herself again. And that was assuming she wanted to give him far too much information—which, maybe, she did. This was so embarrassing. She couldn't let him find her like this.

Before he could pinpoint her location, she crept from the tower and checked to make sure the coast was clear. She didn't see anyone, and jogged across the helipad, feeling like a hunted deer in an open field.

She took cover by the massive generator units. Their hum would mask her racing breath and footsteps.

"Hey, lady." The man's voice carried in the windless sky by the water tower. "You okay?"

Amanda snorted. "That's debatable."

"Just so you know." He laughed, self-deprecating, and seemed closer than before. "I hate being out here."

*Then go away.* This was her refuge and retreat. Why wouldn't he go away? She'd prepared and protected herself from every possible situation for years. Except for this man. How had she gone this entire contract without knowing he existed? A better question might be, how had she gone without feeling the way he made her stomach jump and drop simultaneously?

She waited and didn't hear him. Relief swelled. She scanned the rooftop for a place she could compose herself. Parker or Jared would show up soon. After all, Parker had given the man a direct warning to treat her with kid gloves. *Careful.* Titan wanted to protect her, and she'd run onto the roof like a maniac. Jared would want to have another one of those security discussions...

Amanda maneuvered toward a tiered section and then descended onto a metal ladder. Although the sun was bearing down, the rungs didn't burn her hands. She stepped from the ladder, careful to soften her path through a gravel bed littered with pigeons and thick, corded wires, then stepped onto a metal catwalk that reminded her of chain mail. Despite its strength, she could see through the walkway. It quietly clanged with every step, and if she hadn't been familiar with the bridge that spanned a communication depot of large antennas and dishes, common sense would've told her to stay off.

The birds scattered and resettled as she crossed, drinking in the never-ending view. Her muscles unwound. A steady breeze rolled, and Amanda let it sweep the after-effects of her hysteria. She eased onto the metal catwalk and threaded her legs between the barrier wires. Her feet dangled, and she relaxed, safe, and so very high in the sky. This was the kind of gusty day and beautiful view that could erase the worst of bad days.

Every bird froze. In unison, their heads twisted and swiveled, and the mystery man appeared at the top of the ladder. If she hadn't been seated, her legs would've wobbled. He looked on top of the world, big and broad as a gust tousled his thick hair. Sunlight bathed him in gold.

Her heartbeat strummed in her ears, and the impulse to run melted away. Amanda gave a small wave. "Found me."

"Only so many places to look." His eyebrows knit, surprisingly not in judgment or irritation, but closer to concern. "You okay?"

She wrapped her arms to her stomach and focused on her knees. "You've had to ask me that a lot."

He waited until she faced him again. "I'm not sure you've given me a straight answer."

She laughed to herself, then admitted, "No."

"I appreciate the honesty." The corner of his mouth twitched. "Even when you've been evasive."

"It's a talent."

He glanced at the tiers and ladder, then into the wind. Amanda wondered what was going through his head and if he'd decided that he'd had enough with her shiftiness. She didn't blame him. His frown grew deeper. She bit the inside of her cheek, preparing herself for him to leave, then he descended the ladder.

Her stomach fluttered but she didn't know how to explain herself. The impact of his gaze scared her, and she threw an arm toward the sky. "I needed a little alone time. Just me and the birds."

"I get that." His footsteps crunched on the pebbles. Pigeons fluttered. Their little heads swiveled between the two humans. "And, trust me, if I didn't have a reason, I'd leave you to hang with the birds."

The back of her neck tingled. "What's your reason?"

"That's a hell of a question." He rested a foot on the metal catwalk and gripped the railing. She expected a lecture about the consequences of rooftop falls. But he didn't start in on her. He crossed his thick arms over his broad chest. "You know your way around out here?"

She shrugged. "Do you?"

"No." He shook his head. "I avoid it at all costs—unless we get to fly drones and crash plants."

"I'm not doing either."

"Or, if I need to check on someone."

Amanda bit her lip. "You don't have to check on me if that's your reason. I know my way around."

"Actually." He paused as though he understood the power of patiently letting time slip by. He lifted his palms slightly. The corners of his lips curled. "I don't care if you do or don't." He stepped farther onto the catwalk. The metal walkway shifted under his heavy weight, punctuating the placid stillness that came hundreds of feet in the air. Halfway onto the metal platform, he arched his eyebrows and whistled. "You sure know how to pick a secluded spot."

They were above a pit of antennas, but at the right angle, the building's edge seemed as though it were only feet away instead of the semi-safe distance of several yards. "You can go back inside," she said.

"Then I couldn't tell you my reason." He drew closer on the catwalk.

"Bet I could guess." She fidgeted.

"Actually, it's more like a question."

She could guess that too. *Are you crazy? Are you insane? What's wrong with you?*

"I want to know," he said. "Why aren't you okay?"

She hadn't expected that one. Amanda bit her lip. "It's complicated."

"I like complicated." The metal grates groaned when he took another step. He eyeballed the catwalk and made a funny face, then added, "I like puzzles. It makes me good at my job." He held up his palm. "I won't say another word about work. Even though I know you're dying to ask what I do."

She laughed.

"Nope." He shook his head. "Don't be cute. I'm not gonna share."

Her smile almost ached. "I'll try to contain myself."

"Try." He winked. "For my sake."

The wind picked up again. Goosebumps prickled across her skin as if Mother Nature wanted to make sure Amanda realized her senses had reached a state of hyper-awareness. But with him only three feet away, she needed exactly zero reminders of his presence.

He crouched to eye level. "If I scared you, I didn't mean to."

"You didn't."

He nodded to himself. "I don't intentionally say things to make you want to run."

Amanda grimaced. "It's a bad habit."

"Fight or flight?" He pressed his lips together. "That's a gut-level reaction to keep you alive. Not a bad habit to have in your arsenal."

She side-eyed him. "You don't have to pacify me either."

He chuckled. "Mind if I sit?" He didn't wait for an answer and swung his legs under the barrier like hers. "I don't want to pacify you either, and I mean, you take fight or flight to the extreme—"

She groaned. This was almost as bad as talking to her mother about robots and agitated elements.

"But, I'd rather have you knee me in the nuts than run up here."

Her chin snapped up. "That's insane!"

He lifted his muscular shoulder. The move tightened the cotton T-shirt across his chest. "I'd take a little pain any day over you hauling ass toward the roof, upset."

Her heartbeat stopped dead. The blood drained from her face. "You thought I'd jump?"

"It doesn't matter what I thought—"

"Yeah, it does." Bile churned in her stomach. "Oh my God. I'm an idiot." He'd shown up so she didn't swan dive off the roof. Just like Jared would've. This guy didn't want to chat an arm's length away. He wanted to be able to grab her if she decided to end it all. Amanda reached for the railing to pull herself up. "Thanks for checking on me, but I've gotta go fix the cameras you broke."

"I bet you don't know about the third F?"

She stopped before she reached her feet. "What?"

He extended two fingers. "There's fight, flight, and…"

She hesitated, more curious than she let on. "And?"

"Freeze."

"Freeze," she repeated, feeling memories from a high school science class nudge the back of her brain. *Fight, flight, or freeze.* The body's response to stress. "I'd forgotten about that one."

"Don't blame you. It's the worst of your options."

Amanda sat down again. "I don't recall that explanation from science class."

"Think of it like this," he suggested. "If you can't fight or flee, then you're paralyzed."

She did have the tendency to freeze up, but that had always played second fiddle to leaving or inflicting bodily harm.

"But you don't freeze? Then you're doing better than say…I don't know." He shrugged. "Bambi."

"*What?*" Her forehead scrunched.

"Jeez." He scrutinized her. "Who doesn't know Bambi?"

"I do!"

He laughed. "Think about deer. When they run out onto the road, a car comes, and they see headlights. Some run. Others freeze. Freezing never works out."

"You made your point." She side-eyed him. "But now I can't shake the possibility of Disney horror movies. Bambi versus traffic."

He rubbed a hand over his jaw. "I didn't think you were going to jump because I pushed you about the past." He stared up at the sky, then held her gaze again. "But, I was concerned, and…I wasn't ready to leave."

Doubt and desire wound up her back. Amanda's eyes dropped to the edge of the building instead of the man by her side. The drop was less daunting than the way he looked at her.

Pigeons squawked. They took off and re-landed. She watched them settle, then summoned courage to look at him again. "You said something about recognizing me."

He moved a hand to bat her words away, then stared at the city. "Forget I said it."

Amanda rolled her lips together and wanted to tell him more. She wasn't sure how much or what she was capable of putting into words. "Have you ever wanted to be someone else?"

He leaned forward and rested his arms on a barrier wire, then tilted his head her way. "I wanted to be a video game tester when I was a kid."

Amanda laughed.

"I'm serious."

He cleared his throat and shrugged as though Titan's towers weighed his shoulders to the ground. "There was a time when I wished I could've switched places with someone."

The heaviness of his sadness didn't need to be explained. Even as he tried to hide the pain, his burden made itself known. Amanda wanted to comfort him. To touch his shoulder, to offer a hug. But the rules she lived by, the ones that protected the world from her...they didn't take into account another person's pain and burden. Dylan would've called her out on that—and he was probably the only person who would've been able to get her to see how selfish her behavior had been.

"I wish I could've switched places with someone, too," she admitted. "Though, now that I think about it, I don't think they would've been happy with…" Tears welled. She shook her emotion away. "I only meant to tell you that sometimes I think everything would be better if I wasn't me."

He inhaled and held it for a long time, letting his somberness evaporate. "You mean right now?"

"Yeah, I guess so."

The man tilted his head toward her. "Why?"

Amanda knotted her fingers in her lap and wasn't sure how to elaborate without opening a flood of questions. "Anonymity would be easier for me."

With a half-hitched grin, he shook his head. "I don't know a thing about you, and trust me, you're not making my life easy."

"Hey."

"But I like it," he continued, "and I like you."

Her eyes peeled. "You don't even know me."

"I've been trying, if you haven't noticed." He grinned in a way that made her heart skip. "That okay with you?"

She blushed and nodded, not trusting her voice.

"All right then. Good to know." He repositioned. "What do you want to do?"

"With you?"

"Yeah." He wriggled his eyebrows, intensifying the heat in her cheeks, but he playfully back-pedaled. "In general."

She had no idea *what* possibilities could exist if she took a chance on him. *I want to...make a friend? Jump him in the stairwell?* Was there a middle ground that she couldn't see? Amanda scanned the rooftop like she'd missed a billboard sign. "I don't know how."

"Unless you were someone else," he offered.

She nodded. "I know that doesn't make sense."

"Let me see if I understand what you want." His low voice reverberated down her spine, and she shivered. His eyes danced, tightening at the corners as though he were imagining the possibilities of what she might want. "It'd be easier for you to go out with me if you weren't you."

"Exactly." A nameless night out! But wow, that sounded shady. "I mean..." Her ears and cheeks flamed. "What I meant was—"

"Hang on. I have an idea for you to consider."

She couldn't blame him if he propositioned her to go jump in bed. If he read between the lines, he might see that as what she wanted.

"What if you stay you," he suggested, "*but* we stick to your no-name rule?"

"Really?" Her nerves pulsed with the possibility of opening herself up—actually being herself—without repercussions and preconceived assumptions. Arousal poured through her veins, and this had to be too good to be true. Her stomach plummeted. "Wait, I want to be clear," she faltered, hoping she wouldn't see disappointment. "I don't want a booty call. That's not—"

"I want dinner." His smoldering expression teased. "Though I like where your mind jumped—"

"It didn't!" Oh, she was a liar.

"Trust me." The corners of his lips curled subtly. "My mind's jumped there more than I should admit to you."

Amanda fought to find the right words. Any words. Then she couldn't stop them. "Why would you agree to an anonymous date?"

"Because you're beautiful, and I like the way your eyes light up when you see me."

Amanda curled her finger into the small of her throat.

"Because you know about LIDAR cameras and know the secret way to force Boss Man to walk on eggshells."

This man was too much to be true. She laughed, wanting to cry.

Smooth and confident, everything that she wasn't, he slid to her side. "I want to know why you think you have to hide and what it'd take to convince you that you can trust me."

She swallowed hard. "That's a lot."

"It's just dinner." He waited, watching, protective and circumspect, reminding her of the few patient people she had in her life.

"Dinner." She nodded, shocked that he'd suggested terms that she could accept. She pressed her hand against the drumming pulse in her throat and met his white-hot gaze, almost convincing her that he craved her touch as much as she wanted his. This was trust, and it was an aphrodisiac unlike anything she'd experienced. Amanda smiled. "You're something else, you know that?"

"Actually, I'm Hagan." He held out his hand.

"No!" Hadn't she just swooned over trust?

"I never said I didn't want to be me."

True, but … "That wasn't fair."

"I have a feeling you know that better than most." He waited for her to shake his hand.

Amanda wanted to protest. Compromise had no place when it came to personal and professional situations. But instead of recounting her rules or freaking out, she said his name and shook his hand.

# CHAPTER FIFTEEN

**NINE YEARS AGO**
**GEORGETOWN GRAND HOTEL**

MANDY HID FROM her prom date and the rest of her high school senior class in the last bathroom stall of the farthest bathroom she could find. She hadn't run far enough. The muffled voice of the deejay echoed through the walls. Thumping bass and a muddled cheer answered him. Even with her hands over her face and eyes pinched closed, Mandy couldn't escape the hell of senior prom.

She sat on the toilet. Her knees pinched together, and the thigh-high slit in her black dress mocked her, a pathetic reminder of her foolishness. Mandy sniffled. As if she could act like one of her classmates.

A loud knock pounded on the door, and she knew it was Dylan before he announced, "I'm coming in, Sparkler."

He didn't wait for her response. He never did, and his dress shoes echoed on the bathroom tile before she could yell, "Go away."

Dylan knocked knuckles along the stalls as he strode toward her hiding place. "Do you want to talk?"

"No." She dragged her fingers down her cheeks, rolling her

eyes. "I'm not here. Go away."

The stall next to her opened, then slapped shut. Mandy groaned. He hated when she ran away, and he never let her pout.

"You should leave. I'm really not here." She stood up and retreated to the far wall. Below the stall partition, she saw his shoes and pants as he leaned the same way, opposite her.

"You're not here?" Dylan whistled, low and long. "That's going to frustrate the shit out of McNally. She's been posted outside this bathroom and hasn't let a soul in to pee."

Mandy rolled her eyes. "No one's coming into this bathroom to pee."

"Then, she's cockblocking the bathroom where girls drink from the flasks hidden in their dresses."

"That's more like it." She snorted. "But, whatever, I don't care. It's not like I was going to win a prize as everyone's favorite friend." She smoothed her hands down her dress, then bunched the fabric between her fingers when tears streamed again. "Maybe for biggest fool."

Dylan stepped to their dividing wall, lightly thumping his fists against it. She could picture the pensive way he searched for the right words, never treating her like a kid or sugarcoating his thoughts. Sometimes, though, he'd take forever to figure out what he wanted to say. "Spit it out, please. Then you can leave." She swiped at her tears. "I really want to be alone."

"That guy's a first-class dickhead."

She almost laughed. Dylan had absolutely chosen the right

word. "I should've known better."

"No, you shouldn't have." He sighed. "No one should expect to have their privacy invaded like that."

"Yeah." She snorted. "I think I should expect it." Her cheeks flamed, and she'd never forget the moment she realized her prom date had set her up. His cell phone was already recording before he'd convinced her to slip from the ballroom and into his arms. "What kind of stunt will I have to pull tomorrow to change the headlines?" Surely, they'd run the gamut from *The First Daughter's First Kiss* to *The First Daughter Bares All.*

"Fitzgerald got the kid's phone. You don't have to worry about the video going anywhere."

"Great." She still ached though. Mandy wallowed, crushed because she'd thought he'd really been into her like she'd been into him. "I hate boys."

"You don't hate me," he pointed out. "I'm a guy."

"You're an adult."

"Trust me," Dylan promised. "There'll always be someone you could hate."

"Then I'll wrap myself in a bubble and never come out."

He laughed. "You'd suffocate."

Mandy shook her head. "The more I think about it, the better I like the idea."

"Nah." He leaned back against the stall wall again. "If you think life will get easier when you turn eighteen, go to college, get a job—"

"It will get better when no one cares about the Hearst family anymore." No journalists. No political pundits. No classmates hellbent on ruining her life. "It'll be amazing."

Dylan whistled long and low. "Wrong. Life never gets easier. You just get stronger."

She wrapped her arms over her stomach. "I don't feel any stronger than I did an hour ago."

"You'll see, one day. Anyway," he said, changing the subject, "what's your plan? Are we going to hang out all night in here?"

"Probably."

"Damn, I was hoping you'd let your dad send over an Apache to pick you up." He chuckled. "That'd send one hell of a message to the dickhead."

"No helicopters! I'd rather sleep in this stall."

He chuckled. "I'm going to radio McNally and ask her if she can grab me a plate from the buffet bar—" Dylan snorted, then responded to the agents on their communication line, "Hey, kidding, kidding. Ease up, McNally. Unless, for real, you wouldn't mind—" He laughed again. "Just kidding."

Talk of food broke through Mandy's pity party, and on cue, her stomach growled. "If someone's bringing you a plate, ask them for a fruit kebab for me."

"You got it," he said. "Sparkler wants a fruit kebab. Somebody figure out what the fuck that is and grab me a plate of chips and dip, too."

They waited quietly. Her thoughts drifted, continually coming back to her stupid date. "I thought he really liked me."

The stall partition shifted when he leaned his weight

against it again. "If I had had any idea..." He thumped a fist against the divider. "I would've told you and had a conversation with the little prick."

Dylan was sworn to keep her safe from physical threats, but she trusted him like a big brother. "I know."

"McNally says the fruit kebabs are gone and that she's not bringing me my chips."

"Sucks to be you." Mandy laughed quietly.

He bantered with the other agents for another moment, then knocked on the divider as if he didn't already have her attention. "What do you say we get out of here?"

"Not yet."

"We can go do something that'll drive the press crazy?"

Mandy smiled, not because he would let her run around Georgetown with half-cocked ideas to arouse the suspicion of gossip journalists and politicos alike, but because she appreciated that he'd always be there to help. She moved toward their separating stall partition. "Tell me another story about your boring, normal family."

"Then we can swing by McDonald's?" he suggested.

"Oh, good idea." She could already taste the French fries and nuggets. "But first, tell me a story."

Dylan hummed. "My mom hit up the grocery store last night and couldn't find her favorite brand of tater tots. It caused a family riot—"

"I'm serious, tell me something that'll make me forget about prom." The trouble hadn't only started tonight with her date. When she'd picked her prom dress from Target, political talk shows had volleyed talking points about the true meaning of the purchase. Was her father trying to reach out to middle-class Americans? Did her mother want to soften Mandy's image and make her more relatable?

Had anyone considered that she'd simply liked a dress she'd seen online? That maybe she had clicked on an ad and decided to one-click the black gown for overnight delivery? Not a single, so-called expert considered her purchase to be as benign and boring as it was. "You're not talking yet."

"Give me a minute." He laughed. "I'm sifting through an enormous amount of generic, boring chit chat that might enthrall you." After a minute, he cleared his throat. "All right, here's a little small-town drama for you."

Mandy grinned. Small-town was their inside joke. His family lived in Louisville, a large city in Kentucky, but he promised they acted more like a small town than most small towns. Neighborhoods had names. Bakeries had been passed down through families. High school sports were the focus of the family. College sports were like a religion.

She'd never visited much of the state, and never Louisville, but she envisioned shotgun houses with manicured postage stamp lawns along a parkway, blocks of Victorian mansions turned into college housing, a vibrant and diverse waterfront, and a sprawling suburbia with shopping centers and restaurants that wrapped around the city limits like a familiar hug.

"Last fall, my little bro thought he'd be captain of the football team."

"Of course he did." The best stories were about Dylan's

younger brother and sister, so Mandy didn't feel like the only person on Earth referred to by a code name. Saber, his brother, was her age, and Starbright was his sister. They lived a life she could only dream about. One where no one documented life's ups and downs. Where predictions weren't partisan but grounded in hopes and dreams as simple as the captain of a football team.

"When he wasn't captain, he carried the decision around like a chip on his shoulder throughout the season—which probably made him a worse player, proving that he shouldn't have been captain to begin with, if you ask me."

She laughed. "Bet Saber appreciated your two cents."

"You'd think." Dylan chuckled.

"So what happened?" Mandy asked.

"Nothing. This is a boring-ass story about people you think are normal. Nothing happened. Except," He dropped his voice, "there was a plot twist."

Mandy clasped her hands together. "Tell me."

"Stay with me now," he said. "Starbright's best friend works at the Steak 'n Shake with the guy who was the football captain."

She closed her eyes and pictured their life like a movie.

"Turns out," Dylan continued, "the dude hates football."

"*What?*" She didn't see that coming. "The football captain?"

"Yup. The poor kid busts his butt because his parents bust his."

"Friday night fever," she whispered.

"They had it bad. Now here's the kicker. The kid gets two scholarships for college: a football one and an academic one."

"Wow."

"Guess which one he plans to take?"

Mandy arched her brows. "Not the football one?"

"Not the football one," he agreed. "Full ride, in-state tuition, so long as he picks a major within the Humanities Department."

"Scandalous." Happiness bubbled in her heart for the guy. It was as if she were only a few connections away from Starbright's best friend's co-worker.

Dylan unlatched his stall, walked out, and rapped on hers. "You ready to get out of here?"

She was. Mandy opened the door as Dylan slipped off his jacket and laid it over her shoulders. "Thanks for the story. And for the coat." She pulled it around her. "That's a nice touch, Agent Carter."

"Yeah, some small-town habits are hard to break."

# CHAPTER SIXTEEN

THE WEEKEND ARRIVED. Half-past five with less than an hour to go and Amanda was more nervous than she'd ever been. That was saying something, since her top three peak, nervous spots included an audience with Queen Elizabeth, bungee jumping off the side of a cliff, and telling the leader of the free world, also known as Dad, that she wouldn't return to college after she'd finished recuperating from the explosion.

Amanda shook that fiery nightmare from her head and focused on tonight. In less than an hour, she'd meet Hagan and be on her first date in years. She checked her reflection in the mirror and approved. She'd added a touch of makeup, pulled her hair back into a high ponytail, and appreciated the way her white blouse contrasted against her features. Her jeans were cute, if not practical, but the more she stared at them, the more two-dimensional she felt.

Clothes were a tool to blend in. She didn't want anyone to remember if they'd seen her. But that wasn't a great stylistic foundation when dressing for a date. She flung her closet door wide and saw much of the same. Jeans and khakis, long skirts and dresses that did more to cover her up than make her feel beautiful.

The hangers scratched as she sorted through her options. Nothing would work—a box on a shelf above the hangers caught her attention. She pushed onto her tiptoes and pulled it down. A thin layer of dust had settled on the silver cardboard container. Amanda carried it to the bathroom vanity and lifted the lid.

Her eyes widened. The bright red linen dress remained as breathtaking as she remembered when her Mom and Dad had sent the gift on her first day in Abu Dhabi. The small note card laid on top of the dress that she'd never had the courage to remove from the box. She opened the card and reread her Mom's handwriting above their signatories. *Let the adventure begin.*

Was today that day? It wasn't as if she hadn't seen the world, though, she hadn't necessarily explored it. She lifted the dress. Tissue paper fell away as its skirt fell out, and she whispered, "Wow."

Light creases could be quickly steamed or ironed out, and if it fit, it would be the perfect first date dress.

She laid it flat and switched on both the steamer and iron, then paced, more anxious than before—but also electrified.

Her phone buzzed, and grateful for the distraction, she saw that it was Halle and answered, "I was just about to call you."

Halle waited a beat. "Everything okay?"

Amanda heard the caution in Halle's voice and nodded, grateful that Halle's first reaction was always to prepare for the worst. "Yes. I wanted to let you know where I would be later."

Halle hesitated. "Where will you be?"

Perhaps she should start from the beginning, otherwise Halle might think Amanda was in trouble and forced to recite a story about a date. Danger was far more likely than meeting an unknown man for dinner. "I met an interesting guy—"

"Wait, what?"

Amanda laughed. "I knew you'd say that. But I did. He might think I'm nuts, but—" Nerves exploded in her stomach like fireworks. "He said I was beautiful."

"Like a real, live person?"

Amanda bristled. She knew the idea would sound far-fetched, but couldn't Halle rein in her doubt? "That's what I'm trying to explain."

"You spoke with someone outside your—stop, start over." The hint of irritation enveloped her words. "Brief me from the top."

Her teeth tapped together. "Like I said," She frowned. "I ran into him in a stairwell."

"And you just chatted the guy up?"

Maybe Halle hadn't been the person she needed to speak to before her date. "Yeah. It's what people do."

"Not you," Halle accused.

"You're right. I patted him down, panicked, and then kicked him in the groin." Amanda gritted her teeth and forced a steadier breath. "And he still asked me to dinner."

"Sounds like a winner."

"What's your problem?" Amanda demanded. "I wanted to tell you where I was going. Ya know, to be safe. And, I expected you to be surprised. But not pissed."

Halle didn't respond.

Amanda checked the call. They were still connected. "Are you there?"

"Yes," Halle said. "I'm not pissed. Just—" She huffed. "Do you even know anything about this guy?"

"Honestly?" She cackled. "Not a damn thing, and I can't wait."

"Amanda," Halle softened. "I want you to be careful."

Her fingers clenched. Amanda tried to appreciate Halle's worry, but the past only made her frustration grow. "You're being hypocritical."

"Don't—"

"You introduced me to—"

"Don't say his name," Halle yelled.

They'd never had this argument. Their friendship had been rooted in school and then work before their personal lives. They never talked about the guy Halle had set Amanda up with, that same guy that Amanda had taken a chance on. "William Taylor Morris."

"Stop!"

"I knew his name. His major," Amanda yelled. "I trusted my best friend who set me up with him. I knew everything except how much he wanted to kill me!" Her throat ached, and she collapsed onto the side of the bed. "It should've been me."

The steamer puffed, and the hushed tone woke her the past like a train blew its horn. She wiped at her cheeks.

"Nothing about that went like it should. And Dylan?" Halle choked up. "His death fucked my life up too."

Amanda didn't have the energy or interest to debate her best friend. She saw her reflection in the mirror. Puffy eyes and smeared mascara were good reasons to cancel her date. She retrieved the Bluetooth earbuds that made her think of Hagan and popped them in as the silence stewed between them. "Halle?"

"Yeah?"

She lifted the red dress. "I have a date tonight, and I'm excited."

Halle inhaled and let it out. "I can't wait to hear about it."

Amanda closed her eyes and nodded. "Thanks."

"So…" Halle laughed awkwardly. "Would it be totally inappropriate to run something by you?"

The pressure in her heart untied. They'd always turned to the safety of work. Offering protection to others had allowed them to heal before, and apparently, tonight. "Shoot."

"We received a request from the Lebanese government. I'll forward you the email now."

Her eyebrow crooked. "A request for proposal?"

"Nope," Halle said. "A small job they'd rather keep quiet."

Amanda sat at her vanity and removed the smeared makeup. "Interesting."

"And time sensitive."

She touched up her mascara. "An analysis of some type?"

"One that I'd kill to be the point person on."

Amanda inspected her eyes, then dabbed concealer below the lower lashes. "Then why are you forwarding it to me?"

Halle groaned. "The location. They need someone on the

ground, and you're closer."

Satisfied with her makeup, Amanda moved the dress to the steamer and hoped she could get away without ironing.

Halle continued to talk shop. Amanda methodically steamed. The back and forth motion coupled with Halle's clinical summary helped erase the ugly emotion that had reared between them.

They finished the call with Amanda promising to check her email, then she removed her earbuds and checked the mirror. It was time to shed her dull clothes and see if the dress would fit.

She stripped and stood in front of the dress, then before she could shy away from the bright, bull's-eye color, she slipped it on.

"Oh my…" The skirt swayed softly, and the red made her feel as powerful as she looked. With a decisive move, she pulled out her ponytail and stared, a woman transformed.

## CHAPTER SEVENTEEN

For the hundredth time, Hagan checked his wristwatch. He wasn't worried she'd stand him up, but he had noticed that the minutes now crawled. He crossed his arms to keep from checking the time again and watched throngs of people milling throughout the park surrounded by shops and restaurants.

A slight disturbance interrupted the rhythmic foot traffic. His pulse picked up, and he knew she'd arrived. Then Hagan saw her. She offered a shy, vulnerable smile that left him breathless, and he moved toward her, a man on a mission.

She tilted her chin up as he stepped close. "You're smiling."

"It's a thing I do sometimes." Hagan rested his hands on her side. "I like the way you never say hello."

She laughed. "Didn't realize I did that."

"You look amazing." Her dark hair hung over her shoulder, and she wore a dress the color of poppies. The fabric flowed over her curves and stirred around her legs.

"Thanks." She lifted the side of her skirt and let it go. "I've never worn this before."

"Why not?"

She thought before answering. "I wasn't ready."

Whatever that meant, he was glad she'd worn it tonight. Her eyelashes fluttered. The tip of her tongue darted to her bottom lip. Her eyes searched around them as though she were checking the crowd, then she pointed over his shoulder. "Could we go in there before dinner?"

He turned toward a tea store nestled under the shade of low-hanging trees. "Sure." He might see a small gift he could purchase for his sister.

"I want to get something for my mom," she added.

Playfully, he crooked an eyebrow. "I'm surprised my anonymous date admitted to having a mom."

The corners of her lips quirked. "I wasn't cooked up in a lab."

"Good to know." They picked their way toward the store. She stayed close to his side, and when Hagan opened the heavy door for her, he caught a whiff of her perfume before they stepped into the small, aromatic store.

The door clicked when it closed. Silence transported them into another world. Music with bells and chimes whispered from all round. He rested a hand on her back as they gingerly stepped farther into the store.

She leaned into his side. "I feel like we should whisper."

How could there be so many people and so much noise just beyond the door? The aisles wound this way and that, bending around shelves and displays. Hundreds of teas and trinkets covered every inch of space and dangled from the ceiling. The chaos had a meditative state. It was the perfect start to their night.

Even with the mysticism that danced in the air, he noted the way she assessed their surroundings. It was a familiar habit, and without much thought, they'd both located the entrances and exits and assessed the store for risks and threats. He wouldn't ask her about the habit, instead filing it away as a clue.

"Have you been in here before?" she asked.

"No, but I might come back again."

"Really?" She eyed him. "Shopping for yourself or someone else?"

"My sister."

Interest colored her expression as she led the way. "Can I ask you about her?"

"Sure." He picked up a small box and shook it. "Her name's Roxana."

"What is she like?"

Hagan returned the box and snickered. "She's a pain in the ass, if you want the truth."

"Oh, be nice." She elbowed him.

Hagan pinned her arm to his stomach, holding her long enough to breathe in the scent of her shampoo and feel her warmth. He let go, and his date, this nameless beauty with stealth moves and a history to hide, stayed close enough to kiss. They didn't move. The moment remained fragile. A gust of wind could destroy it—or fan an underlying flame of explosive heat.

The shopkeeper bustled in and stopped. He held a stack of skinny, dark purple boxes in his arms and cocked his head. "I didn't hear you come in. Welcome."

His date assessed the old man. Hagan complimented the store. The shopkeeper pointed to where he would be if they had questions, then he slipped away as quietly as he'd approached.

He wanted to ask if she was okay but instead, Hagan picked up a box and gave it a shake. "My sister's pretty amazing when she's not acting like a pain." He shook the box again. "What is this? Sounds like BBs, but it doesn't have any weight."

"No idea." She took it from his hand and put it on the shelf. "But your sister doesn't want it."

"You don't know that."

She reached for the most expensive-looking item within arm's reach. "I think she wants this because she probably knows you keep calling her a pain."

Hagan laughed, then nearly choked at the price tag. His date threatened to give it a shake, and Hagan took it from her and replaced it on the shelf. "Roxana gives as good as she takes."

"Is it her birthday or something?"

Hagan shook his head. "No, I just like to surprise her with little gifts. She worries, and, hell, I don't know. I figure sending her something nice will help."

"How?"

He shrugged. "I want her to believe my life isn't in danger. If I'm in a place that sells expensive crap that would brighten her day, she might believe that my job is safe."

"That maybe one of the sweetest, most misguided things I've ever heard." She patted his bicep. "But it's cute that you try."

Hagan laughed. "Cute, huh?"

"Very."

Damn, he wanted to touch this woman. "Good to know." He placed his hand on the small of her back again and guided them into another area. Spices hung heavier in the air. They stopped at a row of barrels and glass jars. "Your mom likes tea?"

"We both do." She eyed the intricately designed labels handwritten in Arabic. "She bought new teapots for us on her last work trip."

"Where did she go?" he asked.

She pinched her elbows to her side and concentrated too hard on what should've been an easy answer. "Overseas."

He ignored the evasive answer. "Do you read Arabic?"

"No, but it's beautiful."

Hagan motioned to a placard. "Loose tea. Then it looks like…" He inspected the labels. "Local, grouped by spices."

"You're fluent?"

"Yeah. And over here." Hagan took her hand. "This seems more like a global selection."

The shopkeeper interrupted again, "Looking for anything particular?"

"A gift," she said, and let go of his hand.

"This one." He swept a satchel and scoop off a shelf, shoveled a sample into the bag then into Hagan's hand. "A favorite."

He didn't know what the hell to do with one tea bag's worth, but the shopkeeper stared at him as if there was something Hagan should do. He brought it close to his nose and sniffed. "Damn—" He choked as though he'd shoved cinnamon sticks into his nostrils. "I mean, that's nice." His eyes watered. "Potent."

The shopkeeper beamed, agreeing. "Yes, yes."

Whatever else the man said turned into white noise. The woman grabbed his forearm. The touch cleared his senses like she'd hosed off his face. She laughed and led them away even as he wiped at his eyes one last time. Once they reached fresh air, he knew he'd survive.

"Are you okay?" She giggled and peered at his face like he'd sustained a serious injury.

"My ego's a little wounded." Her infectious laughter tugged at his cheeks. "But yeah. I'll make it."

"Good. I'm not ready to end the night yet."

Damn, he loved when her honesty surprised him. Hagan inched closer. Their eyes connected, and her laughter died. He wrapped an arm around her back and pulled their bodies together. Her smile reached her gaze, and with her in his arms, he felt more of a man than he ever had before. "What is your name?"

"Amanda," she whispered.

Simple. Beautiful. Her name had made her fight and flee. Until now. She'd given it to him, and Hagan took that as a sign of trust. Nothing had made his blood race hotter than her belief that he could keep her safe.

# CHAPTER EIGHTEEN

"AMANDA." HAGAN SLID his hands up her sides, taking his time as if no one existed but them. "Thanks for trusting me."

Revealing her name would have been anti-climactic. Except, Amanda had a front-row seat to the broadest, most genuine smile on Earth.

To be the center of someone's attention for being herself was a great feeling. "How are you this sweet?"

"I'm not." He winked and stepped back.

Amanda moved to his side and slipped her arm into his. The scent of soap and strength made her float. "That might be the first time I don't believe you."

"You got me. I'm a nice guy. Believe it or not."

"Why wouldn't I believe that?"

He eyed her as they walked. "Do you think nice guys exist?"

She scoffed. "In your line of work?"

He chuckled as if he understood. "But—" He gave her a pointed glance. "You don't know what I do."

She had to give him that. "Tell me," she asked, hiding how her question was a bigger step than she let on.

"I do a little bit of everything." He shrugged, confirming that he didn't understand the magnitude of what she had asked. "I know my way around computers and explosives."

Amanda flinched. "Neat."

Briefly eyeing her, Hagan continued as though he didn't feel her jump or hear the quiver in her voice. "If something doesn't make sense, I want to figure it out. That sums up my job no matter where work takes me."

"You like puzzles," she recalled.

They reached the restaurant, and he stopped, standing close. "Exactly."

"I'm not sure if I like that, or if it terrifies me," she laughed.

His chuckle fell short, and his attention focused over her shoulder. Amanda spun. Her stomach bottomed out as though she were a teenager who had been caught sneaking out. Boss Man was an arm's length away, reminding her of a volcano ready to erupt. His dark eyes challenged Hagan. Defensive and uncertain, Amanda leaned back into Hagan's chest, but Jared ignored her like she wasn't there. The two men faced off. It had everything to do with her, and yet Jared wouldn't even look at her. "Hello?"

Jared's chest rumbled. "What did I say?"

Her stomach turned, and she knew his bite was as bad as his bark. He needed to back down. "Forget the contract."

As if a mention of work and their fiercely debated contract broke through his fury, he dropped his gaze to her. "I warned you, too."

"Don't scold me like a child," she snapped.

"Then I'll scold you like the first—"

"Don't!" She only realized that she had surged forward when Hagan gripped her hips and pulled her back to him. Blood hammered in her ears. Amanda didn't know what Jared might say, and she didn't understand what this debacle did to their contract and friendship. Her throat ached. "You wanted progress."

He shook his head. "Don't do this."

Hagan lifted her to his side, then squared off to Boss Man.

Removed from the discussion and understanding that this wasn't the time for contract negotiations, that it was more for two men to settle their concerns, Amanda moved behind Hagan. She knit her hands into the back of his shirt.

"Stand down, Boss Man."

"You've got some fucking balls, son."

*Son?* Amanda curled her fingers in Hagan's shirt. Jared wasn't much older than they were, but he'd crossed the line from protective to patronizing. Pissed-off tears burned the back of her throat.

"Go home, Hagan," Jared growled. "I'll take it from here."

Hagan took a step closer. "Is that an order?"

*Oh, God. They were going to fight.* Each thought they had her best interest in mind. If she had talked to either of them, this wouldn't have happened. But she'd been afraid. Once again, her actions would ruin people she cared about. "Stop it." Amanda rounded Hagan and pushed between the two men. She looked up, willing him to take a breath and meet her eye.

The broad plane of his chest heaved with angry breaths. Amanda clasped her hand on his face and could feel the tension in his jaw. "Look at me." Years crawled by. "Hagan," she pleaded. "We need to walk away."

Jared laid a possessive hand on her shoulder. "I'll take you home."

"Get your hand off of her," Hagan roared.

Amanda dipped from Jared's hold and pulled on Hagan's hand. "I want to go home. Please."

Hagan didn't budge. She realized a crowd of onlookers had formed, as if this couldn't get any worse. "Hagan," she begged. "I'll tell you whatever you want to know. Just please, let's go."

His attention returned to her. Relief swelled at the hope that this would end now. But so did a sickening feeling coiling in her gut. Jared had pushed her hand, and she wasn't ready to share yet.

The muscles in Hagan's jaw ticked. "No."

Disappointment clouded her vision.

He took her hand. "I don't want to know anything that you weren't ready to tell me." He snarled at Jared. "Not because of this."

Too much was going on to fully appreciate what he had just said. If Amanda hadn't been terrified of growing close to another person, that would have been the moment that she fell in love with Hagan.

On his terms, Hagan stepped from Jared and gave a two-finger salute that might as well have said *fuck you*, then he pulled her to his side like she was his to keep safe, and they walked away.

Making her legs move forward almost hurt. Amanda waited for Boss Man to yell orders, but they didn't come. Hagan eased them through the small group that had formed as though he hadn't had a verbal altercation with his boss.

Her panic ebbed, and as adrenaline washed away, she trembled and leaned against Hagan. They moved off the path, under a section of trees in the park, and stopped. His strong arms wrapped around her. Safe and hidden, Amanda burrowed into his chest and breathed him in until she knew that she wouldn't fall apart.

Hagan pressed his lips to the top of her head. "I'm sorry."

She uncurled from his arms. "Don't be." She didn't add that it was all her fault because she didn't have the strength to defend that truth. While they hadn't known each other for that long, it seemed as if they had been through so much together. "What now?"

"No idea," he admitted. But his eyes lit up, and Hagan held out his hand. "But I want to find out. Do you?"

Amanda beamed. "Absolutely."

# CHAPTER NINETEEN

THEY MEANDERED THROUGH the park. Hagan waited for Amanda to reveal another gem. Could she top sharing her name and facing-off with Jared? Hagan wouldn't be surprised. She just needed the choice to be hers.

"I work in security," Amanda admitted, as if on cue.

That didn't surprise Hagan. Dozens of questions came to mind, but gut instinct told him to keep his mouth shut and listen. It was harder than he expected.

"Not the type that Titan Group might do," she offered. "More of the tech side."

"Like Parker?"

"Not exactly," she explained. "I don't know the first thing about hacking or layering technology in a war room situation. But I can design systems that give him what he needs."

"Like the LIDAR."

"Exactly." She nodded. "LIDAR made self-driving cars a real possibility. When I saw how thousands of laser points could read the difference between the shoulder of a road and another lane, I could envision how they could map variables like people."

"And feed them into a database?" he asked.

"Sure, but also, when you add in advancements in artificial intelligence, security systems can make decisions based live-streaming data and extrapolate additional threats." They paused to let a man walk by as he video chatted. She ducked her chin and studied one of her sandals. "Like." She glanced up. "Temperature and respiration readings."

"Like lie detectors?"

She nodded. "Yes. But without asking the question."

"The cameras are taking people's temperatures?"

"In theory," she agreed, noncommittally.

"A little intrusive, if you ask me."

Amanda laughed, that time agreeing. "There's a fine line between ethics and security." Her walk stiffened. "Which is one of the reasons why I'd rather stay away from people. Ethically, it seems like the best option." She scrunched her shoulders. "For everyone involved."

Protecting herself and others? He bit his lip, trying not to push when he could tell she'd waffled on sharing the last bit.

"Anyway." She cleared her throat. "AI has a long way to go. Temperature and respiration readings help correct for biases."

"We updated a heavy-lift drone with temperature readings." But he didn't get what that had to do with bias.

She grinned. "Your plant test?"

Hagan chuckled. "Yeah. Glad we tested potted plants first."

"I saw the remnants of your first attempts on top of Tower Two." Amanda grinned. "But that's a different kind of reading than Titan wanted for their security systems. Parker and Jared understand an AI system is only as good as the information programmed at the start. Programmers have implicit biases, like biases they don't want to make but, because of who they are, they are made."

Hagan nodded. "Like when it made the news that AI systems were flagging people of color as suspicious."

"Exactly, more often than anyone wanted to admit, the initial algorithms sourced material that had been influenced by systematic racial disparity."

"Like arrest and incarceration databases?"

"Yeah." She nodded. "Part of my job is to search out the best programming. Temperature and respirations are more reliable than facial recognition. Parker likes good data, and Jared likes intel he can trust."

"You know Jared well, huh?"

She shrugged. "Yeah."

Hagan waited. That was the only answer he was going to get without pushing. Once again, he bit his tongue, then changed the subject. "Are you still hungry?"

"Yes." Both her voice and body language seemed lighter. "How do you feel about a picnic?"

Hagan glanced over. They'd reached the edge of the park, and though it was well lit, he wasn't sure that plopping on the grass with takeout would score him good-date points. "Is that what you want?"

"Well." Her lips rolled together. "We could grab something to go, and there's this place with an amazing view at my building."

"If that's what you want." He grinned when she lit up,

nodding. "All right then." Hagan pulled out his phone and opened a restaurant app. They ordered, and he calculated it would take the same amount of time to walk to the location as the app said was needed to make their meal.

They left the park and reached a street corner. He noted how her gaze swept their surroundings with far more scrutiny than just checking for traffic. "So, your security company."

"Hm?" They crossed the street.

"Does it offer security personnel?"

She shook her head. "Nope."

"Where'd you learn how to nail such a great groin shot?" He chuckled. "And, you know your way around a solid pat down."

"Oh that." Her forced laughter seemed to buy her time to think of an answer. "What girl doesn't take a self-defense class or two?"

"Since when do self-defense classes teach how to frisk someone with a hundred pounds on you?"

They stopped in front of the restaurant, and she focused on its sign, stalling. "I watch a lot of TV shows."

Hagan snickered and shook his head. "If that's what you're gonna go with—"

She playfully elbowed him.

He captured her arm again and leaned close to her ear. "You don't have to tell me yet."

"Okay," she whispered as quietly as he'd spoken, nodding against his lips. "I'm trying. Honestly, I've never talked about this before." She turned in his arms and hesitatingly pressed her hands on his chest. "I got hurt."

That could've meant anything, but Hagan didn't need to know the specifics for his vision to cloud. He managed, "I'm sorry," when what he wanted to do was demand to know more.

"It changed everything about me. Who I thought I was, how I dressed—"

"How you dressed doesn't allow someone to hurt you."

She pressed her forehead to his sternum. "I was different. Hiding in a way that screamed for people to look at me."

Hagan cupped the back of her head. The remorse in her voice killed him. "You don't have to say anything more."

Amanda took a deep breath and met his eyes. "Anyway." She offered a weak smile. "That was the reason I started my company with my best friend, who saw me through a very dark time." Her smile strengthened. "All that happened, and somehow it led me to meet you." Amanda closed her eyes and laughed to herself. "Sorry—" She pulled away. "This is really too heavy for a first date."

Hell, this didn't feel like a first date. It felt like he'd stumbled upon a missing piece of who he wasn't. *That* would be too much to say on a first date. Hagan caught her hand and led her inside to pick up their dinner. "Then let's pretend it's not."

## CHAPTER TWENTY

Like Amanda had promised, the view was amazing. Hagan stood in the center of the helipad and didn't mind that they were standing on top of Amanda's hotel. When he focused on the way she seemed to drink in the night, Hagan decided he didn't care where the hell they were. "How often do you come up here?"

"More often than anyone knows." She fluffed her long skirt. He set their takeout at the center of the landing pad, and she crouched. "Can we eat here?"

"Why not?" He laughed, taking a seat. "At least until air traffic demands we relocate."

The steamy scent of dinner wafted out when he opened the bag. Napkins and plasticware topped several containers. "No plates."

"We'll survive."

"That's the spirit." And without plates or much discussion, they dove in, sampling the tapas, laughing that their meal could've been awkward. But it wasn't. He could've blamed the delayed dinner, but Hagan decided not to look for a reason.

She set her fork on the edge of a container. "You feel like an old soul."

"I don't know if I've heard that before." He tossed his fork down and wiped his mouth.

"You don't waste time."

He chuckled. "Are you saying old souls make their dates feel like they're moving too fast?"

"No." She smiled and sighed, then boxed up their food. "You don't waste too much time asking why or waiting for someone to read your mind."

He moved the containers, napkins, and forks into the bag and knotted the top, then moved to her side and stretched his legs out. "Never thought about that before."

"It's true."

He eased his forearms back and leaned back. "Do you ask why a lot?"

Wind lifted her hair from her shoulders. "No."

He already knew her answer but chuckled at her tone. "Do you say no a lot?"

Amanda nodded. "No lets you control situations."

"Perhaps."

"No's a safe word that puts constraints on everything that can't be controlled."

That was one hell of a riddle. For the moment, he didn't want anything to do with puzzles. Hagan rolled onto his back on the painted rooftop and tucked his hands under his head. After a minute, he inched up and held out an arm.

She hesitated. There would be a back and forth in earning more of her trust. Even the smallest piece made him crave more, so he waited, attempting to be as unthreatening a presence as he could muster.

A warm breeze rolled over the roof. Amanda shifted her legs underneath her skirt. Hagan left his arm extended for her and reclined. She scooted closer. His heart hammered. Hagan stared at the stars, unreachable, like this woman with terms and conditions that he'd never understand, and he worried. For as much as they'd talked and touched, he'd given her this moment to choose. To control.

It killed him to stay quiet. *Come here* dangled on the tip of his tongue.

Waiting made the worry worse. His jaw ached. Hagan wouldn't tear his gaze from the sky as his heart slammed in time with the building's red warning lights.

Amanda swept her hair away and tucked herself close to his side. Her cheek cradled in the crook of his arm. Her breath skipped across his neck.

Hagan forced himself to swallow. "Look up there."

The softness of her hair slid over his skin.

"A word can't control everything." He gestured to the sky. "Sometimes, you shouldn't try."

Amanda rolled onto her back, resting the back of her head between his chest and arm. "Whenever I am high up …" She shook her head. "I never looked at the sky. At least not like this. I look at the edge. I'm aware of the ground." She took a long breath and let it go. "I know how close to push and where I have to stop."

"Sounds exhausting."

"I've never thought about it like that." She rolled to her

side again, returning her cheek to the same spot that let her breath tease his skin.

He brushed her hair behind her ear. "What do you think?"

Her forehead creased, and then she shook her head. "That I could breathe. That I was free."

"If that's what you need to breathe."

Amanda laid her hand on the center of his chest. Her fingertips rubbed the indentation of his sternum. Hagan sensed that she studied his every breath, and he wondered if she clocked his heartrate speeding like she'd pushed him over the edge.

Her chin pressed against his collarbone. Her lips threatened to nuzzle against his neck, and then she whispered against his eager skin, "I don't know what I need."

Hunger knotted in his throat. "That's too bad."

Her fingertips stopped drawing their languid pattern against his chest as though her touch had been paralyzed by the God's honest truth. Because he knew exactly what he needed. To taste her. To feel her. To explore her body and learn every truth that kept her far away. But he'd settle for a kiss.

She fanned her fingers and then curled them against his chest. "Do you know?"

"What I need?" Hagan nodded. "Yeah."

"What?"

He laughed. "That's a list that would probably scare you."

She propped herself onto her elbow, scowling. "I don't scare."

*Fucking hell.* He hoped that was true. Hagan rolled over

Amanda. His forearm stayed at the back of her head. His free hand threaded into her hair. He'd pinned her under his body, caged her to the rooftop floor, and his mouth touched hers, soft and sweet. Like heaven had been set on fire, a greedy purr vibrated from her lips.

Feverish need drove him. Amanda dug her nails into his back as though she could claw her way for more. Her hips arched to his, and she struggled, finally locking one leg around his thigh.

Kissing this woman would drive him mad. He wasn't sure if he'd bothered to breathe. Hagan struggled to pull his mouth away. The way she moved and kissed and held on like he was the last man on Earth had left him insatiable.

He salivated to take her breasts into his mouth, to rub her wetness against her hot flesh. Hagan vibrated with such an all-consuming urge to bring Amanda to orgasm after orgasm that he wasn't sure how to keep from holding back.

Hagan wrenched his lips from hers and fought to catch his breath.

"You don't scare me," she whispered.

Her breathless taunt, full of bullshit and honesty, blinded him with an animalistic urgency to bring her pleasure until she screamed his name.

Hagan grappled with an outrageous level of lust that had started with the honey-sweet kiss. "But you scare the hell out of me."

# CHAPTER TWENTY-ONE

THE NEXT DAY Amanda wasn't ready for the real world again, but Halle had said the contract was time sensitive. She set her tea mug on her desk and booted up the laptop. It didn't take long to find the forward. She swiped the email open and read Halle's message above the original sender's delivery information.

> *I am so jealous that you're closer than I am. See below.*

Amanda scrolled down. The initial email had been sent to their company's generic inbox. The sender appeared to be a Lebanese government official. Amanda tapped her fingernail on the desk. They didn't have any current clients in Lebanon, and the location alone wasn't enough to make Halle jealous of a work opportunity.

Amanda scrolled to the greeting and formal introduction of Imad Nasrallah, deputy minister of the treasury. Mr. Nasrallah offered a concise explanation of Lebanon's gambling tax earned from Casino de Gemmayzeh. Now she had an idea where this might be going and why Halle wished she could work the gig.

According to Mr. Nasrallah, Casino de Gemmayzeh entertained high rollers and slots aficionados alike, and the country owned a majority share of the casino.

"Oh, that's interesting," she muttered, then mentally noted, *if not a conflict of interest*. The country earned taxes and shareholder dividends, and Amanda bet that combination brought in a sizable fortune. It didn't matter that some countries, like the United States, had a travel advisory on Lebanon. Casino de Gemmayzeh was sure to be a cash cow, as many Middle Eastern countries outlawed gambling. This casino would be able to service a hungry consumer group with few options. "All very interesting, Mr. Nasrallah, but what's your problem?"

Amanda scrolled through bullet points better suited for a tourist agency until their content focused on the year-over-year growth of taxes, shareholder dividends, casino guest headcounts, and total games played.

The final bullet point referred to an attached spreadsheet. She had her computer scan it, and the document came up clean, but she still wasn't a fan of opening attachments from unknown senders. She didn't doubt that Halle and Shah would've checked the email and attachment also, but Amanda opted to follow their overly cautious standard operating procedure. She turned to a second, air-gapped laptop that she kept at the ready, and, after saving Mr. Nasrallah's file to a portable drive that she'd destroy after using, she safely opened the spreadsheet on the separate device.

The spreadsheet had column after column of data. Most of it was unneeded but showed an effort to be transparent. "Boring, boring, boring." She switched tabs and scrolled again, casually reading line items that had been extracted from the country's fiscal budgets. Her eyebrows arched. If the numbers were correct... "*Not* so boring."

Without double-checking Mr. Nasrallah's numbers and without the ability to reference the document's Arabic footnotes, she understood the problem before he spelled it out. The annual income and taxes had grown steadily over the decade; however, within the same ten-year period, that growth didn't keep pace with the steady increase of players and bets made during the same time period. The discrepancy was slight, and nearly impossible for a governmental budget office to notice. Amanda and Halle counted several casinos as clients, and only with that background could she see the red flag.

She opened a calculator on the screen, and, after several calculations, Amanda whistled. For every two months of spot-on expectations, one month stumbled a tenth of a percentage.

Her phone chimed and interrupted her chain of thought. She stood and stretched, hardly giving it a second glance until she remembered giving her number to Hagan. A warm whoosh of excitement made her giddy. She grabbed the phone. Not him. Just Shah. And, as fast as she'd floated from the ground, disappointment leveled her back into place.

"Don't be like that," she scolded and tossed the phone to the desk. Everything always went bad when she let a man distract her.

Amanda stretched and thought through her questions before she finished reading Mr. Nasrallah's email. Any number of factors could explain the discrepancy, from a corrupt comptroller's office to a machine that had failed to report correctly. Not everywhere had the same oversight as the Las Vegas Gaming Commission. What people saw in movies influenced what they assumed to be standard procedure. Amanda and Halle had found that even if the solution to their problem was waiting to be found in the data, they still needed to spend time on the ground to pinpoint where they might look.

She stood and stared at her two laptops. The casino had been screwed out of hundreds of thousands of dollars. Maybe more. Without more time and a full data set, she couldn't say. But her mind drifted elsewhere. Maybe she could text Hagan and ask him about the notes written in Arabic. Or maybe she should run them through Google Translate like normal.

Her phone pinged again. She didn't want to talk with Halle or Shah and needed to focus on how casino grifters might've worked slow and steady, nearly un-noticeably, amassing a fortune of stolen wealth, then come up with a plan for a site visit.

She reached for her mug and saw the notification.

*Got any plans for later?*

*Hagan.* Her stomach leaped. But work called. Amanda reread the message. "Later," she told herself. "You can do later." Couldn't she? Quickly, she responded and hit send before she could backtrack.

*No. I'd like to hang out with you.*

The little word under her message changed from *Delivered*

to *Read*. Every part of her tingled. Three bubbles appeared on screen as he typed. No matter what he said, she'd focus on work. The dancing dots disappeared. Her breath caught. There was nothing worse than a message that didn't arrive.

Her phone rang. Amanda nearly jumped out of her skin, then laughed. "I didn't expect you to call."

His laughter rumbled. "I wanted to hear your voice."

She moved to the couch and curled with him to her ear, unable to hide her smile. "Now, I'm not sure what to say."

"I don't think that's true. What are you doing?"

"Work."

"Very specific."

She laughed. "I'm about to use Google Translate to read footnotes in a budget."

"Exciting stuff. What language?"

"Arabic." She bit her lip.

"You could use me instead."

She flushed and thought of several ways that could be done. "I want to finish before tonight."

"I could help you now," he suggested.

"You're not working today?"

Hagan sighed. "Boss Man and I have avoided each other today."

Shit. That wasn't good. "That's my fault."

"I'll deal with it later. Don't worry."

But she did. Hurting others was her specialty, and now she'd found a new way to cause problems. "Hagan—"

"If I promise to help, I could come over now."

"I'm not dressed yet—"

"Perfect. That's a yes; come on over now?"

She giggled. "I'm *wearing* clothes—"

"Pity."

"Hagan!"

"Should I come over now or later?" he asked.

"Now." He was too good to be true. Amanda couldn't wait.

# CHAPTER TWENTY-TWO

**FIVE YEARS AGO**
**WASHINGTON COLLEGE**

BIOLOGY LAB ENDED, and Mandy shoved her textbook into her bag. Her lab partner acted as though she had something to say. Unusual. Mandy pushed her chair in. "See you next week."

"Wait." Halle scooped her notebook into her arm. "Do you want to get lunch?"

The classroom emptied. Mandy lifted her backpack onto her shoulder, ready to return to her dorm and keep a low profile. "Why?"

Halle laughed. "Jeez. I don't know. Because you're hungry."

"Why are you asking me?" Mandy didn't trust anyone in her freshman classes, and her lab partner, thankfully, hadn't come off as someone who wanted to chat.

"Because you're my lab partner, and I'm hungry. Plus, I know, like, two people here. So I thought I'd see about a third person." Halle rolled her eyes. "Don't worry. I'll keep looking."

Dylan glanced in the classroom and caught Mandy's eye.

He lifted his chin as if to ask if everything was okay, and then saw the other girl. He gave an approving nod. Everyone in her classes had passed the Secret Service sniff test, and Dylan had been encouraging her to make friends. He promised high school was never like college.

"No, we should get lunch," Mandy said, agreeing reluctantly. "Don't mind me. I'm working on my people skills."

Halle snorted. "Aren't we all?"

Dylan fell into line behind them and stayed out of the way when they reached the Student Center. Even though she'd forced herself to join Halle for lunch, Mandy realized that she hadn't forced herself to laugh or have fun. It was as if Halle didn't care who she was. Mandy had never appreciated someone's disinterest so much before.

By the time they'd polished off the chicken nuggets and side salads, Mandy didn't want the conversation to end. A guy approached their table. She focused on her tray and a balled napkin. He was cute, but she didn't want a random saying hello like he knew her from wild stories in newspapers and on trash TV.

But he greeted Halle instead.

Mandy blushed, feeling foolish, then realized they didn't just know each other—they were close. "I'll catch you later."

"Wait," Halle said. "Lemme introduce you to my friend. Then you'll know almost as many people on campus as me."

"I'm that transparent, huh?" Her palms sweated as she tried to laugh. "Hi."

The boy stepped from Halle. His smile shifted in a way

that she couldn't describe, as though from comfortable to purposeful. In any event, it made her weak in the knees. "I'm Mandy."

"William Taylor Morris. My friends call me Billy."

Unnerved by the way he looked at her, Mandy picked up her tray. "What should I call you?"

"Whatever you want." He lifted the tray from her hand and then took Halle's. "My vote's for Billy."

# CHAPTER TWENTY-THREE

THE AIR CONDITIONING blasted over Hagan as he crossed the threshold into the lobby. The place smelled as nice as it looked. A far cry from where his team lived. Though, one day, maybe Titan's lobby would shoot fancy air at their guests once the place was up and running.

He caught sight of Amanda in the far corner of the lobby even though she wore a headscarf that partially obscured her face. She waved and crossed to meet him, suddenly Hagan doubted his ability to focus on work. This very public lobby had done nothing to quell the urge to get her alone.

"Thanks for coming over," she said. "I could really use your help."

Hagan shoved his hands into his pockets. "I don't know that I gave you that much of a choice."

She laughed and fell into an intentionally vague explanation of her project as they moved toward the elevators. Once they were traveling to her floor, she fell quiet, but as soon as they stepped out, her explanation started again. It was far more interesting than he expected, and he had to admit, watching her explain her work with such passion did something to his insides. Sexy and smart. That was a killer combination.

They stopped outside a hotel room door. She paused and glanced at him as though she just recalled they had a very new history. "This is where I work." She unlocked her door and walked in.

Hagan whistled. "Not a bad office."

She pulled off her head scarf and laughed. "It does the job."

If she'd been uncomfortable, it quickly passed. She returned to her explanation, but this time with far more detail, raising his curiosity about what she might uncover for the Lebanese.

For the next hour, they reviewed footnotes. Then they ordered lunch, and Amanda walked him through what she thought and guessed. Dinner time rolled around. He didn't want to leave, and she didn't seem ready to kick him out, though she eyed him when Hagan checked his watch. "I don't want to keep you all day."

"Your work's pretty cool," he admitted and grinned. "Almost as much as you."

The tips of her ears turned red, and a blush followed over her cheeks. "Well." She gestured. "It's never dull. Different clients. New projects. But it's not that interesting. Don't feel like you have to stay."

"I don't feel anything but hungry." He pushed out of his chair. "What about you?"

"Really, Hagan." She tugged her lip between her teeth. "You don't have to stay. Two meals in one day's a lot."

"If you want me to leave so you can work alone, that's

fine." Hagan winked. "I'll survive."

"No. I mean—Gah! I'm not good at this." Amanda groaned and rubbed her hands over her face. "If you can't tell."

"I've learned it's best not to try to read your mind after our first introduction."

She groaned again. "I'll never live that down."

"Besides, I want you to explain." Hagan stepped closer. "What do you mean by *this*?"

She rolled her eyes. "You! As if you don't know how nervous you make me."

"Shit." He cocked his head and chuckled. "That can't be good."

"You know what I mean."

"Tell me, anyway."

Her lips pressed together. "You're cute when you're trying to convince me of something."

Hagan smiled. "Good to know I have a secret weapon."

"It's just—" She pressed her arms to her side but inched closer. "I haven't dated in a very long time, and I don't even think it's a good idea."

"Because?" he asked.

"It's complicated." She winced. "That sounds like a cop-out, but I don't know what to do."

"You don't know what to do about me." Hagan crossed his arms and let his eyebrows inch up.

"Yeah." She pressed her palm to her forehead and shook her head. Then she laughed. "Wow, I feel like a huge nerd telling you this."

He appreciated whatever she explained. One day, maybe he'd get why it was so hard. "I have a feeling you're not telling me even a tenth of what you need to say."

Her eyes rounded, all but confirming his guess.

"But I don't care." He sat down and studied her expression. "Tell me something different that makes you nervous."

She scoffed. "Why would I do that?"

"Don't know." Hagan lifted a casual shoulder. "Then you'd worry about that and not me."

She laughed. "Cute." Then Amanda bit her lip as if she didn't trust herself to share another word.

"How about this," he offered. "I'll order room service again, and then let you in on something that's worrying me."

Hesitatingly, she agreed, and they ordered room service for the second time. When Hagan hung up the phone, he pushed his lips and settled back into the couch. "I'm worried I fucked up with Boss Man."

Her lips formed an O, but before she could apologize or protest, he tugged on her dark ponytail to keep her attention. "I'd have done it all over again."

Amanda hummed. "How'd you join Titan?"

"Good question." He thought to the chain of events that landed him in Abu Dhabi. "I helped a friend of a friend when he needed help to protect his woman."

Her eyebrows arched. "Wow."

"That's when I met Jared." He wished he knew how Amanda and Jared met. Even with what he'd learned about her background, Hagan wasn't convinced they didn't have some type of May-December romance. He'd never thought about how old Boss Man might be, just that he'd earned his place in the world and had created a security firm that had the respect of global leaders. But the guy had to be in his thirties, at least. "Jared offered me a job that was too good to be true. I'd have been a fool not to take him up on the offer."

"Why do you think it was too good to be true?"

"The money," he admitted. "I know people aren't supposed to talk about that kind of shit, but that's the reason. My family needed what Boss Man paid." He shrugged, uncomfortable with the amount of information he felt compelled to share. "I had a steady stream of contract work before that, but joining Titan added a layer of stability."

She seemed lost in thought, and then asked, "Do you like the work?"

"Yeah." He nodded. "I couldn't ask for a better team. The gigs are never dull. We get plenty of downtime. But that's all secondary to supporting my family."

She curled her knees to her chest and gave her complete attention. "That sounds like a huge responsibility."

He could see that she wanted to ask why. Hell, diving into an explanation was something he usually avoided. Even though he had so many questions about this woman, he wanted to explain himself. To a point. Some old wounds were still too raw to share.

Hagan shifted on the couch so that he better faced Amanda. "My dad died when I was a sophomore in college. Heart attack."

"I can't imagine losing a parent. I'm sorry."

"A week later, my brother—half-brother, really, but he'd been my big brother since the day I was born." His throat tensed. "There was an accident at work. He died." Words never seemed to do history justice. Hagan didn't want to spoil the discussion with details that might bring up politics or make Amanda feel she needed to offer heroic platitudes about a situation she could never understand. One day, he might give her more of an explanation. But not likely. Hagan wasn't sure he could ever let go of his anger to do right by his brother's memory.

Amanda laid her hand over his. "I'm so sorry."

Hagan appreciated the sentiment but, if he were going to explain what he'd meant about providing for his family, he had to keep going. "It was too much for my mom."

"I can't imagine," she whispered.

"The funerals were barely two weeks apart." Hagan took a moment to keep himself together. Mom had been stoic through the first funeral; he and Roxana had thought Mom was holding it together for the second. They'd been so damn wrong. They failed their mother, consumed in their own grief.

"Hagan, you don't have to tell me."

He'd come too far to stop now. "Mom had a small stroke during the service for my brother."

"Oh, God."

"We didn't notice." His vision clouded. "It wasn't like in the movies." His voice shook. "She had trouble walking from the church. I took her hand and led the way to the car. She didn't say a single damn word during the procession." He swallowed hard. "Roxana had to help her sit and stand during the burial."

"Hagan." Tears clogged Amanda's voice.

His chin dropped, and he closed his eyes. "We thought—I thought—I didn't know." He cleared his throat and glanced toward the windows, gathering his words. "Later, at home, we realized something was wrong." Like always, the sadness shifted. He ground his molars, hating how much they'd missed, wondering if they could've found help sooner, and, more than anything, cursing the circumstances that left their mother all but a living shell. "She'd had a series of small strokes. Didn't kill her."

Tears streamed down Amanda's face.

"She needs a lot of help. That costs money, and we were nothing but two teenagers, suddenly responsible for a mortgage and mounting medical bills that you wouldn't believe." Hagan took a deep breath. "I needed this job." He licked his bottom lip. "Still do."

Amanda wrapped her arms around his neck and squeezed as though she wanted to pull him to safety.

The truth was that nothing had ever helped. Talking about what had happened only stoked his anger. There were so many what-ifs. What if his brother had had a different job? What if he hadn't felt compelled to protect some tabloid half-twit? Except Amanda's arms somehow soothed his rage.

Hagan didn't understand how. He still hurt. Raw resentment still coiled in his chest. But the way her heart beat next to his… He didn't know what to do, so he gave in to her arms and gathered her as if holding her might heal the ache. Hagan breathed her in and decided that he already knew everything he needed to about this woman. He kissed her forehead and eased back. "It's not an easy story to tell."

Amanda wiped her cheeks with the back of her hand. "I'll call Jared. I'll explain everything, and how it's not—"

"You don't have to. I'll find him later. This is between him and me."

# CHAPTER TWENTY-FOUR

Boss Man threw the door open and stormed into the war room. He saw Hagan and his fists curled. "What did I tell you?"

The same surge of adrenaline that would arrive seconds before a bar fight hammered Hagan's chest. He inhaled and held the breath, wanting cooler heads to prevail. Who the hell knew if Boss Man had heard the word no before? If so, it didn't happen often. "I heard you, and I'm sorry. That's not an order I'll follow." Hagan didn't want to lose his job or Amanda. "She's not the job. It's not life or death—"

"How the fuck do you know that?" Jared strode forward and pointed to a chair. "Sit your ass down."

A knot formed in his throat. Hagan didn't back down easily. He gripped the back of the office chair. His fingertips dug into the black leather. Boss Man glared then pulled out a chair. They managed to sit at the same time.

"I like her," Hagan said. "And if mutual interest remains, I don't intend to stop seeing her."

Jared placed his elbows on the table and cupped one hand over the other. He popped his knuckles, one after the next. Hagan prepared for whatever might come, but by the time the last knuckle cracked, Jared seemed less like an angry son of a bitch and more like he was worried. Hagan would have almost rather dealt with the anger.

"This still gives me heartburn." Jared leaned back and stared at the ceiling, then added, "She hasn't told you anything you need to know."

"How do you know?"

Jared snorted and shook his head. "Trust me, I'd know."

Hagan's heel bounced. He wished he'd opted for breakfast, or maybe not as much coffee. His stomach churned. "I need this job."

"I know," Jared muttered, finally adding, "and I want you on this team." He took a minute to lean back in his chair and scrub a hand over his face. "But this isn't going to end well."

"Appreciate you looking out and all." Hagan shrugged. "But that's on us. Not you."

Jared shook his head.

Feeling more confident than when he'd first walked in and waited, Hagan cleared his throat. "I want to run something by you."

"Oh, this'll be good," he muttered. "Shoot."

"I translated some Arabic for Amanda. A casino project out of Lebanon."

Jared's scowl deepened. "This sounds like you're about to ask me to approve leave for a slumber party with your girlfriend."

Hagan chewed the inside of his mouth. "From everything that you and Parker have said, it sounds like you worry about her."

He didn't disagree.

"And, after listening to Amanda and her business partner brainstorm the best way to approach the project, we think that I should head there with her."

Jared arched his brows. "We think?"

"If there's nothing on the books still." Hagan nodded. "I can partner with Amanda. Get the job done and be back before we suit up for our next assignment."

He smirked. "Did they go into detail about what this partnership might look like?"

Hagan forced a neutral expression. "I was more concerned about how you and I would work things out."

"Yeah, I'm sure *that's* what had your focus, and not the shared hotel room."

"Look, man." His molars ground. He couldn't afford to wonder if they'd shared a hotel room before. "I don't get your problem, and I don't want to know. But if you'd rather send her into a situation alone, when backup is preferred, then we don't understand each other."

Jared grimaced, as if realizing he'd been called out on the hot-and-cold way he treated Amanda. His fingernails drilled against the heavy table, and his jaw sawed. "You know what?" He thumped his fist against the table. "You're right. Bring her in today. Have Halle connect with Parker."

His eyebrow crooked. "That's it?"

Jared pinched the bridge of his nose. "Doesn't seem like anyone's listening to me. You're both sure as shit not sharing what you need to—"

"I'm not?" Hagan asked.

"This will be great." Jared pushed out of his chair. "Or you'll realize you should've listened to me. Keep her safe." He jabbed a finger toward Hagan. "From everyone. Including you."

# CHAPTER TWENTY-FIVE

JARED SHUT THE war room door with an ominous thud that mirrored his hulking, brooding demeanor. He rounded the room and took a seat at the head of the table. Across from Hagan, Amanda squared her shoulders and chin, refusing to shrink from his glower. "Boss Man."

Her stubborn, defiant streak did something to Hagan. He knew it might haunt him one day, but until then, he wanted to clap Amanda on the back and say good job.

Jared's expression tightened, clearly not happy to have been pulled into this job, but he finally greeted her, dipping his head. "Sparkler."

Hagan gripped his chair's armrests and refrained from telling his boss that cutesy fuckin' nicknames weren't needed in the war room. Amanda's gaze clashed with Jared. But as her nostrils flared, she seemed to acknowledge he'd scored some kind of point in their asinine, silent battle.

Angela walked in, unknowingly breaking the tension, and distributed briefing books. Parker joined them and closed the door. After everyone had a booklet, she dialed on the conference call line, briefly speaking to someone before announcing that Halle was on the line.

"The gang's all here." Jared flipped open the briefing. "Let's talk about penetration."

"Don't be a two-year-old," Amanda chided.

Hagan cut a hard glance between them and tried to see Amanda as the head of another security company. This was essentially a joint task force. A joint op. She didn't work for him, no matter that they contracted together. For this job, Jared and Amanda were equals. And, no matter their history or games, right now she seemed ready to remind everyone of that fact.

Jared gestured to Hagan. "Isn't that what we're all here to talk about?"

"No one needs to be an asshole," Hagan muttered.

"Just so we're clear." Jared leaned forward, set his elbows on the table, and eyed them around the table. "I am an asshole."

"This isn't going to work." Amanda stood up and smiled toward Hagan. "Thanks for offering to help."

"Wait," Halle called from the speakerphone. "I've already put things in motion. I think we can all agree that two people are better than one."

Amanda crossed her arms and looked as though she might hang up on Halle. "We're not pen testing their system. Simply scouting for information."

"Too bad," Jared added.

Hagan witnessed Amanda's struggle. It couldn't have been far from how he felt.

"Let me guess." She stiffly returned to her seat. "You plan

to be as obnoxious as possible until we go our separate ways?"

He smirked. "How's my plan working?"

"All right you two. Enough," Halle demanded.

Hagan glanced at Angela and Parker. Angela didn't seem to know what was going on, and Parker seemed to orbit somewhere between laughing his ass off and standing in solidarity with Jared.

Jared held up his hands. "No more talk of penetration testing."

Despite the dynamics of the room, Hagan almost laughed. He bit the inside of his mouth and prayed that he could show the smallest slice of control. He'd never claimed to act mature. The nature of his job forced him to find humor in the shittiest of situations. This meeting wasn't the shittiest situation, but it had to be the most uncomfortable. Lord, give him strength to finish this meeting without fighting his boss or laughing out loud.

"If you can't control the urge," Amanda said, "you just say pen testing. It'd be less of a distraction, Boss Man."

"Noted," Jared grumbled.

Something that sounded suspiciously like choking laughter came from Parker. Hagan wondered how he'd gone his entire life without attending a meeting where someone had said penetration. That had to be impossible. Off the top of his head, he recounted a half-dozen missions in the last six months that required him to breach a line or infiltrate enemy barriers, and yet today that word sounded as inappropriate as … finger.

Hagan dropped his chin and pinched his eyes shut, knowing damn well that if he were to look up, he wouldn't be able to keep it together.

Shuttlecock. Diphthong. Dreamhole. Hagan rubbed his temples. Innocuous words from long-finished crossword puzzles had come back to haunt him. His dirty mind did one better, ensuring that he somehow heard words like kumquat, dongle, and angina in Amanda's voice.

"Everything okay over there?" Jared demanded.

Hagan's thoughts had transformed into weirdo pervy word lists. Hell, his grandma had had angina. This meeting might ensure his place in hell if he weren't careful. "Yeah. Fine."

Jared opened his booklet again and flipped a few pages. Everyone else took it as a sign they could get down to business. Hagan skimmed the first pages and stopped cold. *Newlyweds*.

He glanced up. No one seemed shocked as they read the briefing contents. Was he the only one who hadn't put two and two together? Amanda and Halle had discussed the benefits of a cover that operated as a couple. In theory, he'd digested that information. But to see the details of their coupledom written in black and white. Newlyweds, no less. As if he wouldn't have had sex on his mind already. But that word equated into lots and lots of sex.

Angela pushed a shoe-box-sized container toward the center of the table. Hagan realized that he'd spaced on the discussion. Amanda reached for the box and extracted three smaller boxes. She opened the first, and without much fanfare, shut it and slung it across the table to Hagan.

Hagan eyed the box, not ready for what was inside. How

the hell could he face off with his boss over a woman but let a fake marriage make him feel as cagey as a captured lion?

Amanda settled in her chair again. Two unopened boxes remained by her side.

Hagan refocused on the briefing and turned to the details of their joint operating agreement. Nothing much to see except for legalese.

He turned another page and skimmed. The summary read a little wordier than Titan's usual mission briefings, but nothing out of the ordinary. Then Hagan read the first details of their cover. He'd never worked a job like this before.

Pieces of their cover surprised him. Hagan glanced up, confirming, "You'll stay Amanda?"

She nodded. "And you'll stay Hagan. There's too high of a risk that the casino's security system might register an unacceptable time variance if we interacted with different names."

"You're saying a fraction of a second could blow our cover?"

"Yeah," Parker agreed. "We've kept what we have to and slightly adjusted everything else."

Hagan reviewed his information. "We live in Bardstown, Kentucky."

"Right," Parker said.

"Because I grew up in—"

"No!" Amanda held up her hands. "Don't share anything with me unless it's on this paper."

Jared sighed. "That ship has sailed."

She ignored him. "Are we on the same page?"

Back to this again. Hagan ground his molars. What choice did he have? Then again, until Jared started poking him with a stick today, Hagan had been okay. He studied his profile. "Got it. I'm a pilot for UPS."

She relaxed. "You know how to fly?"

"Says so right here." Hagan tapped the briefing book.

Jared sighed.

Angela set another box on the table. This time, Hagan grabbed it first and dumped the contents onto the table. A flowery cloth purse and a well-worn masculine leather wallet fell out. Hagan slung the purse toward Amanda, then flipped open his new wallet and inspected his ID and credit cards.

The briefing wrapped in a matter of minutes. Jared and Parker left when Angela picked up the phone line and chatted with Halle. Only Hagan and Amanda remained. He scooped his new gear and moved to the seat at her side. "Time to check out the good stuff, huh?"

Her business-as-usual attitude had disappeared. "Guess so."

Hagan gave his box a shake. It was heavier than he'd expected and required him to tug off the top. Amanda opened her two boxes and placed them in a row with his. Inside the velvet-lined boxes were his-and-hers earpieces and mics, an engagement ring, and two matching gold bands.

# CHAPTER TWENTY-SIX

THE CONTENTS OF the boxes weren't a surprise, and given the way Jared had led the meeting, Amanda hadn't been focused on the jewelry as much as she'd wanted to make it through the briefing without strangling him or exposing her personal details.

Still, with Hagan at her side and their wedding bands waiting to be slid into place, her stomach jumped.

Hagan looked to her and nodded back to the boxes. She laughed at his expression. It was as though his stomach had not only jumped but also run for cover.

"Guess this is par for the course," he said.

A knot lodged in her throat. Amanda gripped the strap of her Vera Bradley bag and nodded. "Goes with the gig."

He picked up the box with the engagement ring and shifted it to catch the light on the diamond. "Do you use the same ring every time?"

"No."

His eyebrow crooked. "Is it real?"

"Yeah."

Hagan removed the engagement ring from the velvet. The delicate band seemed so small in his large hands. He laughed nervously. "Not something I see every day."

The moment felt far more intimate that it should have. "Halle and Angela have good taste."

His head tilted, though Hagan didn't pull his eyes off the ring. "Do you like it?"

"Sure." Keeping her thoughts in a rational place took an enormous amount of mental strength. Maybe she'd made a huge mistake. After working alongside Hagan all day, with their natural chemistry ... acting like a couple didn't seem like a big deal. But now it felt far too real, and she wanted to tell him things that would let him see who she really was. Amanda bit her lip. It was one thing to kiss and touch him, to tell him that he made her nervous. But giving him personal information? *Wanting* to give him those little details that she'd kept hidden away for years? It was too much to explain.

Besides, he didn't want the real answer. Her real answer would be way too much to say. *Oh, it's a beautiful ring, but not for me. I like rings that tell a story. So, yeah, that's a pretty solitaire. But it's not nearly as complicated as love and life can be, and that's what I'd want in an engagement ring.* "Maybe we stick to what our covers like."

He caught her eye, and for a terrifying moment, she wasn't sure Hagan would let her off without a battle-hardened plea for his mercy. "Then I guess we should skip to the good part." He took her left hand. "May I?"

He took her hand and slid the ring onto her finger. Amanda couldn't breathe.

"Amanda?"

She lifted her gaze to his. "Thanks."

They'd talked about their chemistry. About how they could play a couple because they were exploring what that might mean. But the sparks that she'd planned a mission around singed her nerve endings.

Hagan's thumb caressed over her knuckles then slipped away. "Looks nice."

The diamond glittered, and though it was intentionally chosen not to be memorable, she admired the ring as if it weren't a prop for their cover. After a second, she laughed. "Okay, try yours on."

Hagan removed the larger band and slipped it on his finger. "Fits."

She put her band on also. "Though, I think I'm supposed to put the band on first."

"Why?"

She gestured. "I don't know. People say that it's closer to your heart?"

Hagan laughed it off. "People can kiss my ass." But he lifted her left hand and switched the order of the rings. "Better?"

"People would say so."

She'd never wanted him to kiss her so much before. "That's what we're doing. Convincing people."

He lifted her from the chair and set her on the edge of the massive war room table. "We don't need rings to convince people."

As though they hadn't sparred with Jared or didn't have

secrets that should keep them apart, Hagan pulled her ass to the edge of the table, wrapping her legs around his. His mouth took hers. They didn't have to prove anything to the world. People could see what she could feel, him hot on her body, hungry for her mouth. Her locking her arms over his broad shoulders, clinging to his corded neck.

She worried they'd get caught until his tongue parted her lips. Then Amanda did nothing except pray for more. Hagan nibbled, kissed, and rubbed against her. Her hands clawed into his hair, knowing there had to be a hundred cameras in the room and wishing every single one would lose their connection. She wanted to feel Hagan's skin. She needed his weight to cage her to the table.

"Hello," Angela called as she opened the door, then retreated. "When you have a minute…"

Hagan smiled against Amanda's mouth, and if the urge to hide and die of embarrassment had surfaced, his quiet laughter kept it away.

"Busted," he whispered, then softly kissed her one more time. Hagan waited until Amanda had thrown herself into the chair, attempting to look like she hadn't been begging Hagan to jump her on the table. He kissed her one more time, still smiling. "We have a minute."

Angela swooped into the room, looking everywhere but at them. "Jared had a question for you."

"Then Jared could've come down instead of sending you." Hagan sat next to Amanda and crossed his arms over his chest. "Or Jared could've picked up the phone and called."

Angela grimaced as though she'd figured out why Jared had done neither. "Your plane tickets."

Amanda grabbed the folder that Angela slid over. "These are for today?"

"Yes." Angela nodded. "Halle said that would work with your schedule."

Hagan eyed the tickets and checked his watch. "Wheels up in less than six hours."

"Please touch base with Jared before you go." She reached for the door. "He said something about staying looped in on this job. I think he just wants to know how your day is going."

Amanda understood that Boss Man still wasn't comfortable with any of the liberties she'd taken. "We can do that—"

Hagan rocked in the chair. "The day that Jared cares about *my day* is the day that grenades learn to toss themselves while I drink a cold-ass beer."

*Or not...* They weren't going to get out of the building as easily as she'd thought.

"Hagan." Angela had the kind of smile that appeared perfect, but underneath screamed for compliance. And for Hagan to shut up. Amanda could tell that this wasn't the first time she'd used it on him or his teammates. "What do you want me to tell him then?"

Hagan scooped the boxes, briefing, and tickets into one hand and grabbed Amanda with the other. "Tell him my day's going great, but I had to catch a plane."

He ignored Angela's incredulous glare and sauntered across the room, with Amanda promising she'd touch base soon.

"You know that won't work," Angela called as they passed her and walked down the hallway.

Amanda squeezed his hand. "We don't need to irritate Jared more than we already have."

He winked then looked over his shoulder. "Tell Boss Man I grabbed my new wife and will check in from the honeymoon sometime after I land."

# CHAPTER TWENTY-SEVEN

Casino de Gemmayzeh was everything that Imad Nasrallah had promised—beautiful and busy. The ambiance welcomed Amanda and Hagan as newlyweds as much as it did high-rolling casino whales. A bellhop had whisked their luggage from sight as soon as they'd arrived, and if she didn't look carefully, it'd be hard to tell that anyone ever left the hotel.

Hagan rested his hand on the small of her back. A firework of prickles ran up her spine. He was playing a role, but he'd touched her like this before, nonchalantly telling the world that he had a claim on her. Color warmed her cheeks, ensuring that onlookers would see that just-married connection. She played her part, touching him as if they'd known each other for years. Except, she wasn't acting. Unlike any time where she played this role, Amanda didn't have a mental list of action items. Smile. Gaze. Touch. Everything with Hagan was natural.

They reached the registration desk. Hagan checked them in as she scoped the security and registration system, peppering the conversation with unobtrusive, fact-finding questions. The man behind the registration desk told them about their room and collected payment. Casino de Gemmayzeh's system and procedures left little room for error and raised questions about their gaming systems. If they were anything like the simple check-in process, Amanda knew they'd have to dig deep.

The hotel registrar returned Hagan's falsified identification and credit card along with key cards to the honeymoon suite, adding, "One second, please. I believe there's one more thing."

Curious, Amanda leaned against Hagan and watched the man disappear into an alcove behind the front desk. Her job was harder than she expected with Hagan rubbing his fingers along her hip. She ignored the way he made her feel like she had been walking on air and twisted in his arms, surreptitiously stealing a glance at the computer screen.

The registrar returned with an enormous bouquet of lilies and struggled to place them on the counter. "You had a delivery."

Her stomach dropped. "Aren't those beautiful."

Hagan eyed her as if he knew lilies were associated with funerals and death, then read the card and handed it to her.

*Best wishes on your speedy escape.*

Oh, man. Jared was pissed.

"It's from the office," Hagan volunteered to the man, then added to Amanda, "Isn't that sweet."

"So thoughtful, too, but ..." Her eyebrows arched. "It's too bad I'm allergic."

"Forgot about that." He crushed the card in his hand and turned the man behind the counter. "Do you know anyone who might enjoy these?"

His brow furrowed. "Are you sure?"

"Absolutely," Hagan confirmed.

Amanda didn't know if the man was genuinely surprised to have the flowers turned away or didn't want to deal with the hot-air-balloon-sized arrangement. "Please," she urged. "As much as we'd love to take them, I'd be bed-bound with an allergy headache."

The man hefted the vase off the counter. "We can't have that." He signaled to the bellhop captain that they were ready for their room, and with a final congratulations, Hagan and Amanda were directed to meet the bellhop who'd initially retrieved their luggage.

"Death flowers, huh?" Hagan's lips lingered near her ear. "Bet Boss Man had to do some Googling to come up with that."

"Or he had Angela take a page from her mother's playbook." They'd never reached the acquaintance level of interaction, but Amanda understood more about Angela's life with a mother like the infamous Senator Sorenson than most.

Hagan snorted. "Don't remind me of that old witch." He smoothed his thumb along the indentation of her spine, then managed an easygoing conversation with their attendant as they made their way to the elevators and boarded.

The elevator quickly rose to the ninth floor. Hagan held her hand like they'd had years together, and when the doors opened, he strode in front of the bellhop until they reached their suite.

"I'll make sure everything is to your liking," the bellhop offered, unlocking the door with a key card and stepping aside.

Amanda took a step. Hagan hauled her back, and with a shiver-inducing half-grin, he winked. "I'm supposed to carry you over the threshold."

*Have mercy.* She needed his arms around her again.

Hagan caught her gaze and held it, lifting her into his arms.

It felt so right. There wasn't a single word that explained how he made her feel. A distant voice in the back of her head warned her that they would both get hurt if she let this go too far. But she'd already had and was fast wondering how deep she could fall for this man.

He carried her into the suite and spun Amanda around. "Does this work for you?"

In so many ways. "Think so."

"Me too." Hagan kissed Amanda and set her down.

She didn't let go, not trusting her legs. Blood rushed in her ears, and vaguely aware of Hagan conversing with the bellhop, she fought against the deliriously amazing fog that his lips could create.

The door shut. They were alone. Hagan placed his hands on her hips and pulled her to him. "I like playing pretend with you."

She swayed into him, feeling herself come alive. His thick erection pressed between them. There were things she had to do. Standard operating procedure required her to sweep the room and inspect their luggage. But Amanda didn't care. "That makes me very happy. She caressed his bulge. She unfastened the top of his jeans, teased the zipper down, and slid her hands under the denim. "Because I like playing with you, too."

"*That's* playing with fire," he warned.

His black briefs were soft to the touch and painted over his muscular physique, and her mouth watered to pull his erection free. But first, she teased. Amanda followed the cut indentation of muscle to the top of his thighs, back to his hips, and then to his firm ass. Her fingernails bit into the hard flesh, and she sank to her knees.

His jeans piled at his feet. Hagan cursed when she tipped her chin up. The fire in his gaze made her tingle. "You're too much for me."

She rolled his boxer briefs down and freed his long, smooth length. "Liar," she whispered against his crown. Her tongue darted out. Amanda licked the thick ridge of his cock, taking her time to feel his body tense before her lips opened over the top of his shaft.

"I lied," he groaned. "You're perfect for me."

Amanda grinned, wrapped her hand around his thickness, and briefly pulled her mouth away. "I agree."

She took him into her mouth again and worked her hand on his shaft. She needed more of him. Her eyes watered. There was a power in bringing his cock to her throat. Her terms. Her man. She pulled back and drank in oxygen, hungry for him to fill her again.

Hagan flexed and growled, nearly shaking to hold himself back. She wanted him to let go, to find what he needed with her—in her—as she was finding it with him.

Amanda gagged. He jerked back. Her hands grabbed for his ass. She willed him to understand that she was okay, that she enjoyed bringing him this much pleasure. Sucking him, tasting him, she'd found a way to own the moment, and it was more freeing than standing on top of a building.

Her mouth encircled his crown, and then she pulled back. Her lips nuzzled against his blunt head. "I need this." Her tongue curled and swiped away a bead of precum. "I need you."

The keycard and hotel brochure fell from his hand as though he couldn't focus on anything but her. She cupped his sac and let her tongue play on his crown. She took him and teased him until any resistance had disappeared. Hagan flexed and thrust into her mouth. She took him, deep and hungry, until she couldn't breathe, then again and again, crying for more, choking on the need to feel him throb and shudder.

His hands grasped the top of her head. He gasped her name in warning. The guttural cry electrified her body. She'd never needed another man's pleasure like this before. Hagan's orgasm thundered. He cried her name and trembled. In the middle of their newlywed suite, their luggage to one side, the key card at her knees, she drank him in until he eased away.

Amanda fell back and grinned. Her lips were numb, and her pussy soaked. "You look like you enjoyed that almost as much as me."

It took Hagan a second to laugh. Then he kicked off his shoes and pants, hooked her under the arms, hauled Amanda to his chest, and kicked open the double doors that led to their bed.

## CHAPTER TWENTY-EIGHT

THE BEDROOM DOORS opened, and Hagan stopped short. Amanda wriggled to see what had frozen her half-naked man, and then she gasped. "Wow."

He half-laughed. They both gaped. Their hot-and-heavy hurry had been doused with a saccharine explosion of cliché.

"If this isn't romance, I don't know what is." Hagan carried her to the massive bed and set her down amid a thick blanket of white rose petals. "What more could my new wife want? Her man without pants, and the world's largest stuffed bear." He grabbed a large pink teddy that took up most of the bed and tossed it to her.

Amanda batted the bear away and propped herself up in the pile of rose petals. "This is a bit extra." She kicked off her sandals and tossed a handful of petals at him, then noticed the placard on the bed. *Welcome and Wishes for a Life Full of Love.* "It's the thought that counts?"

Still half-dressed, Hagan inspected a bottle of chilled champagne on the nightstand. "People need this to deal with that."

She laughed and swiped away the petals until she reached the white eyelet cotton bedspread. "If you want to get your pants or—"

He cut her a quick look. "Like hell." He lifted her off the bed and tore off the top layer of covers. Thousands of white petals fluttered onto the dark carpet. "Betcha room service doesn't get paid enough to deal with this bullshit." He shifted her to his other arm as though she weighed as much as the blanket and then set her on the bed. With a crooked grin, he tore off his shirt, crawled to the center of the bed, and pulled her to his bare chest. "If I'd guessed, I would've thought red or pink roses petals for the happy couple."

"They'd mess up the sheets," she pointed out.

His eyebrow crooked. "We're gonna mess up the sheets."

Amanda laughed until he unbuttoned the top of her blouse. His knuckles grazed over her collar bone. Hagan unfastened a second button. Hyper aware of her breaths, she anticipated his next move. As fast as he'd made her laugh, he'd turned her on again. Hagan didn't touch her skin. Goosebumps still jumped.

After the last button, he spread the shirt. Air wicked over her skin, followed by the cataclysmic heat of his strong hand smoothing over her stomach.

"You shouldn't wear clothes to bed."

The idea of sleeping next to Hagan, naked and wrapped in his arms, made her almost jump. She wasn't sure that was an intimacy she was ready for. But this was. Their eyes met, and it was as if he understood what she wanted, needed, and had to ignore. Hagan found the zipper on her hip, stripped away her pants, and stared.

She caught herself from apologizing for her scars and wished she'd put the kind of thought into this trip of a woman traveling with her man, not a security analyst looking for a clue. Her cotton bra and panties were comfortable and a far cry from sexy, yet he acted as though she were a feast for a starved man. Arousal dampened her ordinary underwear. Her tight nipples pressed into the white cotton. It didn't matter what she wore or wanted to hide. His erection hung heavy, thickening at the sight of her. She was overcome by that same urge that had swelled in her when the door shut and they were alone. She needed to him to fill her body as much as he occupied her mind.

Hagan inched the cotton off her hips then unclasped her bra, laying it at her side. Amanda wrapped herself to him. She was skin-hungry. It wasn't romantic or seductive, but it was so needed. He cocooned her and nuzzled her neck until she'd had her fill of closeness.

Her mouth found his. Their tongues tangled, sweet and slow. His hands explored, touching and testing, studying every reaction as he mapped a path from her breasts to her clitoris. He stroked her sensitive skin and spread her arousal in a teasing game until her legs spread, vagina reaching for his touch. "Please."

His fingers circled her entrance as though he enjoyed making her beg. When she couldn't wait another second, the heel of his palm pressed to her clit and his fingers penetrated her body.

Her head rolled back. But the instant satisfaction of pressure wasn't enough. He read her body and stretched her open. Another finger. Another angle. His hand stroked and slowed and fucked until she squirmed.

"Come here." He jerked himself upright and hauled Amanda's back to his chest. One of his powerful arms belted her in place. The other threw her legs wide. She trembled, vulnerable and needy, squirming for contact and writhing in his impossible hold. Desperation caught in her throat. His fingers curled into her again, and she almost cried. "That's what you need."

She nodded. *Take everything. Take control.* He plunged in and out of her body with a ferocious speed that made her legs shake. Hagan hooked his ankle over hers. Just the same, he pinned her other leg. She bucked against his hand, needing a climax so bad it hurt. Amanda choked on his name again. It caught in her throat.

The hand over her chest moved to her neck. "I've got your body." He growled. "Trust me with everything else."

Her orgasm rolled over her like a volcano erupting. Waves of seismic force echoed as she called his name. The deafening roar of her climax blinded her senses. Amanda trembled and gasped, falling against him. He'd released her legs and curled her to his chest. She floated, pussy still quivering, as aftershocks stole her breath.

Her head met the pillow. Hagan pulled a sheet up and cradled Amanda to his chest.

"I didn't know I could feel like this."

His quieted laughter rumbled. "That makes two of us."

Amanda didn't explain because she couldn't. An unhurried sense of euphoria coaxed her eyelids closed. She didn't fight to stay awake and jump into work. She simply accepted that the world would still be there when she got up.

# CHAPTER TWENTY-NINE

NIGHT HAD FALLEN when Hagan awoke. Vibrant lights peppered the view out their window, illuminating their bedroom. Amanda slept by his side with an ankle hooked over his shin, her dark hair spread over her pillow. She slept soundly. He'd never seen her unaware and unprepared. How exhausting were her burdens to carry?

Hagan shifted to his side. Amanda murmured when her foot fell from his leg, then burrowed herself against him. He tipped his head to the side and wondered what he could do to lighten her torment. The urge to protect her was fierce, but years of security jobs and black ops hadn't prepared him for a fight he couldn't see.

Amanda stirred and nuzzled against his bare skin. Satisfaction burned in his chest. Hagan was content to let her sleep because he had no doubt that when she woke, there'd be business to attend to.

"You're awake," she whispered.

His fingers trailed down her shoulder. "I wanted to let you sleep."

She sighed and snuggled. Peaceful. He wondered how she slept alone and if this was different with him. A possessive part of him assured Hagan that it was. True or not, he wanted to quiet her demons again and again.

"I have a few things to do."

His hand ran down her back as she stretched. The arch of her spine and swell of her ass gave him a quick reminder of the things on his list. It was a very physical list—and should've been the first thing on his mind when he woke up with a naked woman clinging to his side.

He'd process that later, watching as Amanda became more alert. Her watchful guard settled into place; then she rolled away, wrapped a sheet around her breasts, and left their bed.

Reluctantly, Hagan did the same, sans sheet, and redressed. He found Amanda pressed to the window that overlooked the sea-green water of a shimmering, lighted pool. "The view's not too shabby."

"I usually don't take time to notice the pool."

He massaged her shoulders. "Now that you have, want to go for a swim?"

She leaned back. "I don't know why I did tonight."

"Because your subconscious wants to go swimming with me."

She turned and wrapped her arms around his neck. "This is very comfortable."

"I noticed that."

She pressed her cheek to his heart. "Is that a problem?"

His definition of a problem didn't lend itself to the lush way she molded to his body. "Why would it be?"

Her shoulders bunched. "What if this trip blurs what's real

and not?"

He hadn't given a single thought to what their cover had been. Had she? Hagan touched her chin and lifted her gaze. "Did you want me to touch you?"

"*Yes.*"

"Then explain what you meant."

"When we go home, back to normal …" Amanda nibbled on her lip and then squared her shoulders. "I have to work. Want to help?"

"Sure." He'd circle back to home and normal later. "What do you need me to do?"

Amanda held her finger to her lips and walked into their suite's living room. She extracted two devices from her suitcase and handed one to him.

He recognized the technology used to sweep for listening devices and bugs. "The fun begins."

If there was a bug, he doubted she'd remove it. Better to know someone was listening than to tip their hand—even if that meant he and Amanda had offered an earful.

They moved methodically through the honeymoon suite as though they'd been a team for years, quickly finishing without a single concern. She tucked the devices into her suitcase again.

"What other tricks do you have hidden in there?" Hagan leaned on the counter and sifted through a pile of sightseeing brochures.

"You'll have to wait and see."

Hagan whistled. "No wonder Boss Man and Parker keep you stashed away. You're their secret weapon."

She quietly laughed. "I do have a serious thing for surveillance and security."

"And for keeping secrets," he said. Then he added, "You know what we should do?"

Annoyed, she eyed him. "What?"

"Eat."

Her brow furrowed. "I don't know if you're changing the subject because that was a cheap shot or because you're always hungry."

"I'm a big guy." Hagan laughed, then found a leather-bound booklet that highlighted the casino and hotel offerings. "And you make me burn a lot of energy." He took a seat on the couch, perusing the dining options. The casino and hotel had several restaurants, and he immediately disregarded two that required a tie and jacket. "We haven't even broached the good stuff yet." He glanced at her wide eyes, then winked.

"I …" She dropped her chin and shook her head, then laughing, asked, "What are we doing about dinner?"

Damn, she was cute. He turned to their dining options. As much as he wanted an overstuffed pita with the works, he decided that ordering at a counter and waiting for their receipt number to be called wasn't the way newlyweds should spend the first night of their honeymoon.

Finally, he found something between the two extremes. The restaurant promised the full Lebanese experience, and the menu made his mouth water. "There's a place called Zikrayet."

"Let's go there. I like their menu."

Of course she'd already read the menus. "Good deal."

"Give me a minute to change." She pulled her bag into the bedroom. "I need to freshen up."

Hagan threw himself on the couch and flipped the hotel book open again. Amanda had probably memorized it. He needed to catch up. He read through the hotel amenities, then checked his watch. "I could've showered and redressed in the amount of time that it takes you to freshen up."

"Tough cookies," she called.

Hagan returned to the hotel book, pausing at the list of spa services. He calculated the US dollar exchange rate, then double-checked his math. "If I ever need a new career, remind me to look into giving expensive-ass massages."

"What?" She stepped through the double doors.

Hagan glanced up. His mouth opened. Nothing came out. He jumped onto his feet, shut his slack-jaw, and gaped at his pretend wife. "Damn."

Amanda's dark hair cascaded over her shoulders, contrasting against a cream-colored, high-necked blouse with long, airy sleeves. His gaze dropped to the sharp-fitting, slim black pants that hugged her legs, cutting off above her ankle. And those shoes. The black high heels were simple but threatened to steal the show. Hagan had had no idea he was a shoe guy. "Wow."

Her eyelashes seemed longer. Makeup, he guessed. Barely noticeable. Except for her lips.

Nervously, her tongue darted to her bottom lip, stained the color of berries. "We should go."

He crossed the room and kept himself on a short leash. "I

don't want to go anywhere but back in bed."

"Don't be ridiculous."

"Trust me, babe. The only ridiculous thing is that you're still on your feet."

A smile tugged at the corner of her lips. "But work calls."

He almost argued they should quit and become masseuses, but when she held out her hand, he took it.

# CHAPTER THIRTY

Walking down the hall with Amanda on Hagan's arm was almost as good as staying in and diving under the covers. Or maybe even better. That logic didn't add up. He should've been climbing the walls to strip her of everything except those shoes. But that kind of satisfaction could wait, because having Amanda by his side gave Hagan a new type of gratification.

"What's that look?" Amanda asked.

Hagan called the elevator. "I'm glad we're headed to dinner."

"You're always hungry," she teased.

"True."

She glanced as though she knew there was more. "But?"

"I'm damn lucky to be with you tonight." He dipped his nose to the curve of her neck and inhaled. "You make me feel ten feet tall."

Her hair fell away when she arched. "And you make me feel safe."

"That's everything I can ask you for." The mechanical sound of the elevator approaching refocused Hagan. "And, I'll try to remember we're here to work." His hands moved to her backside, sliding over the silky black pants. "I don't know how good of a job I've been doing."

"I don't know anyone who could pretend to be my man"—her breath hitched—"better than you."

Pretend? His palm moved to the small of her back and toyed with the delicate blouse. The fabric was so thin he could feel the warmth of her skin. His fingers caressed the indentation of her spine.

The elevator dinged and the doors opened.

"Time to work," he whispered and led the way.

The trip to the main level went fast, and they exited into a flood of bright lights and people. Cigarette and hookah smoke hung in the air. Distant bells and trills called from the casino floor.

She took a deep breath despite the smoky air and shook away the subtle distraction that had softened her to his side.

They followed the well-placed signage to a row of restaurants and stores. He sensed a change. Amanda's steps weren't as smooth. Her hold felt too practiced. He wrapped his arm around her waist and dipped his lips close to her ear. "Everything okay?"

"Just taking it all in."

"You're tense."

Amanda shook her head. "Something's not right."

Hagan steered them from traffic and found an intimate space between two planted trees. His fingers trailed over her jaw, then down her neck. "Do you see something wrong?"

She nuzzled his neck. "I see something new."

"Don't know what that means." He skimmed his hand across the small of her back. "Keep moving or stay still?"

"Just …" She touched his side. "Get my back to the wall."

"Like I said, whatever you want." He tried to keep a certain level of decorum in mind as he nestled them away. Hotel casino or not, this area wasn't as forgiving of perceived vulgarities. "Good?"

Amanda hummed as though she didn't like what she saw. "All right. Think so."

He stepped back. "You sure?"

Uncertainty clouded her gaze. "Only that I need to move on."

What the hell did she see that he could not? "Let's go."

Hand in hand, they walked by a jewelry store and a shop dedicated entirely to purses. Amanda pulled him from window to window on the way to dinner. She gushed about all that glitter and sparkle. He wondered if she actually cared at all. Finally, they reached an arch of purple lights spotlighting the entrance for Zikrayet.

The host manned a matching podium illuminated in purple. "Can I help you?"

Hagan stepped forward. "Table for two."

As fast as they were welcomed, they were shown to a table. Their waiter approached with water glasses, greeting them with congratulations. How closely aligned was security and hotel hospitality? Hagan thanked the man, and they selected the seven-course chef's dinner.

Once alone, Amanda scoped the room in a similar way as

he had when they'd walked in. She seemed less interested in the restaurant's occupants than he would've been, but they followed the same protocol.

"Nice choice." She took a sip of her water and leaned back into her chair. "I think this will be a nice meal."

"And what do you think of their security?" he asked. "Lots of cameras?"

She grinned. "Yes, but not as many as there should be."

"Maybe you can't see them."

Amanda rolled her eyes. "Doubtful."

He snickered. "You're right, ya know."

The first course arrived. Hagan picked up what the waiter had called 'wisps of aged cheese topped with pancetta' and swallowed it in one bite.

"Good?" Amanda asked.

Hagan decided that Camden's killer cheese-sticks-and-bacon casserole could've wiped the floor with the chef's tiny dish. "Tasty."

She laughed and tried her cheesy bacon bite, agreeing as the next course arrived.

Plate two involved a bowl, but Hagan didn't point that out. Plate three was a misnomer, as a tiny plate arrived to 'cleanse their palates' just before it. He would call that plate 2B if forced to include the 'gelatin made of citrus water with hints of celery' in their debriefing report. "I don't suppose plate four or five will be a ribeye."

"We can only hope."

He snickered. "Are you a slots girl? Or do you like the table games?"

"I like whatever I can beat."

Hagan thanked the waiter for the Jell-O and ignored Amanda's kick under the table. "The house always wins."

"Someone's winning." Two lines creased her forehead. "But I'm still not sure who."

"Want to talk about it?"

She shook her head. "Not yet."

A ribeye didn't come with the next course, but he appreciated that it was more substantial. Hagan still finished it faster than he would've liked.

"Can I ask you a question?"

He shrugged. "Since when do you ask?"

"It's a nosy question," she warned.

He wiped his mouth and leaned back. "Try me."

"Why don't you have a girlfriend?"

His grin hitched. "Why don't you?"

"I'm serious." She gestured. "You already know that you're a catch."

His cheeks warmed. Hagan wasn't sure if he'd blushed before. "Not sure that I've thought about that."

"Have you ever had a serious relationship?"

He rolled his bottom lip into his mouth. "Does playing your husband count?"

"*Hagan.*"

"No—I feel like this is a test." He made a face. "Is there a right answer?"

She cringed. "No, and now I feel ridiculous for asking."

"Don't." He sipped the wine pairing.

"I do anyway. Sorry. Ask me something equally as silly."

With an opening like that, Hagan didn't have to think. "You and Boss Man." He set down his wine glass. "Did you two ever date?"

# CHAPTER THIRTY-ONE

AMANDA CHOKED ON her tongue and had to reach for her water as Hagan's eyebrow arched. After a few sips, she set the glass by her plate. "That's ridiculous."

Their fifth course arrived.

Hagan barely glanced at the plate or the waiter. "You know Boss Man pretty well."

Amanda couldn't wrap her head around the idea of dating Jared. Of doing *anything* with Jared. They were too far apart in age. She almost looked at him like her father. Though he'd kill her for that. Maybe a younger uncle. They'd always had a good rapport. But the idea of her and Jared Westin? Impossible. "He's terrifying."

"I can see he scares the crap out of you," Hagan deadpanned.

"We ..." She had no words. Hagan really believed that it could be true? "No."

"If you say so." He stabbed a julienned carrot.

"Are you jealous?"

"Of you and my boss?" Hagan grimaced. "Considering what happened in the war room? It'd make things awkward."

"I can't believe you think he's my type."

Hagan's gaze narrowed. "What is your type?"

She'd never had one until he'd pestered her away from her rules. "You."

His lips parted, and his posture changed. Now he was the one without something to say.

Their waiter arrived with the next set of wine pairings. Neither of them had touched the most recent glasses. Wine accidentally sloshed, and the waiter overcorrected. The glasses collided, spilling red wine, drenching Amanda's blouse. She jerked back, knocking her water glass into her lap.

Hagan came to his feet. Ice-cold water soaked into her pants. A hush fell. Every table stared. The waiter apologized again and again as the host and manager appeared. She wanted to hide her face and cry but heard herself laugh.

Hagan handed her his napkin. His face cracked. "You might need another."

Dozens of eyes were on Amanda, and she didn't even care. They might recognize her, they might not. For the first time since gossip bloggers had made their living reporting her blunders and faux pas, she didn't care, laughing into Hagan's protective arms.

The manager interrupted with promises their meal was free and her clothes would be replaced. Everyone must have thought they'd lost their minds.

Amanda pulled herself together and lifted a palm to the side like a model striking a pose. "This can't be your type."

"Trust me." Hagan nabbed her arm to his side again. "It absolutely is."

They thanked everyone for the help, and Hagan grabbed a tablecloth on the way out. He cloaked it over her shoulders to keep prying eyes away from the wet, thin fabric.

"Where to?" Hagan asked as they joined the general flow of foot traffic. "You're not going to let see-through clothing and wet pants keep you from the casino, right?"

She tipped her head back to look at him. "You're crazy."

He grinned. "Shower, then bed?"

"Yeah. It's been a long day."

"Ten-four, beautiful." Hagan directed them toward the closest elevators.

She couldn't wait to peel off her clothes and go to bed. *In their bed.* Nervous energy skipped down her spine. What would happen later? She hadn't expected earlier, and she wasn't sure what she was ready for.

They rode alone in the elevator, staying close, but her thoughts were already in the bedroom, wondering what he expected and wanted. It had been so easy when they'd first arrived. Spending time with Hagan should only have made it easier.

They made it to their floor without running into another guest, then walked to their room hand in hand. He opened the door like a perfect gentleman.

"Thanks for tonight." She walked in and stood at the same place they had before when she'd been certain of what would happen next. "We did a good job tonight."

"Easiest gig I've ever had." Hagan broke away and headed for the couch, pulling his shirt over his head. The move wasn't to show off his jaw-dropping physique as much as he needed to strip away their day. Amanda gawked at the rippling display of muscles as he slung the shirt onto his shoulder. "I'll stay out of your way until you're done in the bathroom."

"All right." Moving toward the shower required her concentration. She'd felt his body before, but she apparently hadn't taken time to appreciate it.

She kicked off her high heels and unbuttoned her blouse, tossing it in the trash. The pants stuck to her legs and took wriggling to get off, and she left the wine-stained bra and underwear on the tile floor.

Hagan knocked on the door.

*How about that timing ...* "Yes?"

"I forgot to ask what bothered you earlier."

She cracked the door and stuck her head out. Butterflies swarmed at the sight of him.

"You're busy," he volunteered. "I'll come back."

"There's a store I didn't recognize on the spreadsheet."

"Okay." He backed away. "So long as it's not a big deal."

It was actually a huge deal, but her explanation went hazy. "I was worried about coming back to the room."

His brow furrowed as though he'd missed a threat. "Why?"

"I have no idea." She let the door open.

Hagan raked his gaze over her curves like he was a starving man. "You better figure that out before inviting me in."

"I didn't know what would happen."

His erection strained against his pants. "Now you do?"

"I hope so." She bit her lip, then reached for the top of his pants.

He covered her hand with a fist. "It's your move. So, you're in control."

Now that he pointed that out? Maybe so. The blow job. The bathroom. But it wasn't like she'd mapped out a plan. "I don't know."

He lifted their hands but didn't let go. "Why don't you tell me what you want, then we'll work that out together."

"Sounds like you have way more control than I do."

"Not a chance." He pressed her hand to his cock and sucked in a sharp breath. "What do you need, Amanda?"

"I need you."

"You already have me." He stroked his length with her hand. "What do you need?"

"Is that the same thing as what I want?" She wanted to use his body and trust in his soul. A primal hunger swept over her nerve endings.

"No." He squeezed her hand. "Wants? Who the fuck cares?"

A greedy intensity swelled in her belly. There wasn't anything about them that she could throw away. "But needs…?"

"That's the good stuff." His grin could've melted the sun. "What do you need?"

The truth was as obvious as her breathlessness. "To feel you inside me."

Hagan took her mouth like she'd struck a match to kerosene and lifted her from the cold tile floor. He sucked her bottom lip and whisked her into their bed. "That's what I need, too."

Grinding and groping, she unfastened his pants, and he tore them off. Amanda knotted her fingers in his hair, pulling him on top of her again. She needed his skin, his kisses. Completely without control, she needed more from Hagan than she understood.

Their kisses weren't easy. Their touches stoked their fire. They only paused for a condom, then she let him take command. Hagan teased and toyed with her until she begged for more. Then, as if he knew the moment she couldn't survive her needy pain, he pressed into her body.

Amanda gasped. Eyes closed. Mind numb. She couldn't get enough. He stretched into her slick tightness as she clawed his back.

Hagan flexed and kissed her. Their tongues dueled, coaxing her to ask for more. Her hips lifted. Hagan thrust, then thrust again. His name intertwined with desperate cries on her lips. Hagan drove her to the brink. She clenched around him and cried out as beautiful, painful pleasure blinded her with a climax.

"That's what I needed," he growled, slowing and stroking, riding her body. "To feel you cum like that."

But she needed his orgasm more than hers. Amanda locked her legs around his hips and arched, opening herself for him to take. Together, they climbed closer and closer, fighting for an all-consuming avalanche.

His orgasm released with the cry of her name. Her pussy rippled again. Their hoarse voices mixed in an unrestrained storm until they collapsed, spent.

Carefully, he moved her to his side. She wasn't ready to let go and buried her face into the pounding pulse in his neck. Then she realized that even when they left this bed, she wouldn't lose him.

# CHAPTER THIRTY-TWO

THEY ORDERED BREAKFAST in bed and spent the morning under the covers, with a laptop perched on the nightstand next to half-finished plates of pastries and mugs of coffee. Amanda hadn't completely slacked off of work. To be honest, she didn't feel any guilt at all, though she waited for it to show up between bites of Lebanese French pastries and rounds of lovemaking like they were newlyweds.

Draped over Hagan's chest, she wondered if this was balance. Work. Life. She wasn't sure, because her life revolved around work. Hagan traced the indentation where her backside met her leg, unhurried and at ease. She noticed the distinct smoothness of the wedding band around his ring finger whenever his palm flattened on her ass.

Of all the things to notice, that one seemed impossibly trivial, yet profoundly intimate. It was as though she'd stumbled onto a secret of married couples. Wearing rings while undercover had never connected her to a partner until Hagan had made her step out from the routine of her life.

His hand stilled. "We should get up."

"It's your turn to be the voice of reason?" She repositioned her cheek on his pec and let her hand slide along the muscles that covered his ribs.

His laughter rumbled against her ear. "Guess so."

Amanda gave him a quick kiss and rolled off his body. "What table games do you like?"

"None of them." The mattress shifted when Hagan threw his legs over and sat on the side of the bed.

"I thought you liked puzzles."

"I do." He stretched, then walked toward the bathroom. "Puzzles always have an answer. Gambling is a losing race against odds."

She'd never compared the two before but agreed. "Puzzles are fixed."

With a toothbrush in his mouth, he brushed naked as a blue jay and mumbled, "Yup." He held up a finger, went into the bathroom to rinse his mouth, and came back easier to understand. "The end point's always good, like the happily-ever-after in a fairytale."

"You're blowing my mind a wee bit."

He laughed and shuffled through his luggage. "I'll try to make that a habit."

"Please." She grinned but was still thinking about gambling and puzzles and the role each played in her life.

Hagan threw his clothes onto the bed and picked up his phone. He scrolled and read and scrolled again, finally tossing the phone onto the mattress. "Do you want to get in the shower first?"

He'd processed emails or the daily news, and she still hadn't moved on from what he'd said. They were surrounded by puzzles and gambles. Some were easy answers. Others offered satisfaction. Whether she wanted to get into the shower first would either be yes or no—a fifty-fifty shot like flipping a coin with no discernable risk. Still, he'd lost complete control the moment he'd asked when she wanted to shower.

She hadn't had enough coffee or sex to make sense of how this applied to her life—or maybe she'd had too much. Either way, it was clear that she'd drastically changed the way she lived, subconsciously betting against the odds—and herself. Amanda beelined for the bathroom. "I'll jump in first."

She busied herself, not sure if she wanted to find clarity or clear her thoughts. The shower warmed as she brushed her teeth. Steam shaded her reflection in the mirror, and Amanda stepped into the water, comb in hand, working the bedhead knots out of her hair.

Was she a puzzle or a gamble? A definite answer didn't come to mind, but she clearly played the odds in the way she lived. Amanda didn't want a high-stakes score. But she was certain that catastrophe was only one move away.

The hot water rained over her as she reached for a bottle and shampooed her hair. What about Hagan? Was he either a puzzle or gamble, and did he live life that same way?

Thick, soapy bubbles slid off her shoulders, landing on her feet. Amanda stepped under the spray. The shampoo suds sluiced down her arms, and she lathered a washcloth and massaged her skin. Squeaky clean and in no rush, she decided Hagan was neither. She wouldn't box him in the way she boxed in everything else.

Amanda twisted the temperature knob and waited until the water felt as if it had been pumped from the artic. Freezing water didn't offer clarity, and she jumped out. With a towel hastily wrapped around her breasts, she searched the hazy mirror and swiped the steam away until her reflection appeared.

"You're a gambler." She studied her image and ignored the remnants of mascara. "You might need help." What did people say? Knowing the problem was half the battle? That was why she was in Lebanon, after all. Or had she gone cold turkey? Meeting Hagan. Falling for him, too. She'd grown close to someone, breaking every rule.

Did that mean she'd stopped gambling, or unwittingly come to accept higher risk?

Amanda rubbed her temples. How had she not realized that odds dictated her life? At least until Hagan had shown up and changed the damn game. Or had he clarified the terms?

Hagan knocked on the door. "Your phone's been blowing up."

She blinked to clear her head. Instead of shaking away her thoughts, she'd seen everything with more clarity. "Thanks. I'll be out in a second."

Amanda refastened the towel around her chest and wrapped another around her hair. She knew the caller had been Halle. Shah would've texted, and if her parents had called, they'd only have had the time and patience to reach out once.

Hagan stepped into the bathroom as she came out. "Must

have been quite the shower."

She looked at him curiously. "Hm?"

He hooked a towel near the shower and twisted the knob. "You've got a little skip to your step."

She felt that way, too. The corners of her lips quirked. "It's been quite the morning."

Hagan managed to shower and dress before Amanda had blown out her hair. While she put the finishing touches of her outfit together, he mapped out where they would go from the list of items she needed to review.

They played baccarat and blackjack, then took a break near the cashier's booth. She and Hagan split up before lunch, studying shift changes and the behavior patterns of dealers, bosses, and floor managers. They reconnected with mental lists of what might need a second glance. They weren't on the premises to uncover the mechanics behind the crime. They only needed to spot areas that needed thorough mining for data. Intel forensics always led Amanda the right way.

After a quick meal of overstuffed pitas, they swung through the business hub of hotel operation. Amanda hadn't seen anything unusual, and that in and of itself piqued her curiosity. That, and a peculiar feeling that someone was watching her.

Obviously, someone was watching her, and likely Hagan also. Even if their behavior hadn't triggered a security system's red flag, there were hundreds of cameras and sensors tracking everyone within the building. She'd get the specifics from Mr. Nasrallah once she and Halle had a good idea what they needed.

They played craps and roulette. Amanda couldn't shake the shivers. But her stomach growled as well, and if she was ready for dinner, Hagan was starving.

Only slots remained on their list, and luckily, they wouldn't have to play. There were too many variables with row after row of blinking, singing machines that promised quick payouts. The gaming commission would have specifications that she could reference when cross-checking for problems.

Amanda leaned into his side, tired and ready to take her shoes off. "I'm ready when you are."

"You sure?"

She nodded and laced her fingers with his. "Aren't you hungry?"

"Always." He snickered. "But you look like a bloodhound on a trail."

Hagan had noticed her reaction, not the sense of a tail. She didn't like the way that felt. What did it mean if this uneasy sensation that still needled her was wrong? She'd done nothing different except loosen the hold on the rules and contracts she lived by.

It'd be ridiculous to think that spending time with Hagan had dulled her abilities ... right? Her hand pressed against the bottom of her throat. Rules allowed for her safety. They protected the ones she cared for—like Hagan. "I think I need to go to the room before dinner."

"Amanda—" He caught her arm and pulled them from the busy flow of people. "You okay? You're a little pale."

"Low blood sugar." Paranoia made her suspicious. She

tried to focus on Hagan but couldn't stop searching those who walked by. "I think I screwed up."

"How?"

"I ..." She shook her head, not knowing and terrified of losing control. "I just want to lie down for a few minutes."

His jaw ticked, and he sucked his bottom lip into his mouth. "No problem."

Simply walking toward the elevators was a relief. She'd confide in Hagan upstairs. It wouldn't be easy. Hell, it'd be embarrassing. But she'd made decisions that had repercussions, one of which meant she'd have to ask for help.

# CHAPTER THIRTY-THREE

HAGAN PUNCHED THE elevator call button, then returned to Amanda's side. He'd lost track of the afternoon while walking the slot machines. Their constant, calling whine and lights had given him a headache. Too many people milled through the corridors, like they were part of a never-ending churn.

An elevator on their far left arrived. But they'd wait for one going upstairs. Several casino guests got out, and all but two who'd been waiting took their place.

"I'm so tired." Amanda snuggled her way under his arm.

Hagan held her close and kissed the top of her head. "We'll order in."

"Good plan."

Their elevator arrived. The man to Hagan's side walked in first, never glancing from his phone. The other man held out his hand, politely offering for Amanda to go ahead.

"Thanks," she said.

The elevator bounced when he followed her in, reminding Hagan of how he'd jump right before an elevator would stop with his sister and brother. Their mother had sworn they'd break the cables. One day, they had jumped. The elevator had gotten stuck. They'd never done that again.

The other men didn't look like they'd be jumpers. Amanda would be too tired to surprise him with a move like that. Still, apprehension shivered across his skin.

Amanda rolled her shoulders back and stood tall, glancing at the man with his phone. Hagan wondered if anxiousness could travel like a yawn. It sure as hell wasn't going away.

"Slow, huh." She moved next to him and locked her hand with his.

Their floor would be the next stop, but she was correct. The phone guy stepped toward the door. Amanda squeezed Hagan's hand. Something wasn't right. She felt it too.

"Hey, man," Hagan said as they approached their stop. "This your floor?"

Because it wasn't the number he'd pressed.

The elevator stopped. The man held his phone to the doors. It attached like a magnet.

"Shit." Hagan yanked Amanda behind him. Cornered.

The doors whirred each time they tried to open. The high-pitch squeal of an alarm warned there was a problem.

"We're leaving with the girl," the man at the door said. "She won't be harmed."

Behind him, Amanda stepped out of her heels like she was ready to run. His fists curled by his sides. "Like hell."

The second man removed a plastic tube. Hagan took a second glance. Who brought a straw to a fistfight? Then his stomach bottomed out. A pressurized tranquilizer triggered in a dart. He had no choice but to leave Amanda exposed. Hagan lunged for Dart Man.

Speed had always been an asset. But even with that, Hagan didn't have the upper hand. Everything he knew about tranquilizer darts had come from Sawyer's obsession with veterinarian docudramas. The Whale Wrestler. King of the Cobras. Whatever else. If those crazy-ass doctors heralded tranq guns as their most dangerous waiting accident, Hagan didn't like his odds against a camel tranquilizer.

He smashed Dart Man's arm overhead. Phone Dude attacked from behind, wrapping a chokehold around Hagan's neck and drilling a fist into his kidney. Blinding pain paralyzed him. His dominant hand weakened on Dart Man's wrist.

Hagan gasped for air and slammed his skull back. Phone Dude howled and cursed. A broken nose wouldn't give him too much of a reprieve, but at least he could breathe.

Dart Man struggled to aim. Hagan wrenched the straw arm until the shoulder dislocated. The tranquilizer dropped. Hagan crushed it under his heel.

"Hagan!"

He spun. Phone Dude yanked the cap off a tranquilizer dart with his mouth and spat it—Amanda used her high heel shoe to whack him in the face. The dart whizzed through their cramped quarters and pinged against the ceiling, plummeting toward Hagan and Dart Man.

Hagan dove. Dart Man grabbed his knee. Hagan twisted and caught the man's head between his knees and squeezed. Oxygen depleting, Dart Man still thrashed. The passing seconds moved too slow as the other man reached for Amanda.

She held her arms out to block the attack.

"Amanda!" Hagan released the limp man and rolled over, staggering to his feet.

Her arms collapsed under the man's weight. He pinned her to the wall—then Hagan understood. Amanda gripped his shirt and pulled, driving her knee into Phone Dude's groin. Like Hagan, he hadn't expected the shot. Phone Dude buckled and stumbled. Hagan finished him off with a right uppercut.

"Talk about teamwork." Hagan tore away the phone that connected the doors.

Amanda stepped over the bodies. "Think you did the heavy lifting."

The elevator doors slid open, and the alarm turned off. Two janitors with a ladder and tools gaped, slack-jawed as Hagan and Amanda ran by.

"That shoe move, though."

She laughed. "I can't believe you're making jokes."

"Comes with the job." They stopped at the newlywed suite. He pulled the keycard out of his wallet and let them in. "Though normally I know who's trying to kill me."

"Guess that's the difference between you and me."

They shoved the few items that weren't already packed into their suitcases, erased anything that could identify them and hauled ass for the airport.

AMANDA AND HAGAN walked into the airport, hand in hand, like their covers and like lovers. After a hasty pitstop to change, they'd all but obliterated any hint of the ordeal they'd been in. Blood-smeared clothes and disheveled hair were gone. They seemed like everyone else, ready for a trip. But no one's mind raced like hers.

She had too many questions. Who and why should've been on top of the list. But she couldn't stop thinking about the store with the different name. She had no idea what the connection was, and she wouldn't be able to discuss it with Hagan until they made it through security.

They stopped in front of the ticket counters. Hagan searched for a way out of Lebanon on his phone, keeping a hand on her as if she might float away until he needed to reach for his wallet.

"I won't go anywhere," she assured.

"I know." He kissed her forehead and purchased the tickets, taking her hand as he directed them to an airline carrier. "Texted your ticket. We have ninety minutes until wheels up."

The sweetness of his lips made her insides melt like marshmallows. "Thanks, Hagan."

He smiled as though he could tell she was turning into goo. "Let's check-in and drop the bags."

Her phone beeped with the flight details text message, and she read their itinerary as they approached the desk. "We're going to the US?"

Hagan smiled at the attendant. "Two headed for Washington, DC." It wasn't until they showed their identification, left their suitcases on a conveyor belt, and moved into the security queue that he added, "After what happened, where else would we go to debrief?"

Her stomach churned. Adrenaline still made her tremble. She hadn't even thought about where they would go. Trauma wasn't letting her think straight. "Titan has a perfectly suitable war room."

And that suggestion was all the proof she needed to confirm that her mind was scrambled. Neither had suggested they should call Jared. Amanda didn't know Hagan's reason, but she had a pretty big justification to avoid Jared at all costs: he'd never let her be without security again.

That wasn't a great situation for a woman with a security company. But, it was an even worse problem for America's First Daughter who had exercised her right of refusal—Secret Service would never put themselves in the line of fire for her again—and had effectively managed to reach a hermit level of reclusiveness. Not even the press recognized or cared about her anymore.

"I want to have a conversation with Halle," Hagan muttered.

Amanda bit her tongue until they'd presented their tickets and identification. "Why?"

"I just do."

Hagan could have all the conversations with Halle that he wanted. None would make sense until he knew who Amanda was. God! Why hadn't she told him sooner? This situation was like her name. It hadn't mattered. But had she learned her lesson? No!

This omission would matter. She'd kept Hagan in the dark

and put his life in danger. "I have to tell you something."

Hagan still hadn't let go of her hand. "What?"

Even if they hadn't escaped an attack, she needed to tell him because it was the right thing to do, and—her heart exploded—because she needed to say *I love you.*

# CHAPTER THIRTY-FOUR

"I DON'T KNOW why I pictured a state-of-the-art office building made of glass and steel." Hagan pulled their suitcases through the door that Amanda held open. "Cameras following our every move, taking our temperatures and respiration."

She laughed for the first time in hours. "Your only points of reference are Hollywood blockbusters and Titan's real estate portfolio."

"True." Except he was only aware of the Abu Dhabi buildings and the headquarters in Virginia. Hagan didn't put it beyond Jared to own safehouses across the globe. What else would a real estate portfolio include?

They walked into a generic office built sometime in the seventies when architectural influencers had somehow convinced builders to erect windowless concrete monstrosities. If Hagan had to wager, he'd guess that the overhead florescent lights had been there since the original construction.

"We like to call her old Bertha."

"Her, who?" The worn linoleum floor matched the baby-shit green wall color. "The building?"

Amanda stopped at the first office door they came to.

"Yup."

"Bertha the building." He wanted to laugh but decided Bertha suited the place. Unflappable. Unmovable. That sounded like a Bertha, and Bertha would give zero fucks about the color of her walls. If someone didn't like it, Bertha didn't care. "Bertha's kinda badass."

Amanda placed her palm against a nondescript sensor, then turned the handle. "She's pretty techy, too."

They stepped into a small alcove with far better lighting. The entry door shut and caged them in the tight space. "Nice and cozy."

Amanda entered a code on a number pad and leaned in for a biometrical face scan. The door released with a swoosh. They walked into a sleek reception area several degrees cooler than the outer access point. A receptionist's desk sat empty and seemingly unused.

Hagan walked the room. "This is more like I had in mind."

She tapped her finger to her chin. "Didn't you once ask about a tour?"

"Yeah." He laughed. "Think I did." Something other than their problem in the elevator had been distracting Amanda. But with her last few quips, he hoped that she'd let it go. He needed her smile. "Are you my tour guide?"

She pointed to the empty desk. "This is the front of our office."

He leaned against the wall. "Very official looking."

"It's never used. Completely for show."

"I see." He stroked his chin and tried out a Sherlock

Holmes face. "Making the company look totally benign and legit."

She grinned. "We can leave the suitcases here."

Hagan dropped them by the desk and followed. They passed another security checkpoint and moved into a hub of operations. Several people had their heads buried in cubicles, not glancing up. Amanda led Hagan to a circular room lined with screens. A central desk served multiple purposes, and a man sat on a backless rolling chair, tapping a pencil on a notepad as he talked to himself.

Amanda caught the man's attention. "I'm back."

He pulled buds from his ears, offering a genuine smile. "I didn't know you'd be here so early—" The man locked on Hagan. "You brought home a souvenir."

"I did." She smiled and made introductions. "Shah, Hagan. Hagan, Shah."

They shook hands. Hagan would have been more comfortable if they could exchange nicknames or call signs, or even if they went *only* by last names.

Amanda pressed on with the tour. "Let's go this way." She led them to a far door.

Hagan found himself in the first hallway that they'd started in. At least, it looked the same. He had a feeling that nothing was as it seemed. They crossed to an unassuming door he'd have guessed a janitorial closet, but Hagan stepped into a dark room lit only with LED lights along the baseboards and computer screens.

"Our office," Amanda said.

A woman leaned over a large table and scrutinized architectural plans. She held up a hand, warning them not to talk, then circled part of the diagram and turned. "You're here?"

"Hello to you, too." Amanda sat on the edge of a desk, offering the same style of introductions with Halle.

Exchanging pleasantries with Halle had made Hagan's conversation with Shah feel like chatting with teammates over a beer. If Amanda had rules and secrets, Halle had ultimatums and inquisitions.

By the end of the conversation, Hagan had learned that Halle had thought he was "smaller like Shah" and that Amanda's loose hair was so wild that, "the next thing, you'll be wearing short skirts."

Amanda jabbed back, but the tension lingered. "Let's debrief. I'm exhausted."

Halle called Shah into the room, and they sat at the table.

Amanda gave a rundown of her findings, focusing on the store name and the fact that she couldn't find anything else that rubbed her the wrong way. Notably, she didn't mention what sent them hightailing from Lebanon to the US.

Hagan waited until he was sure she'd finished, then crossed his arms. Why had Amanda hidden the crux of the problem?

Halle thought she shouldn't have left until touching base with the office and confirming that she'd unearthed every possibility. Shah didn't say much, though he muttered to himself. Deep creases now crossed his forehead, causing Hagan to wonder if he'd been party to clearing the project.

Amanda and Halle spoke over each other, neither grasping

the other's point. Hagan had had enough. "Listen." Their faces snapped to his. "The assignment could've killed Amanda."

Her eyes rounded. Halle's narrowed. Shah's neck nearly snapped when he turned to Amanda.

"Theoretically speaking," she amended. "Bad intel leaves a body count, and—"

"I'll figure out what happened," Shah promised. "And I agree with Hagan. Walking into a situation blind can be deadly."

Halle's nostrils flared as though she wasn't into the dramatic discussion of what could've happened. "But everything was okay?"

"We're here, aren't we?" Hagan rolled his shoulders.

"Yeah." Halle scrutinized him as if he were the theoretical link that could've endangered Amanda.

"Then, I guess that's settled." He noticed that neither woman suggested they loop in Boss Man. "Unless you need to ask again."

Halle turned her ire toward Shah. "Are you hungry?"

"Already ate."

Hagan wasn't sure he believed Shah but couldn't blame the guy.

"Well, I need a break." Halle crossed her arms and stared like she could make Hagan disappear. "What about you two?"

He and Halle weren't going to get along. So, he gave her a big grin. "I could always eat."

"We have to go," Amanda agreed.

Halle smirked at him. "Pity."

Halle grabbed her purse, then left, and Amanda grabbed his arm. Shah muttered as he made notes. Hagan wondered what their office rules said about overprotective displays of affection because he wanted to grab his woman and drag her out of this place. Why hadn't Bertha belched Halle out already?

"I thought you were tough to get to know." Hagan shook his head. "But Halle's something else."

"It takes time for her to warm up," Amanda said.

"Yeah, but she's been like that for weeks." Shah flipped his pen and let it fall. "Something about her boyfriend is sick. I don't know. You know how she is."

Amanda sighed. "Like a vault."

HAGAN STILL COULDN'T pinpoint when Amanda had changed. The taxi pushed through the throng of shoppers and tourists crossing from M Street to Wisconsin. Hagan hadn't spent much time in DC but sensed this wasn't his neighborhood. The location didn't strike him as reflective of Amanda. Part of him wanted to shrug it off, questioning what did he know about her anyway? She'd transformed into the ice queen he first met somewhere over the Atlantic Ocean. This could just be who she was. But the other part of him shouted for him to look down.

Ice queen or not, she had a death grip on his hand. The woman he'd first met wouldn't do that, and not for the first time, he understood that he didn't know nearly enough to make assumptions. "You're a Georgetown girl?"

"You can turn there," she directed the driver, then added, "It's what I know."

"Did you grow up around here?"

She licked her lip. "Sort of."

Hagan clamped his jaw and waited. A new nugget of information always followed, but his patience was waning. The shrouded mystery act had lost its appeal mid-flight. This was a woman he could fall in love with. Hell, maybe he had. But Hagan only knew what she allowed. Did that make a difference? What did it matter where she'd grown up? It didn't. Except that it apparently did.

"Where'd you go to school?"

Amanda dug into her purse and removed a rubber band, then tied her hair into a ponytail so tight he was sure it'd hurt. "Washington College."

Her clammy hand returned to his, and she closed her eyes. "Do you get car sick?"

"No."

"I grew up in Florida. Near Alabama. We lived in a beach house on Perdido Bay." The past trembled in her voice. Slowly, she opened her eyes. "I thought I was a mermaid until second grade."

Hagan rubbed his thumb over her knuckles and tried to imagine a carefree Amanda as a kid who believed in magic and fairytales. "What happened?"

"My mom's a science professor." She laughed, and whatever memory had crossed her mind allowed for a smile to warm her face. "She'd only let that go on for so long before explaining DNA."

Hagan chuckled. "Fish and people don't mix."

"That, and she sprung the birds and the bees on me around the same time."

"My mom and dad couldn't keep their hands off each other." Hagan squinted and made a face. "And my brother was way older than me. He gave me the rundown. Not scientific in any way."

Her grip relaxed, then Amanda leaned forward. "There's an alley at the end of the block. You can drop us off there. It'll give you an easier way to avoid one-way streets."

The driver thanked them and eased off the gas.

"I grew up in Kentucky," he volunteered.

She didn't balk.

"Louisville," he continued.

Amanda settled against him. "I've heard that's a magical place."

Hagan snorted. "It's something, all right. No mermaids, though."

"I know we need to talk about work." She rested her chin on his shoulder. "But I want to talk about this stuff, too."

Perdido Bay and mermaids, the kind of details he needed. But he'd been wrong. He wanted to know more, but she was the good stuff. Having her against his arm was what he needed. He needed to keep her there, safe and sound. "I want to figure out what happened in Lebanon, and then we can take all the time you need."

"Thanks." Her shiny eyes blinked quickly, then she straightened. "This is good. Right here."

The taxi stopped between two dumpsters. The deteriorating backside of mid-rise brick apartment buildings wasn't what he expected after cruising Georgetown's posh streets. But that was life. Perspectives changed. The view wasn't always the same. Hagan swiped his credit card as the driver popped the trunk. Amanda hopped out.

"You need a receipt?" the driver asked.

"No, sir." Hagan returned the card to his wallet. "We're good. Thanks." He joined Amanda in the narrow alley, took his suitcase out, and shut the trunk. The driver let off the brakes, and Hagan took her suitcase as well and followed Amanda while scrutinizing the alley. Large dumpsters aside, it was open and allowed for a clean line of sight in both directions.

They stopped under an awning. "This is it." Her fingers swept over the security box, punching a long code. The door clicked, and she pulled it open for him to bring the bags in. They came to another door, and from what he could tell, she entered a different code that buzzed them into the apartment lobby. "You'd think I'd shy away from elevators after today."

He snickered. "I think you don't shy away from much."

"Oh, ya know. Except for things I need to say."

His grin hitched, and he had to give her that.

She called the elevator. A woman in a power suit walked through the front doors, never glancing up from her cell phone. The elevator opened. Two men stepped out. Both looked past them like they were ghosts.

The woman and Amanda stepped into the elevator. Both pressed for their floor without acknowledging one another, and he realized why Amanda liked the appeal of DC living. So many people were so involved with their self-importance that most didn't look around to see what they might miss. Or, at least, that was Hagan's hot take.

They arrived at Amanda's floor and walked down an L-shaped hallway. After they turned the corner, her apartment and an exit for the stairwell were the only doors within view.

Instead of a door lock, she had another punch code and sensors that he hadn't noticed on other apartments. "High tech."

Her grin waffled. "Uh-huh."

They entered, and she disabled a security alarm. The still air felt untouched. Hagan pulled their bags into the living room and parked them against the wall. Amanda approached him as though she were walking a tightrope, but at an arm's length away, she turned—"I need to check something"—and hurried down the hall.

"All right." Tension balled his blood again. He paced the living room. Books with cracked spines lined shelves around a television. Hagan looked for pictures and found none. "How long have you lived here?"

"Since after I left college," she called from another room. "Halle was my roommate for a while."

"Huh," he muttered under his breath, "bet that was fun."

Amanda returned but pinned herself to the wall. "The store

name."

It took him a moment to reframe his thoughts to work. Hagan nodded. "The one that didn't match up."

She skirted the room and sat on the edge of the couch. "The footnotes didn't say anything about the change."

"Right." They'd double-checked over breakfast in bed.

"It doesn't make sense, and I can't let it go."

He sat on an armchair and repositioned a throw pillow. He frowned. The store's name seemed a distant second to the attempted abduction. "Of our two headaches." Hagan shifted the pillow again, then chucked it across the room. "I've gotta admit, that's not the one I care about."

"If they're connected—"

"They are." He'd considered the entire job a farce. They'd found nothing, and someone had tried to grab Amanda. God only knew why. "I feel like you're forgetting someone tried to—" He pinched the bridge of his nose. "I'm not the expert here, but it feels like you're stuck on who, and I haven't moved past why." He stopped cold. "You already know why?"

Her lips parted as wide as her eyes. Fear rolled off of her in waves.

Hagan jerked the armchair toward the couch and sat on the edge of the cushion, leaning closer, damn near begging her to open her mouth. "Amanda."

She barely nodded.

"Before." He licked his lip and tried to regulate the bristling anxiety knotting in his neck. "What did you have to tell me?"

She swallowed hard. "You have to know—"

"Yeah, babe, I have to know," he growled.

Amanda shook her head and gasped like the threat had clogged her throat. She wiped her hands over her cheeks. They trembled as she pulled them away. "Before anything else. I have to tell you—" The color drained from her face. "I am in—"

The door buzzer rang, and a man's voice called from a speaker in the hall, "Coming up, kiddo."

"What?" she screeched and spun. "*No.*"

# CHAPTER THIRTY-FIVE

**FIVE YEARS AGO**
**FLOYD LIBRARY**
**WASHINGTON COLLEGE**

THE OVERHEAD LIGHTS hummed. Mandy flipped her spiral notebook over and pretended to study her chicken scratch, highlighter poised as though she were preparing for the midterm and not eyeing Halle leaning way too close to Billy.

"Maybe we should take a break." *Maybe* Mandy's best friend and boyfriend should steer clear from hushed conversations over a shared biology book. Or, maybe, Mandy needed to chill. Her new relationship was just that. New. Halle and Billy had known each other forever. She didn't think she was the jealous type. Then again, she'd never had friends who acted like friends.

Billy leaned back in his chair until he balanced on two legs. "I'm okay."

Mandy tapped the highlighter on the table, glancing out of the study room's glass partitions. Dylan leaned against a pillar quilted with campus flyers, Greek life announcements, and work-study job openings. McNally tapped a pencil against her temple and ignored the three-ring binder open in front of her.

Not many students remained in the library. Those who did

were spread among the silent reading tables, doing a much better job at studying than Mandy was.

"Actually." Halle stood and stretched. "I have to go to the bathroom."

"You're sure?" Billy's throat bobbed.

Mandy rolled her eyes. "Yeah, I think she knows if she has to go."

"Right." The overhead lights caught on Billy's forehead as though the tiny room was too warm.

Soon as Halle left, Mandy would ask Billy what the hell was going on. Or, should she ask Halle after they wrapped up tonight? After pushing Mandy to take a chance on Billy, Halle had gotten weird. Then again, what did Mandy know about friends and dating?

Halle opened the study room door. "Everything will be fine."

Mandy scowled. "I didn't think we were that worried about mid-terms."

"I'm not." Halle snickered, then glided away as cool as the surge of fresh air that flowed into the tiny study room.

"She's not," Billy muttered as if he'd realized that mid-terms were about to throw him into the fire. If not mid-terms, then feelings for another woman?

Suspicion beat a slow drum roll at the back of Mandy's skull. High school had been cruel, but she refused to fall back on assumptions based on those so-called friends. Whatever Billy's problem, he'd made clear that his romantic interest was Mandy. She leaned across the table and scooted Halle's notebook to the far end.

Billy straightened. "What are you doing?"

"What does it look like?" Mandy smoothed her platinum hair behind her ears, then caught her reflection in the glass. Heavy makeup. Angry clothes. The façade weighed her down like waterlogged Doc Martens, but it protected her in the same way. She could be bold. She *would* be. "I'm moving next to my boyfriend."

Billy gripped the edge of the table and nodded. "Good." He wiped at his brow, then patted Halle's chair. "Sit next to me."

She relocated her bag next to Billy's. His legs bounced under the table. On top of the table, his stranglehold on his pencil threatened to break it in two.

"Are you okay?" she asked, telling herself everything was okay. He liked her—and if he didn't, he wouldn't dump her while studying for an exam.

The pencil snapped. Billy jumped. "Yeah. Fine." He pushed the chair out and rummaged in his bag.

Mandy bit her lip. "If you need another pencil, I've got you."

His pencil search took all of his attention, but without finding a new one, he zipped it shut and shoved it under the table again. "I have to go to the bathroom."

Her eyebrow went up. Billy hustled out and let the door slam. Dylan straightened and looked her way, but she couldn't read his expression.

Her gaze dropped to Billy's backpack. A strange urge to

snoop pushed Mandy out of her chair. She reached for his bag and hefted it onto the table. Its surprising weight made the back of her neck tingle. She pulled the bag open. *Canisters and wires.*

She froze and couldn't scream. Movement blurred outside the glass room. Dylan and McNally appeared. But Mandy couldn't run or even point.

Dylan ripped her from the backpack. "Damn it."

McNally yanked Amanda over the table.

"Go, go," Dylan bellowed. "Run."

If her feet touched the ground, Mandy couldn't remember. They ran until Dylan plowed them to the ground, a bulldozer protecting the peace. The explosion tore over their bodies. Thunder and fire rained. Her vision wouldn't focus as the building shook.

McNally rolled from under Dylan but couldn't stand. Mandy didn't try to move. More pain might kill her.

"Sparkler?" Dylan labored. "Still with me?"

Sulfur and smoke burned her eyes. Blood seeped everywhere. Pain devoured her disjointed thoughts, but she whispered a groan. "Yeah."

"We made it longer than anyone expected." His breaths gurgled as the fire alarm blared. "Think—" The gurgles became an agonizing wheeze. "S'my time to go."

Mandy couldn't move, but she needed him to be okay. "Dylan?"

"Sparkler...it's been an honor..."

"Dylan! No!" He wasn't fighting. Her fingers found his

body; Mandy clutched his clothes, trying to shake him. "Don't leave me!"

"…and a privilege."

# CHAPTER THIRTY-SIX

*K*IDDO? HAGAN GOT to his feet, unsure which had left him more surprised—the arrival of an elusive parent or the way Amanda pivoted toward the door, arm extended as though he were an oversized dog to keep back. "Who's that?"

"They do this sometimes," her voice cracked. "I'll explain everything. Give me a minute to send him away."

Hagan frowned with a sour taste in his mouth. "If you don't want me to meet your folks." He shoved his hands into his pockets. "I'll go."

"You can't. Not yet."

A light knock rapped on the door. "Sweet pea?"

"They're both here." Amanda pressed her fingers to her temples, processing as though simply answering the door wasn't the obvious choice of what to do next.

Hagan cleared his throat. "I'll go. You don't have to introduce me."

"It's not that—damn it. I will explain everything."

He crossed his arms and nodded. He could handle an awkward greeting with her parents. Truth was, given the high drama, he wasn't even curious. He couldn't reason her reaction. Wanting privacy was one thing, ignoring the past another. But blocking him from her life as it literally knocked on the door...yeah, that wasn't making him feel warm and fuzzy on the inside.

She marched toward the door, then braced herself against it, barely inching it open. "Hi."

"Surprise," her dad said. "Are you going to let us in?"

The voice struck Hagan as familiar. The tension corkscrewed in his chest.

"You didn't call," she said.

Her dad laughed. "Then it wouldn't be a surprise, would it?"

"Are you okay?" Concern edged her mother's voice. "You don't look well."

"It's been a hard day." She relinquished her spot at the door and glanced at Hagan, miserable and apologetic. "I have a guest."

The door swung open. The blood drained from his limbs, and sweat prickled on his back. Hagan's mouth dried as a nightmare unfolded. Her parents walked in, hugging their daughter, giving Hagan the missing piece so that everything made sense.

Dad and Mom were the President and First Lady. Hagan's respect for their offices and the love of his country held him in place. He wanted to hate them, to yell or throw a chair. But it wasn't their fault. They hadn't played a part in destroying his life. Only their daughter had that burden, which she hadn't yet claimed.

The President straightened from hugging his daughter. The

First Lady smiled as though she'd stumbled upon a happy moment.

"Mom, Dad." She faltered. "This is Hagan—"

He strode forward, refusing to look at Amanda, and held out his hand to the First Lady. "Hagan Carter." Then stepped toward her husband. "Sir."

The President swatted his formal behavior away, then cocked his head to the side. "You said your name is Hagan Carter?"

"Yes, sir."

President Hearst glanced at Amanda, hesitantly adding, "Any relation to…"

A kaleidoscope of memories collided in Hagan's chest, and it was as if he could see everything at once: The morning his brother passed his driving test; they spent the afternoon driving nowhere. That time Dylan had tricked Hagan into climbing an impossible tree only to spend hours coaxing him down so Roxana wouldn't rat them out. Hagan remembered the day he went to college. Their mother sobbed. Their dad pretended not to choke up. Then that day Dylan came showed off that shiny Secret Service badge attached to his waist. Hagan had told every single kid in his class that he'd be like his big brother one day.

"Dylan Carter." Hagan cleared his throat, nodding to the President. "Yes, sir. My brother."

Amanda gasped. Hagan's gaze jerked to her, furious at what she'd tried to hide.

"I'm sorry," the First Lady said. "We cared deeply for Dylan."

The jovial atmosphere disintegrated as if everyone understood what she hadn't told him. "If you'll excuse me, please."

Amanda sounded miles away.

Hagan waited for the commander in chief's dismissal.

The President silently lifted his chin.

"Thank you, sir." Relieved from hell, Hagan strode out the door, refusing to stop until he understood how this happened.

## CHAPTER THIRTY-SEVEN

THE APARTMENT DOOR shut behind Hagan, and heartache exploded deep in Amanda's heart, pinching so tight she couldn't breathe.

"Honey." Mom shook Amanda's shoulder. "Are you okay?"

She collapsed into her mother's arms. "*No.*"

Dad came up behind them and petted her hair. "It will be okay, kiddo."

She didn't have the strength to remind him that not everyone had it as lucky as her parents. Amanda sniffled and wiped her eyes. "How did you know I was home?"

"Halle emailed and said something happened on your trip, that you came home." Mom's eyebrows inched up. "Anything you'd like to share?"

"Not right now." Amanda could only deal with one crisis at a time. "That was thoughtful of her, I guess."

Mom gestured toward the luggage parked against the wall. "We weren't aware that your friend was involved."

It was only a matter of time before Mom would break out science analogies amidst her questions. Amanda had no choice but to give them more details. "I didn't know that he was

Dylan's younger brother."

"If you didn't ask, and he didn't say..." Dad frowned. "Why would he think that you knew?"

She stared at the ceiling. "It was obvious Jared Westin and Parker Black knew." Tears burned the back of her throat. "And that I was the reason they didn't speak up."

Dad's cell phone chirped, and he quickly unclipped it from his belt and read the screen. "I'm sorry. I have to get back."

They'd been here longer than she could've expected. Besides, if they left, no one would remind her how stupid her contracts and rules had been. "It's fine. I'll come over for lunch soon—"

"I'm free for the rest of the day," Mom volunteered.

"How'd you manage that?" Dad asked.

"Someone phoned in a threat to free the test animals in the science building."

"*Mom.*" Amanda scowled. "You test animals in the labs?"

"No." Mom scoffed. "I suspect someone wasn't ready for an exam. If so, they got their wish. Campus is closed for the day."

The cell phone chirped again. "That's my cue. I have to run." Dad hugged Amanda. "Bye, kiddo." Then he laid a smooch on Mom that made Amanda turn away.

The majority of the security detail left with Dad. Mom's detail remained in the hallway and outside the building. Once the entourage had left, Amanda fell apart again. Mom coaxed her onto the couch and went into the kitchen to set a kettle on the stove.

She returned to Amanda's side. "Dylan's younger brother—"

"Hagan." She wrapped her arms around her knees and hugged them to her chest.

"He's the man you kicked."

She pressed her forehead into her kneecaps and moaned. "Yeah."

Mom sat down and rubbed Amanda's back. "He's a handsome guy."

"I know." Amanda leaned against her mom. "It turns out I'm not a robot."

Mom sighed. "So, you liked him?"

"That's an understatement."

"You like him a lot?" Mom put an arm around Amanda. "Something more?"

Amanda translated into a language her mother might understand. "He agitates my molecules."

Mom laughed. "That's a good thing, baby."

"Not really, Mom."

"Miscommunications won't ruin agitation." She crossed her leg and hummed, quietly teasing, "If that's not an example of scientific law, I don't know what is."

"We're pretty far beyond a miscommunication." Amanda sniffled. "He hates me, and I don't blame him."

The kettle whistled, and Mom stood. "If he's part of Dylan's family, he's got a good head on his shoulders. You two just need time."

"I wish I had your optimism," she muttered.

"Maybe it comes with age." Mom lifted her hands, then walked into the kitchen. The kettle stopped whistling. The mugs clanked on the counter, and she called, "Why don't you call Halle? She could always use a girls' night in."

Halle was surprisingly easy to convince, and an hour later, she arrived with three pints of ice cream as Mom opened the microwave to make popcorn. Amanda queued up her Netflix, and they settled in with their junk food.

Seven o'clock rolled around, and like clockwork, the Secret Service's shifts changed. Amanda didn't recognize the agent but found comfort in their routine. Same stations, same rotation, no matter who worked the detail.

Maybe that was the problem with her rules and contracts. The presidential detail allowed for a routine with moving parts. Amanda never allowed for deviation, believing she'd never change. *Got that wrong...* This was an awful way to learn her lesson.

Halle excused herself to take a call near the end of the movie. Mom had fallen asleep on the couch sometime after that. Amanda made it her duty to finish off her mom's ice cream and pick at Halle's popcorn until she returned, somewhat more sour than normal.

Amanda paused the movie. "Everything okay on your call?"

"Yeah." Halle waved for her to turn the movie back on, then struggled to find a comfortable place on the floor, fidgeting until the credits roll ended.

"Maybe I should call Hagan," Amanda mumbled and tossed the remote on the floor. "Or maybe not."

"That's my vote," Halle added. "Let him wait."

Amanda frowned. "It's not like he's in the wrong."

Halle shrugged. "So long as it's just us tonight."

That made Amanda smile. Just like they avoided guy-talk, they generally didn't stretch girls' nights in. Halle was too high-strung to sit around and do nothing. "Maybe we should do this more often."

Halle didn't look well. "Maybe."

Mom stirred and stretched, yawning. "Did I miss the end?"

"Not by much," Amanda said.

"That's okay, I've seen it a time or two." Mom checked the time. "Later than I thought." She turned to Amanda. "Are you doing better?"

"Yeah, I think so. It's been a long day." Mom's yawn was contagious. "Woke up on the other side of the world today."

"I'll head out then." Mom picked up her phone. "Let me give the guys a heads-up...that's weird."

Amanda wished Hagan would've texted her. Maybe he thought she should be the one to reach out. She stared at her phone. *No service?*

"I don't have any service," Mom murmured.

Amanda's stomach turned. "Halle, your phone worked, right?"

Mom slipped her shoes on again and walked toward the apartment door. Amanda held her phone at different angles, watching for the service bars to change. Mom gasped. "Oh, God!"

Halle and Amanda jumped to their feet and rushed to

Mom.

"What?" Amanda asked.

Halle glanced into the hallway. "Oh, shit." She slammed the door shut. "Breach. Man down."

"What?" Amanda pulled Mom down the hall. Who would know where the First Lady was? "Stay here." She checked the security system base, unable to request the screen change. It wasn't disabled. Frozen? Hell, it didn't matter. "We don't have a way to communicate."

"We have to get your mom out of here." Halle hurried by Amanda.

She followed into her guest bedroom and loaded weapons from her closet. It wasn't as if Amanda had an arsenal at her place. They just had to protect Mom and get to the agents on the perimeter. "Let's go."

Mom shook on the couch, and it was the first time Amanda had seen her mother frightened. "Who would do this?"

"Dr. Hearst." Halle reached for Mom's hand. "Doesn't matter right now. We have to go."

"Where?" Mom asked.

Halle eyed Amanda. "Fire escape?"

That'd drop them close to a perimeter checkpoint. "Yes."

Halle gnawed on her lip. "Shooter could be out there."

"The shooter could be anywhere…" Amanda fumbled to make sense of the delay. "But we're certain where they've been. We take the fire escape and keep moving."

"Better than waiting, sitting ducks." Halle led them toward Amanda's bedroom, edging around the corners.

Amanda opened the window, and they crawled onto the rickety platform. It groaned under their weight. They stayed close to Mom, searching for the threat and climbing as fast as they could move together.

Halle stopped on the third floor. "Stuck." Her eyes widened as if this was the one thing she might not be able to control. "Too far to jump."

Amanda eyed the alley and agreed.

"Why don't they see us?" Mom cried.

Amanda had no idea.

Halle attacked the rusted ladder with a fervor Amanda had never seen until the old thing dropped, panting, "Go."

They hurried down the ladder until they reached the alley and ran with their arms around her mother. Amanda's stomach twisted. Agents should've jumped out, weapons drawn. Nothing happened. They reached the checkpoint SUV.

"Fuck," Halle cried.

Amanda's stomach revolted. Two dead agents still in their seats. "Not again…"

Halle ripped open the driver's door and removed the downed agent. "Amanda! Get your mom in."

Tears fell as Amanda pushed her mother into the back seat, then she rushed to the passenger side and fought against the dead agent's weight, removing him from the seat. "I'm so sorry."

"Damn it, Amanda," Halle yelled. "Get your ass in the car."

With one more apology, Amanda jumped in.

Halle floored the gas before Amanda closed the door. "Call someone."

Amanda fumbled for her cell phone. "No signal?" She searched the comm system and computer attached to the dashboard console. "Disabled. What's going on?"

Halle made a sharp turn and checked her mirrors. Amanda twisted to Mom but had no idea what to say.

"Your father will fix—" Mom's voice cracked. Tears spilled free. "Those poor men."

The SUV made a hard turn. Amanda and Mom fell to the side. Halle braked. Amanda looked out the window, not seeing why they'd stopped. "What's the matter?"

Halle opened the center console. Smoke exploded inside the SUV. Amanda choked on the instantaneous slap of gas. Mom coughed and sputtered then keeled to the side. Halle covered her face with a mask.

"What are you doing?" Didn't matter. Amanda had to get out. The door wouldn't budge. The window wouldn't lower. She could break it, but her arms were too heavy to reach for her gun. Amanda fell toward Halle, begging for help, but saw her best friend, unmoving.

Everything went black.

# CHAPTER THIRTY-EIGHT

**LOUISVILLE, KENTUCKY**

THE TURNING SIGNAL clicked too loud. Hagan slammed his fist onto the center console. He didn't like the rental car he'd picked up at the airport, but the idea of being without his own transportation and an exit plan made this day that much more hellacious.

The drive from the rental lot was a short one. He sped onto the interstate, and just as fast, yanked the steering wheel to exit on Eastern Parkway. Sometime during the flight from D.C. to Louisville, he'd managed to believe that going home would fix everything. As soon as he hit the brakes at the stoplight, Hagan realized he was dead-ass wrong.

The light turned green. His head still pounded. Hagan drove through the familiar neighborhood. The road curved one way. Then the next. Everything was the same. Everything was always the same. A blessing and a curse. But it should've helped with the pain.

He slapped the turn signal and gnashed his teeth as he made one turn and then another until he could see his end goal. Three driveways until he was home. He eased off the gas pedal and wished to hell that the half-bottle of antacids he'd downed would do their job.

He pulled into the driveway, glared at a man in their small yard holding a rake, and threw the car door open hard enough to bend the hinges. Before either man could say a word, the front door flew open, and Roxana launched herself off the front porch.

"You're home!" She tackled Hagan in a blunt-force hug he barely felt. "You should have called."

"Will next time." He wrapped his arms around his sister, waiting for the pain to go away, then lifted his chin to Roxana's boyfriend, who was warily watching from the edge of their postage-stamp-sized yard.

Jason threw the rake to the side and approached with caution. "Good to see you, man."

Hagan grunted.

Roxana tightened her hug, then abruptly let go. "Wait—why are you home?"

He forced his teeth to separate. "Felt like it."

Knowing bullshit when she heard it, his sister scrutinized. "You're hurt?"

"No."

Her sharp assessment ran from his face to his limbs and back. "You certainly aren't pleasant. What's wrong?"

Hagan worked his jaw. "I had a job on the East Coast. I wanted to stop by home."

Roxana clapped her hands on her hips. Jason wrapped his arm over her shoulder. "Give him a minute before you interrogate the poor guy."

"*Fine.*"

Jason made a face that warned Hagan he was on his own after they got inside. "Can I get your bag?"

"I didn't bring one."

His answer didn't offer a reason for Roxana to ease up. "Let's go inside. Mom's in the kitchen."

"Give him some room, babe." Jason cajoled Roxana toward the house.

Grumbling, Roxana let them up the front porch stairs. "Mom," she called, "Hagan's home."

Hagan tossed his keys on the well-used entryway table and took a deep breath. Home always smelled like dinner and laundry. Today was no different. He guessed a roast was in the crock-pot. The farther he walked into the long, narrow shotgun house, the more certain he was that what had happened with Amanda would be a distant memory.

Except, he stopped in the living room and felt sick. The walls on either side of the large picture window were blanketed with family photos. Dylan's honors gleamed in the warm glow of fall's afternoon light.

Maybe he shouldn't have come home. Hagan turned for the kitchen. The dark hardwood floors creaked in the same spot. The same quilt was laid over the same couch. Why did Hagan think home would help him see his way through this level of hell?

His steps quieted on the worn hallway runner until he stepped into the kitchen. The linoleum creaked under his feet. His mom sat in her wheelchair at the kitchen table, and he found it near impossible to form words.

"Hey, Mom," he managed and bent in front of her gaze. She'd never smile or say hello again, but part of Hagan believed she knew he was there. He kissed her cheek. "I was in the neighborhood."

Roxana clucked from the counter, dicing carrots.

He ignored his sister and crouched next to Mom. Hagan laid a hand on top of hers, then straightened the gray-and-yellow crocheted blanket draped across her legs. "I like your shirt," he added, touching the sleeve of the blue Kentucky Wildcats T-shirt layered loosely over another shirt.

"Blasphemy," Jason called from the living room.

"This will always be a house divided," Roxana reminded Hagan as if he'd been gone too long to recall that she'd attended the University of Kentucky like their mother. Jason had gone to the University of Louisville like their father had.

Hagan smoothed his mother's shirt. "It was a big game this weekend, huh?"

Roxana dumped the carrots into the crock-pot. "Every game's a big game."

Football banter and family. This was what he needed. But his anger was only diluted. "That's what you always say."

Roxana placed the cutting board to the side and wiped her hands. "And they always are."

"If you say so." He found her rock-solid faith in the Wildcats endearing, especially when she was convinced everything would always go wrong for them—and maybe she was right. He hated Amanda Hearst.

Roxana took the handles of Mom's wheelchair and led them from the kitchen. "Will you be around for the rest of the weekend?"

Hagan trailed. "I don't know."

"What's your plan?" She parked Mom next to the coffee table and sat next to Jason on the couch.

Hagan sat on the stuffed chair next to their mother. He repositioned, unable to find a comfortable spot in a chair that had never been comfortable to begin with. "I don't know. Just sort of found myself here."

Roxana picked up a Big-Gulp-sized Wildcats tumbler, positioned the straw to Mom's lips, and let her take a few sips. After a moment, she set the tumbler down and wiped a linen napkin over her chin. "You might as well start talking, Hagan, or I'm going to start asking."

Where to begin? He could share that he'd slept with the woman who'd ruined their lives. That he'd jumped through hoops that only *Mandy* Hearst could've thought up and let his guard down. Hagan rubbed a hand into his hair.

"Does this have anything to do with the *gorgeous* woman you mentioned last time we talked?" Roxana casually asked. "What? Did mediocre sex send you running for home?"

Hagan choked and stole a glance at his mother like he was a teenager busted with condoms in his wallet.

Roxana rolled her eyes. "If that's it, I'm going to—"

"Give me a break," he snapped.

"Did she hurt your feelings?"

*Hurt his feelings?* He had to laugh because, with one revelation, Amanda had obliterated everything he thought he'd had. "It's not that simple."

Roxana clenched her fist. "I'm not above—"

"I know. I get it. You're the product of two older brothers." Hell, it was probably against the law for Roxana to joke like that. "Let's move on from bodily harm." He steered the conversation with a safer answer that wouldn't send his sister to jail. "Things became complicated."

"*Complicated?*" She turned to Jason. "Is that manly, macho-guy talk for feeling butt hurt?"

"All right." Hagan rubbed his temples. "This might've been a bad idea."

"Coming home?" Roxana pouted. "I'm—"

"*Listening*," Jason suggested.

Hagan appreciated the help, but he didn't know where to begin. The stairwell pat-down? The President of the United States knocking on the door?

"Earth to Hagan," Roxana snapped. "Are you sick?"

No, but he might get sick. Nothing good would come from the truth. But it would be worse the longer he waited. "I slept with Mandy Hearst."

"I don't understand." Roxana jumped to her feet and waved her hands in front of her face. "Wait. What did you just say?"

Hagan had never been the type of guy to kiss and tell. But in this parallel universe, he had to call a spade a spade. He'd thought he'd fallen for that woman, but she'd been a wolf cloaked in lambswool.

Roxana fell back to the couch. Her arms hung as limp as their mother's. Jason put his hand on Roxana's back. Hagan didn't know how much the guy knew, but he could tell it wasn't good.

There wasn't enough oxygen in the living room. Hagan bound toward the window like he might throw it open.

"I don't understand." Roxana's eyes welled, and she pressed a hand over her mouth.

He didn't either. He rubbed the back of his neck.

Roxana stormed to her feet. "How could you?"

"I didn't know."

"That's insane," she cried.

Jason reached for her arm. "Babe."

"Don't babe me!" She swatted him away, turning her wrath back to Hagan. "Lie to me again."

Looking back, he saw what he had missed—the differences in her hair, no makeup. Mandy Hearst hadn't spent as much time in the news during college as she had during high school. They'd always worried about Dylan. He'd always said they didn't understand. Mandy wasn't the teenager gossip hounds made her out to be. But that was no excuse for missing Amanda as Mandy.

Roxana's eyes brimmed with explosive tears. "You fucked her, or you fell for her?"

"Roxana," Jason snapped.

That time, she let him pull her to his side.

The truth hit Hagan like sniper fire. "Both."

"You're disgusting." She pulled from Jason and rushed for

their mother and wheeled her to the kitchen.

Hagan paced the living room, then dropped into the uncomfortable chair again.

Roxana returned, fists curled at her sides, eyes welling with tears. "Of all the dick things you could do." The tears spilled. "If Mom could understand a single thing you just said, you would've killed her."

Another sniper round lodged in his chest.

Jason walked to her side. "You need to take five."

"No," Roxana snapped. "You show up here, angry or sad or whatever you are, and *she's* the reason?"

A swell of cold anger prickled down his neck. "Ease up, Rox."

"Are you kidding me?" Roxana demanded.

He closed his eyes and pictured Amanda. Her smile. Her laughter. He couldn't explain why he hadn't seen the truth, and now listening to his sister rage the same way he had…he missed Amanda. "You're not even listening."

"You haven't said anything worth listening to."

His throat tightened. One second, he understood Roxana's disgust and condemnation, and the next, he recalled the pain in Amanda's face when she connected him to Dylan. The image vibrated with as much pain as he felt—which was impossible. Amanda Hearst wasn't allowed to act shocked and hurt because she had known from the day they met: Mandy Hearst was responsible for his brother's death.

"Hagan," Roxana pleaded. "We hate her."

"I know." Except he didn't hate Amanda. He hated the

gothy, glorified party girl who the press loved to track as much as she loved to taunt. Dylan's reminders struggled to find their footing. He'd always said not to believe what they saw.

He scrubbed his hand over his face and met Roxana's fury. "Mandy's the reason I flew home. But Amanda...I don't know what to think right now."

"I'll tell you what to think." Roxana jabbed her finger, then threw her arm toward the kitchen. "If it wasn't for a headline-addicted twit, then Mom wouldn't be living a life like that."

Jason seemed confused but knew better than to confirm Mom had had a stroke. Clearly, Roxana hadn't given the guy the nitty-gritty details. Just like Hagan hadn't with Amanda. He'd called Dylan's death an accident at work. What did that say about his problem with her secrets and omissions?

Roxana curled into Jason's arms and cried.

Hagan's head pounded. He laid a hand on his sister's trembling shoulder and listened to her sob as though it might serve as penance. That atonement wasn't nearly enough.

# CHAPTER THIRTY-NINE

Tiny, carefree clinks of a wind chime and a crick in Amanda's neck urged her to wake. Her head ached. She blinked, trying to place the little tree fairies kicking chimes in her skull.

The dark room smelled of gasoline, and when she moved, her skin pulled like it had stuck to the seat. She sat up. Her head swirled. What had happened to her—the dead agents. Halle driving. "Oh, God."

She was still in the car? Her hand reached for the door, her stomach threatening to throw up. The armored door swung wide, but Amanda turned for her mom.

Mom laid over the back seat, and Amanda reached over the center console. "Mom." She pressed her fingers to her mother's neck, relieved at the steady pulse. "Mom, we have to wake up."

Then figure out what the hell was going on. Mom didn't wake. The wind chime's song danced in the night. Amanda checked for her weapon. *Gone.* She studied the surrounding area. Rusted tools haphazardly covered the uneven floor. Moonlight poured through the open garage and cast a gauzy light over the shiny black SUV that had every window rolled down.

"Halle?" Amanda called.

Only the wind chime and the whisper of rustling leaves answered.

She returned to the backseat and shook her mother. "Wake up."

"You're up?" Halle called.

Amanda turned to the garage opening. "What the hell is going on?"

"Is your mom awake?" Halle stepped into the moonlight.

Unlike Amanda, she had her weapon, and by the looks of it, access to a militia's payload. "Where are we?"

"Home." She leaned against the garage. "Where we grew up."

"We?" Her thoughts struggled to catch up.

"Amanda?" Mom called.

"Right here." She jumped into the backseat of the SUV and helped her mom sit up. "Are you okay?"

"I've got a hangover from hell," Mom muttered. "What's going on—"

Through the shadows, Amanda saw as her mother recalled the events that led to where they were now.

"Where's Halle?" Mom rubbed her temples. "Halle, can I have a word?"

"Mom," Amanda hissed for her mother to be quiet, though she didn't know why. It wasn't as if Halle wasn't watching them from behind. "This isn't something you can lecture us about."

Her mom waved Amanda aside then slid from the

backseat, somehow with her usual grace. "Halle?"

Amanda waited to hear, *Yes, Dr. Hearst.* Or something else oddly normal that would make no sense. Not one to be ignored, Mom grumbled and trudged toward Halle until they faced each other. "Young lady, what is this about?"

Mom and Halle danced around the situation, getting nowhere, and Amanda tried for a plan. Short of getting Halle's weapon and shooting, nothing came to mind. Queasiness and lack of intel didn't help.

"Enough questions. Time to take it inside." Halle directed them with the barrel of her gun as though they'd been out for a nice hike that had gone wrong. "That way."

Amanda locked arms with her mom and followed the directions that led them into the cabin lit by a handful of candles. Shadows danced on the exposed timber walls and bent over the ceiling beams. Old family photographs hung on the wall. Some frames and glass were cracked. Cobwebs hung over lamps. A pair of sneakers waited by the closet door.

Amanda pivoted and took in the small space: living room, dining table, and kitchen. A once blue-and-white checkered tablecloth had been dulled with a thick layer of dust. It must've been years since anyone had stepped foot in this cabin. "You lived here?"

"Not all of us grow up in the White House."

Amanda shrunk back.

Mom stepped between them. "That's not Amanda's fault."

Amanda pressed her hand to her throat. "Where are your parents?"

"In prison."

Since when? Reality snapped, and Amanda realized nothing had been true. "Why?"

"It doesn't matter."

"It does." Amanda stepped forward.

"Because," Halle snapped, "we believe nothing that you do."

A shiver ran down her back. Billy had said those same words, filled with that same venom, during his trial. "Beliefs won't put you in prison."

Halle lifted her chin, proud of whatever had jailed her parents. "There's no progress without sacrifice."

Hadn't Billy's lawyer said similar things? Amanda wasn't sure. She'd been recovering from burns, mourning, and hopelessly depressed. But she recalled the headlines that screamed: Homegrown terrorist. Nationalized extremist. Hate in the name of God. "You're one of them?"

A photograph of Halle caught her eye. Dust and cobwebs had been wiped clean, and in the candlelight, Amanda could tell that the picture frame had been picked up and put down dozens of times.

She picked it up and stared at Billy and Halle. By the looks of this picture, they were far more than old friends … "I don't understand."

"You never will," Halle snapped.

"Why are you doing this?" Amanda threaded a hand into her hair and pulled until it hurt. "Because of *Billy*?"

Halle pursed her lips. Her nostrils flared.

"He's why? You did all this for him?" Amanda shook the frame and threw it onto the floor. "This isn't progress or sacrifice. It's insane."

Glass crunched under Halle's shoes. She crouched and lifted the frame. Glass shards fell, and her eyes glistened. "He has cancer."

Amanda hadn't known. What was she supposed to feel? Joy? Compassion? Her mind had gone numb, and she simply muttered the only thing she knew for certain, "He's in prison."

Halle's anguish rolled in waves. A tear slid down Halle's cheek. "And they won't let him out."

Mom moved to Amanda's side. They watched Halle pick the broken glass from the photograph. She dropped the pieces to the floor.

"Halle," Mom whispered.

Halle held up the photograph as if that were what Mom had asked for. Part of Amanda had always understood that Halle and Billy had a bond, but to see them so young, sitting hand-in-hand on a porch swing, and to know what they both believed… The truth clarified doubts that Amanda had tried to ignore from the first lunch in the cafeteria to the last night at the library. "You loved him?"

Halle swallowed hard. "He's dying."

"I know," Mom said. "And, I'm so sorry that he brought it upon himself."

"Shut up!" Halle said.

Amanda twisted to her mother at the same time. "What?"

"He has lung cancer."

Halle shook her head like it wasn't true. "We didn't know the explosives would make him sick."

"But you knew it could kill people," Mom added softly. "And it did."

Amanda trembled. "How do you know any of this?"

Mom took the picture frame from Halle then set it where it had been. She stared at the photograph and shook her head as if everything made sense. "Someone filed a compassionate release request on his behalf."

Halle's lips trembled. "It was denied."

"No, honey," Mom said, almost heartbreakingly sad. "Whoever made the anonymous request failed to include who they were and how to contact them."

"So what …" Halle's voice cracked.

"The warden and federal medical center never offered a decision. They needed financial support details. A confirmation of care."

"He would've been." Quiet tears fell from her cheeks.

"Mom," Amanda whispered, "how do you know?"

"That boy tried to kill my child." The evening breeze carried through opened windows as the wind chimes sang. A tear slipped down Mom's cheek. "I made it my job to stay informed."

"I'm bringing him home," Halle snapped as she hardened into the stony friend who Amanda had always known. "I'm going to work on that now." She removed the gun from her side holster and jammed the barrel into Amanda's chest. "Get on the couch."

Amanda hadn't come up with a magical escape plan, so she and Mom followed orders. Dust plumed when they sat down. Halle bound their hands and feet, then tied them to a hook on the wall.

"Go to sleep," she demanded, then disappeared the way they'd come in.

The muffled sound of a phone call filtered through the wind. She and Mom couldn't distinguish a single word. Two phone calls came in after that.

"Don't worry, sweet pea," Mom said.

"Give me a single reason why we shouldn't worry."

"No matter who she's called or what she's planning, your father will be one of the first to know."

That offered some solace, but Halle's betrayal and haunted thoughts of murdered agents kept her spirits down.

What seemed like hours later, Halle returned with a blanket and pillow. She set up camp on the dirty floor and tucked herself into bed with Billy's picture and a shotgun by her side.

# CHAPTER FORTY

HAGAN WOKE TO Roxana shaking his shoulder and tearing the covers off. "What the hell?" He covered his face with a pillow. "Go away."

"Get out of bed," Roxanna demanded.

"Now," Jason added.

He ripped the pillow away, glare bouncing between them. The hard edge in Jason's voice had sent shivers down Hagan's back. Their looks brought him to his feet. Hagan ran a hand over his face and realized he'd fallen asleep in his clothes. "What?"

Jason stepped aside, and Hagan followed his sister into the living room, feeling as though they'd roughed it for miles. The television's volume played on low. Like his nightmare years ago, the on-screen banner served a sucker punch.

*First Family Under Attack*

He snatched the remote and turned it up. Hagan collapsed on the couch. Roxana sat by his side.

"—only just now learning that FBI negotiators are already on the scene."

Grainy surveillance still shots showed Amanda, Halle, and

her mother. A timestamp clocked the date and time as last night.

"What's happening?" Hagan didn't recognize the sound of his voice.

"Something about Mandy—" Roxana winced. "Amanda and her mother. The business partner was never who she said. I'm not sure." She rested her hand on his forearm. "I'm sorry. About this—and yesterday."

His mind spun to catch up. The news cut to a mugshot. Acid churned in Hagan's stomach.

"Authorities have confirmed that this may be related to the explosion at Washington College five years ago. William Taylor Morris was convicted to life in prison for his role in the terrorist organization that injured Amanda Hearst and killed US Secret Service special agent Dylan Carter."

"Confirmed that it *may* be related," Roxana snapped. "What kind of reporting is that?"

The news continued, "Morris is reportedly in a medically-induced coma as his late-stage cancer requires the use of a ventilator."

"Am I supposed to feel sorry for him?" Hagan couldn't watch anymore; he needed to talk to Boss Man. "Where's my phone?"

As if on cue, he heard it vibrate on the kitchen table. Hagan hustled down the hall and grabbed it. The caller ID said *War Room*.

Hagan answered, "Yes, sir."

"Are you ready to move out?" Jared demanded.

Questions flooded his mind, but he managed the only words that mattered. "Yes, sir."

THEIR ORDERS WERE clear. Get in. Eliminate the possibility of a catastrophe like Ruby Ridge. Get out. No one would be able to tie the ACES team to the scene—except for the First Lady and Amanda. But they wouldn't.

The helicopter blades silently sliced through the night. Hagan didn't need to see his teammates' faces to know they had concerns. They still watched him under their night-vision goggles, wary and reticent about what to say since they'd rendezvoused. The lead-lined tension promised that Jared had offered a colorful explanation of how Hagan was to blame.

The full force of the federal government, an alphabet soup of labor from the Secret Service to the National Guard to FBI negotiators, had coalesced as one unit on the side of a Shenandoah Mountain, ready to assist with the hostage negotiations and facilitate a prisoner exchange.

If all went according to Titan's plan, the Feds wouldn't have to raise their weapons, and Hagan would forever be in Jared's debt.

"Hagan, if you want…" Camden stomped his boot and ground the floor like he'd crushed a cigarette. "I'll take care of the asshole for you."

If anyone would put their hands on William Taylor Morris, Hagan had first dibs. He cracked his jaw and ignored the offer. Too much hung on the line to let his concentration break.

"I mean," Camden's voice crackled over their comms. "After this is all said and done. Just say the word—"

"Shut up," Chance growled into his mic. "Get focused."

*Stay focused.* Hagan dropped his head and replayed the plan.

"Midas, do you copy?" Parker called from Titan Group headquarters.

"Roger that, Zulu," Chance answered.

"Ground force commander's continuing to hold their position."

Hagan rubbed the back of his neck. Their success depended on ground command's patience. They had to have faith in the negotiators. The negotiators had to believe what they were doing was right.

"Boreas," Parker spoke to the pilot, "target vehicle approaching, westbound."

"Roger that, Zulu." Boreas gained altitude. "No visual." They hovered above a rest stop west of Charlottesville and waited to sight the ambulance. Once in view, it wouldn't be hard to miss, even without flashing lights. The US Marshals followed closely, facilitating the prisoner's transportation down the interstate in the middle of the night. "Possible visual." The radio garbled the transmission. "Zulu, one bus. Three JPATS. Target confirmed."

"Copy that. Stay with 'em," Parker said.

"Already am."

Hagan hadn't felt the forward propulsion and imagined the

stealth copter was invisible to the fleet of news choppers that had followed the ambulance from afar since it left Butner Federal Medical Center.

"Smooth skills," Camden mumbled.

"That's why they call me the wind god." Boreas chuckled as though this were any normal black op job. "Sit tight and enjoy the ride."

If Hagan hadn't been about to face his brother's killer, he might even have smiled.

"BamBam Rescue," Parker announced. "Ready to deploy."

ACES unfastened and stood. Each checked for last-minute gear adjustments. Chatter between Boreas and Zulu crackled. Their altitude decreased, and the hatch opened for the low-altitude drop. They had precisely ten seconds to land five men on the ambulance as it rumbled over Mechums River on a bridge the length of a football field.

"BamBam Rescue, to the door."

Liam handed Sawyer and Camden a line, kept one for himself and Chance, then handed the third one to Hagan.

"Ready, BamBam Rescue?" Parker asked.

"Affirmative, Zulu."

"Boreas?" Parker said.

"Traveling steady," the pilot answered. "JPATS remain close."

Hagan had no idea what the prisoner transportation officers would do when ACES descended, but he'd been told not to worry.

"BamBam Rescue, you're a go."

"Copy that," Chance said.

They fell into the night like black knots on a weighted thread. Inch by inch, they lowered to the base of the line. Hagan held his post and stared down. The broken white lines blurred as the headlights groped ahead. No one knew that ACES would rain in from above.

"JPATS slowing," Parker called. "Pulling back."

"Copy that."

Anticipation mounted. The interstate dipped into a valley and climbed. The Shenandoah Mountains weren't too far ahead. The ambulance rounded a bend.

"Zulu, JPATS outta sight," Boreas announced. "River's dead ahead."

"Green light," Boss Man commanded. "Go."

Hagan sighted the bridge in the ambulance's headlights. The Black Hawk dropped. If he pointed his toes, he'd touch the roof.

"Midas," Parker called. "At your command."

"Romeo One," Chance directed their next move.

They released the safety carabiners that attached them to the line. Hagan's blood rushed. His muscles contracted. The bridge was almost under their feet.

"Mike, Mike, Two," Chance ordered.

They dropped like rain on the roof as the ambulance rumbled over a joint expander. Road noise echoed over the bridge.

"Go, one," Chance counted their moves the same as he counted down the seconds. "Two."

Sawyer and Camden went right. Liam and Chance left.

They stayed in the blind spots.

"Three."

Hagan crouched center line, above the ambulance doors.

"Four."

Liam and Sawyer dropped to the back of the ambulance as it roared over the highway.

"Five."

They opened the back hatch.

"Six."

Hagan rolled over the roof, dropped inside, and double-checked the metal partition that separated the prisoner from the ambulance cab. The driver and attendant couldn't see the patient except through a video feed that Parker had already doctored and played on a loop.

Chance hoisted himself inside the ambulance on Seven. Camden dropped inside on eight.

"Nine."

Hagan secured the door. The ambulance jostled over a pothole and another bridge joint expanded.

"Ten."

Outside the ambulance, Sawyer and Liam were to reach for the Black Hawk's dangling lines.

"Airborne," they announced.

"JPATS headlights rounding the bend," Boreas warned.

"Copy that," Parker said. "Get over and out."

Hagan caught his breath, decompressing from the exertion, and it wasn't until he turned in the tight quarters and saw William Taylor Morris comatose that he remembered how to be human again. The worst of humanity roared to mind. Hagan tasted revenge. This man had stolen Dylan's life. In a way, he'd taken Amanda from him, too.

"Two minutes," Parker announced.

The ambulance slowed and exited the highway. Road noise mixed with the slow-and-steady suck and whoosh of forced air into the man's lungs. There wouldn't be much time left, and Chance and Camden hadn't said a word. Hagan's heart slammed against his ribs, and a cold sweat broke out on his back the same way it had when he'd testified at the sentencing hearing, promising that life in prison wasn't enough.

Hagan could hold Chance and Camden back if they tried to stop him. He could simply flip the ventilator's switch, and it would be done.

"BamBam Rescue, hold your position," Parker ordered. "JPATS falling back."

The ambulance slowed, stopped, then crept forward again.

"Field coordinator waving you through," Parker explained.

Hagan tried to picture the compound on the side of the mountain where Halle had taken the First Lady and Amanda and how Halle thought this would end. What would she do with her dying partner? He didn't know how they could escape and survive.

Then it struck him. What Boss Man hadn't explained. What his teammates already realized. Halle had no intention of going anywhere. ACES wasn't only ensuring the safe delivery of the first family, but preventing an additional murder-suicide.

## CHAPTER FORTY-ONE

THE AMBULANCE RUMBLED as it climbed the moonlit mountainside. Rocks skittered under its tires. Chance and Camden perched against the back doors.

"On our mark," Parker called.

Chance unlocked the back doors and held them ajar. Time ticked by as they crawled up a hill.

"Now," Boss Man said as if he'd pulled a trigger. "Go one and two."

Chance and Camden stepped from the climbing vehicle onto a curving makeshift road along a steep embankment. The ambulance maneuvered around an uneven bend, and Hagan's teammates disappeared into the sharp angle of the woods as he caught then secured the doors.

He closed his eyes and pressed his forehead to the cold metal. Every federal agency had tucked themselves onto a side of this mountain, ready to descend through the forest like wolves. They didn't need a prisoner to exchange. They could save Amanda and her mom without handing over his brother's killer.

Alone, Hagan turned and moved to the side of the stretcher. The ambulance stopped. The warning cry of its reverse sirens wailed. The ambulance veered as if lost footing. It quickly lurched forward, jostling Hagan. "What the hell?"

"Can't get eyes on you," Parker said. "What's going on?"

They stopped on a steep incline. A back wheel spun without traction then lurched hard enough to knock Hagan to his knees. "Car trouble."

Supplies rolled on the floor. The suck and whoosh stopped. He turned toward the stretcher. Morris's body struggled as his machine didn't make a damn sound.

Hagan felt everything that Morris stood for, everything that he took away—then Hagan saw a plug had been knocked loose as supplies fell. A switch hadn't flipped. The grim reaper hadn't called. A goddamn unconnected wire had left William Taylor Morris's life in Hagan's hands.

Suffocating gasps sputtered, and Morris strained. Hagan waited for satisfaction to soothe the anger in his heart as he watched the killer struggle against death.

It didn't come, and instead of relishing in the retribution, he found a harder task than murder—a single, undeserved act of mercy. Hagan reconnected the plug.

The suck-whoosh returned. The strangled dying ceased. Hagan held his breath until his lungs burned and let it go when he was certain that had been the right thing to do.

The ambulance stopped. The parking brake applied. The heavy vehicle settled into place.

"Target is on the move," Parker said.

Hagan listened for what would come next. With Halle outside the home, Chance and Camden would move in.

"Twenty yards and closing," Parker reported.

"Sparkler and Scientist found," Chance reported. "Happy and healthy."

"If not pissed," Camden added.

The corner of Hagan's lips quirked. "I bet."

"She's ten feet and running, strapped as if she's going to war."

Hagan heard his heartbeat as he waited for Halle to arrive. The ambulance driver and his partner had been instructed to let her enter from the back and wait for federal ground command to approve the exchange. Halle didn't deserve to see her man. She'd turn around and realize her hostages were now well-guarded.

The doors flung open, crying, "Billy—"

Hagan blocked Halle. "Surprise."

Her head snapped back, and she gasped. Her face showed one emotion after another like falling dominoes. Shock. Distress. Disappointment. Anguish. Exhaustion. Fresh tears spilled. She didn't raise a weapon. "Will you let me see him?"

Her anguish stabbed Hagan in the back, and a million pinholes of pain radiated from his heart. His jaw clenched. "You helped him kill my brother."

Despair twisted her features. Hagan didn't see a single slice of regret for Dylan, for what she'd destroyed, only what she couldn't have. Her chin quivered. "Please…"

"You're not even sorry," he demanded.

Misery and martyrdom clouded her face, and she whispered, "I don't know."

The truth pummeled Hagan. He wanted to shove Halle from the ambulance and deprive her of the last moments with someone she loved. "You don't deserve mercy."

Like the truth had sentenced her to an understanding of her cruelty, she staggered back. Hagan hoped she hurt. He prayed for her misery. His chin lifted high, and he drank in a deep breath, but it soured in his gut. Life never made sense. Humanity wasn't always good. But he was and wouldn't devalue his own pain by denying hers.

Hagan had lived through pain too similar to Halle's. Sick to his stomach, he extended his hand.

Disbelief tugged her gaze to his. "Why?"

"Because…" He stepped from the ambulance and methodically disarmed her without a fight. "People I love wouldn't have suffered if someone had shown you there's another way." Hagan helped her into the ambulance and zip-tied her hands next to Morris's. He locked them together and turned toward the cabin. The sour taste in his mouth was gone. Hagan walked away, at peace.

THE PITCH-BLACK SKY had softened to a gray-purple, and Amanda had no idea what was going on. She'd only slept in spurts, most recently waking to find Halle gone, replaced by two men in tactical gear who paused long enough to assure that she and Mom were still alive. No matter how many times or how loudly Amanda asked, they wouldn't untie their wrists or share who they were.

Mom yawned. "I could use some coffee."

Amanda rested her forehead on the back of her bound hands and worried that Mom had brain damage from whatever Halle had gassed them with. "I wouldn't mind a knife and a gun."

The men appeared again, this time with an armload of security equipment that they dumped on the blue-checkered tablecloth table.

Amanda scowled as they walked by again. "If you're going to fleece the place, can you find a minute to cut us loose?"

One guy laughed. The other pushed him to get back to work. She eyed the equipment that looked as if it had been removed from their office. Halle had amassed quite the stockpile, and before Amanda could wonder, the men returned with their hands full of weapons. She kicked and twisted to get loose. "A little help?"

No answer.

*Of course.* Amanda tried to stomp her feet but only succeeded in pulling her ankle binding tighter. She wouldn't make the same mistake as she had last night when attempting to tear the hook out of the wall. That rustic piece of metal was anchored to the cabin with voodoo magic. "Did you arrest Halle?"

They ignored her and worked through the pile, dismantling and organizing like they were the booby-trap-evading-evidence fairies that had come to childproof a crime scene.

"Try to relax," Mom suggested.

Amanda stared at the Zen-shade of purple in the sky and

wanted to scream. "How are you this calm?"

"I'm not, sweet pea." Mom sighed. "My heart hurts for Stephen, Brooks, and Juan. I'm tired, hungry, and in pain."

Guilt threaded into Amanda's chest. She hadn't asked Mom about her detail. "I'm sorry."

"Me too, and I'm angry." Her mom leaned against Amanda. "It's okay to be more than one thing at a time."

The two men walked out again. Not even a nod as they passed. This time, Amanda didn't yell for their attention. "This was everything that I tried to avoid."

Mom nodded. "I know. But you can't control the world."

"I know."

"I'm not sure that you do." Mom wriggled against the couch. "You have to try."

"Why would I do that?" Amanda asked, then braced for a science pun when Mom grinned.

"You'll figure it out."

There were too many other things to figure out. "Right. I'll get on it—" The sound of a truck reversing wailed from outside the cabin. "What is that?"

The two of them craned to see out the window. Spinning lights refracted through the trees.

"An ambulance," her mom explained.

The lights stopped. The reverse warning beeped on and off. Why would Mom assume an ambulance? Then Halle's words from last night replayed. *They won't let him out.* "She's exchanging us for Billy."

"I think that might be her plan," Mom agreed.

"It will never work." Amanda temples pulsed. "She's an extraordinary planner. There's too much risk—"

"I don't think Halle sees a choice."

Amanda turned to Mom. "Did you know about her?"

Mom shook her head. "Not in a million years."

"I should've seen—" The missing pieces from Casino de Gemmayzeh lined up. Halle had planned and executed. It'd been an inside job to lure Amanda away from the protective reach of Titan Group. Billy was dying, and Halle needed a bargaining chip. "She planned Lebanon."

Mom's brow furrowed. "What?"

"I had a job in Lebanon. It went wrong." She pressed her fingertips into the corners of her eyes, exhausted. "But I didn't know why."

"How'd it go wrong?" Mom asked.

Considering their current circumstances, Amanda wondered how big of a deal would her mom see an attempted abduction. Probably a pretty big deal … She decided to save that for later and bore Mom into a new subject. "The casino's fiscal budget showed irregularities. I didn't realize the numbers were doctored until I saw a store listed with an outdated name."

"So?"

Mom didn't sound the least bit bored. "Well …" Amanda chewed her lip. "A little Googling explained that the store's parent brand had filed for bankruptcy. But unless you were in the know, it would've been missed."

"Why would Halle create a bogus job?" Mom asked.

Amanda bit her lip then leaned against her mom. "I didn't want to worry you."

Her mom snorted. "Take a look around, sweet pea."

"Hagan and I botched a paid attempt to grab me."

"Amanda." Her mom took a heavy breath. "You've had a very rough few days."

Amanda snickered. "Don't make me laugh."

"I'm not trying to. What else have you neglected to mention lately?"

"I don't know." She bit her lip. "If I had just kept it together after Dylan died …" She shook her head. "None of this would've happened. I would've seen what was happening. Or, better, said something about—" Her stomach churned. "I don't know."

Mom sat up and gave her a look. "Said something about what?"

Amanda looked away. She'd never told anyone how Halle and Billy had been before the explosion. At first, she forgot. Then with Halle by her side at the hospital, Amanda thought the memory had been a delusion.

"What didn't you say?" Mom demanded.

She shook her head. "I thought there was something between Halle and Billy, and it turns out that I was right." Amanda waited for her mom's lecture or, at the very least, reference to a science project gone wrong. But it didn't come. Neither did the shame she should've felt for being duped.

"You can't take on all of this, Amanda," Mom whispered.

Her protest caught on her tongue. Exhaustion weighed her

shoulders down. She was so tired of taking responsibility for the burdens she continued to carry. "You're right."

Her mom wriggled until she could hold Amanda's eyes. "I know that. But, really, do you?"

She'd never claimed to be a saint, but the differences between right and wrong were suddenly clear. Other people had been assholes. Classmates who talked to the press. Journalists who picked her apart. A boyfriend who blew up the library. Their issues had pulled Amanda underwater so many times—and she was done carrying the load. "I do."

Then her tears came. She'd created every rule, contract, and teenage attitude problem in reaction to others, and that had cost her the one thing that she really wanted: Hagan.

Heavy footsteps came closer. The two men reappeared, and this time, faced them. Amanda wiped her cheeks, not using one iota of energy to glare.

"Ma'am," one said, as though apologizing for leaving the First Lady tied up. "We—"

"You never saw us," the other added. "We were never here."

The first guy smacked the other one on the back of the head, then gave a quick salute.

"Thank you," Mom said.

The men disappeared the way that they first came in, giving Amanda one more quick glance.

"What are you thanking them for?" Amanda managed once they were gone.

"Don't forget, your father's the commander of the free

world. *And a lame duck.*"

Amanda blinked, trying to see what Mom saw with her term-limited father, the longest-serving US president in history, never running for office again. "So Dad sent spec op guys to screw around until the cavalry arrives?"

"A particle attracts another particle with a force that's directly proportional to the product of their masses."

Amanda squinted. "Come on, Mom. I'm too tired to think."

"He'll move heaven and earth to safely get by my side." Mom grinned. "Your dad's my particle."

"Oh, God." Amanda dropped her chin and shook her head. "I think Newton just rolled over in his grave."

"Newton, huh?" Mom beamed. "Guess my little quips have made an impact over the years."

"You mean traumatized," Amanda said. "I haven't forgotten our heartwarming birds-and-bees discussion."

Mom patted Amanda with her bound hands. "You remember when we made jelly-filled donuts."

She gagged. "I haven't had a jelly donut since second grade, thanks to you."

"Oh, come on, sweet pea." Mom chuckled. "How boring would life be if my advice was simply trust in your man to find you."

The large shadow of a man stepped in from the far side of the cabin. Amanda's heart stopped. "*Hagan.*"

"He found you," Mom whispered. "That's a good man."

Amanda had so much to explain and didn't know how to

ask for his understanding. She wanted to tell him that she wasn't a puzzle or gamble, but simply a survivor. But above everything, he needed to know that she loved him.

Unlike the other men, Hagan's face wasn't covered. Triumph and heartache pulled at his expression. His long legs crossed the room like a man on a mission. Then, Hagan nodded to her mom, "Dr. Hearst," and then swung his fierce gaze to Amanda. "You're okay?"

She nodded. "Yeah. Where's Halle?"

Hagan ran a hand into his hair. "Locked in the ambulance with—" His eyes darted to her mom and back as if he'd said too much.

"With Billy." Amanda's chin dropped. Even if she refused to carry the guilt and anger that Halle forced on her, the betrayal still stung. "We've solved a mystery or two while tied to the couch."

"None of this is your fault." Hagan touched her chin, then lifted her face. "I know that."

"I want to explain," she promised. "I'm sorry—"

"I'm sorry. I shouldn't have left like that." He shook his head. "We can—" The corners of his lips tightened at the sight of her scratched wrists. "This'll be another thing you won't be able to explain to the feds." He pulled a knife from his thigh and sliced their bindings.

Mom rolled her hands. "To go with our imprisoned captor and disarmed cabin."

"More importantly." Hagan focused on Amanda. He took a deep breath and let it out as if he'd held it since they'd parted way, then dropped onto one knee. His gaze swept the ground before he met her eyes. "I can't untie your feet."

Mom sighed. "That's not what you should've said."

Hagan's forehead creased as if he didn't understand her lifetime of hoping Amanda would fall in love and live happily ever after. Or, at least, remember that she wasn't a robot and find someone to have sex with.

"*Mom.*"

"I can't take all their fun away." He double checked the bindings hadn't cut into their skin, then sheathed his knife. "In less than five minutes, a battalion's worth of federal agents will swarm up the mountain to save the day."

"My particle," Mom said as if Amanda needed the reminder of who might be the commander in chief.

"You know where Halle is," he continued, "every trigger and trap has been removed. There will be no surprises when they arrive."

"You're leaving?" Amanda asked.

"We were only here to mitigate risks that bureaucracy might create."

That had to be code for doing whatever was necessary to keep everyone alive. "Okay."

He checked a large watch strapped to his wrist and hesitated. "If you hadn't thought about it yet. There'll be plenty of press—they wouldn't know what to do with themselves with that smile."

Her heart twirled. "I'll try to remember that."

"I like this boy," Mom added.

Hagan grinned. "And when the feds come rolling in, try not to knee anyone in the—"

Mom gave her best science professor look. "'nads?"

"Yes, ma'am." He winked at Amanda. "We'll talk soon. Figure out what needs to be said."

"Sort of like starting over?" Amanda bit her bottom lip, not sure she was ready to forget everything that had grown between them.

"I don't know. I'd like to avoid groin injuries and squaring off with my boss." Hagan's grin hitched. "Maybe we just review the basics?"

Her heart melted when his smile grew, and she held out her hand. "I'm Amanda Hearst."

"Hagan Carter." He shook it and traced the gold wedding band on her left hand. "Still got it on." He lifted his hand. "Me too. How about that?" Hagan rechecked his watch. A muscle in his jaw ticked as though he didn't want to go. "When this sorts out, let me take you to dinner?"

She beamed. "You're asking me on a date?"

His eyes danced. "Maybe Majboos?"

Back together and with an inside joke that made her insides go squishy … "I'd love to."

"Good." Hagan bent down and kissed her cheek, whispering, "Because I'm in love with you."

# EPILOGUE

BLUE LIGHT GLOWED from the flat screens that streamed mission control and hotel security data. Amanda took the last sip of her tea and set her mug down, ready to be done for the day.

Shah stopped tapping his pencil. "Where are you going?"

She stretched. "I don't know. Nothing's going on—"

The red blinking light indicated a call from Titan Group headquarters.

"Famous last words," Shah chuckled and returned to a notepad of calculations.

"Parker," she answered and slipped back into her seat. "What's going on?"

"Not Parker," Boss Man boomed.

"You sound so insulted," she laughed. "Have you tried meditating? It might help with your cheery—"

"It's a good thing you're good at your job."

Amanda leaned back in her chair. "I learn from the best."

"Don't suck up to Parker," he groused. "He can't save you."

"I wouldn't dare—wait a minute." Her eyebrow inched up. It had been almost a year since Parker handed her the reins. In that time, she'd managed the nerve center with her partner Shah, overseeing hotel surveillance and mission control. Neither Parker nor Jared indicated she wasn't up for the job. "Save me from what?"

"Nothing," Jared grumbled. "There's something up with a sector in tower one."

Her eyebrows arched. "Says who?"

An alert pinged, and a pulsating rectangle zeroed in on a stairwell. Amanda reached for the keyboard and reviewed the alarm code. *Unclassified and/or other.* Amanda pulled up the live feed and found an empty staircase. "Since when are you in the business of telling the future?"

Jared snickered. "Since the beginning of time."

Amanda rolled her eyes and reviewed recent footage. "Nothing's there."

"Double-check for me."

She checked the time on her Fitbit and considered lobbing the request to Shah, but his calculations held his complete attention. Besides, Hagan wouldn't be back until tomorrow; she didn't have anywhere to be. "Only because I haven't got enough steps in for the day."

Amanda touched base with a new analyst then headed for the elevators. She rode up and stopped a few floors early, reaching the stairwell in question when her Fitbit notified her the day's work was done. *If only it were that easy.* She checked the security sensors. All were in perfect working order.

A distant echo beeped like her watch. She froze, but the noise had stopped. Amanda checked her wrist—her watch hadn't beeped—and a shuffle of footsteps made her pivot. "Hagan?"

He jogged up the flight of stairs. "Hey, beautiful."

"You're home early." She met him halfway down the flight and wrapped her arms around his neck.

"Surprise." He lifted her feet from the ground and carried her to the stairwell landing. Pressing her against the wall, he warmed her lips with a kiss hot enough to melt the sun.

He tasted like mint and smelled like heaven. She didn't know how he'd found her but suspected that Boss Man had something to do with it. Whether Jared liked to admit it or not, he enjoyed being in the mix.

"This is the kind of welcome home we should plan more often." Amanda slid to her feet and tangled her hands with his. Then she looked around and laughed. "Do you realize where we are?"

Hagan studied the stairs as if he'd just noticed. "Think so."

She slid under his arm and walked to the center of the landing. Not much had changed except a few coats of paint. Amanda smiled and relived the best parts, blushed at the worst, and shook her head at how far they'd come. "Can you believe—" She turned and saw Hagan waiting on bended knee.

"I believe anything when it comes to us."

Every fiber in her body hummed, unable to believe life had led her to this man. "Hagan…"

His smile grew until his eyes burned like fire. "Every time my heart beats, I swear it says your name."

"Same," she whispered.

"And every time that I say, 'I love you,' what I mean is that you're my life." He reached for her and grasped her trembling hand. "Let me be your husband, Amanda. I need you as my wife."

Hagan slid the intricate diamond ring on her hand.

"Of course." She remembered the night two years ago when they had removed their fake bands and promised never to pretend again. Their first words to each other after that vow had been, "I love you." She'd known they'd be together for the rest of their lives. "You're the best thing that I never planned."

## ACKNOWLEDGMENTS

Every book has a story of how it comes together. This one started with a challenge that I couldn't have predicted—a viral storyline questioning a fictional governmental response. It required substantial rewrites to maintain my goal to transport readers into an exciting world where they could escape the day-to-day.

As one of many working single parents suddenly thrust into the enormous responsibility of academic teaching, I can say that distance learning brought more challenges. It's hard to write a sex scene when someone needs their second breakfast or can't remember their Zoom password.

This book wouldn't be what it is if it hadn't been for unexpected situations and the people who helped me through it. My heart is grateful for my resilient children and for my partner Scott who never let me forget that my most important job is to raise good human beings.

I am eternally thankful for teachers and school administrators. Leslie, Gayle, and Ana, I can't imagine how hard you worked to maintain the vibrant learning community that we loved. Anthony and Allyson, thank you for keeping us off our butts. Keri, I appreciate your patience. Nicole, thank you for inspiring little scientists to ask questions. Jade, when their world seemed too large to understand, art focused on tiny details that they could grasp. Julie, thank you for the gateway to magical lands and lessons learned; I've always appreciated your talent to match kids with books, but it was your no-nonsense command of Zoom sessions that elevated you to sainthood. Kathryn, you calmed my heart. Jalene, thank you for the joy, love, and grace that you freely give. I have never met a more inspiring person than you.

Erin and Avi, Xiao and Bryan, thank you for acting as my sounding board and refereeing distance and masks during playdates.

Mom and Dad, I am always grateful for you! But when I had a very tough decision to make, those hours of questions over the phone helped me see my way.

A huge thank you to the team that made this book shine, including cover designer Kim Killion of Hot Damn Designs, editor Dylan Garity, and early readers and proofers Gabriela Almeida, Khatina Brunson, Jenn Burgess, Karyn Doran, Erin Park, and Bettye Underwood.

# ABOUT THE AUTHOR

Cristin Harber is a New York Times and USA Today bestselling romance author. She writes sexy romantic suspense, military romance, new adult, and contemporary romance. Readers voted her onto Amazon's Top Picks for Debut Romance Authors in 2013, and her debut Titan series was both a #1 romantic suspense and #1 military romance bestseller.

Connect with Cristin! Text TITAN to 66866 to sign up for exclusive emails.

The ACES Series:
Book 1: The Savior
Book 2: The Protector
Book 3: The Survivor

The Titan Series:
Book 1: Winters Heat
Book 1.5: Sweet Girl
Book 2: Garrison's Creed
Book 3: Westin's Chase
Book 4: Gambled and Chased
Book 5: Savage Secrets
Book 6: Hart Attack
Book 7: Sweet One

Book 8: Black Dawn
Book 9: Live Wire
Book 10: Bishop's Queen
Book 11: Locke and Key
Book 12: Jax
Book 13: Deja Vu

The Delta Series:
Book 1: Delta: Retribution
Book 2: Delta: Rescue*
Book 3: Delta: Revenge
Book 4: Delta: Redemption
Book 5: Delta: Ricochet
*The Delta Novella in Liliana Hart's MacKenzie Family Collection

The Only Series:
Book 1: Only for Him
Book 2: Only for Her
Book 3: Only for Us
Book 4: Only Forever

7 Brides for 7 Soldiers:
Ryder (#1) – Barbara Freethy
Adam (#2) – Roxanne St. Claire
Zane (#3) – Christie Ridgway
Wyatt (#4) – Lynn Raye Harris
Jack (#5) – Julia London
Noah (#6) – Cristin Harber
Ford (#7) – Samantha Chase

7 Brides for 7 Blackthornes:
Devlin (#1) – Barbara Freethy
Jason (#2) – Julia London
Ross (#3) – Lynn Raye Harris
Phillip (#4) – Cristin Harber
Brock (#5) – Roxanne St. Claire
Logan (#6) – Samantha Chase
Trey (#7) – Christie Ridgway

Each Titan, Delta, and 7 Brides book can be read as a standalone (except for Sweet Girl), but readers will likely best enjoy the series in order. The Only series must be read in order.

Made in the USA
San Bernardino, CA
29 July 2020